THEN THE FISH SWALLOWED HIM

A NOVEL

AMIR AHMADI ARIAN

HARPERVIA

An Imprint of HarperCollins*Publishers*

THEN THE FISH SWALLOWED HIM. Copyright © 2020 by Amir Ahmadi Arian. All rights reserved. Printed in the United States of America. No part of this book may be used or reproduced in any manner whatsoever without written permission except in the case of brief quotations embodied in critical articles and reviews. For information, address HarperCollins Publishers, 195 Broadway, New York, NY 10007.

HarperCollins books may be purchased for educational, business, or sales promotional use. For information, please email the Special Markets Department at SPsales@harpercollins.com.

FIRST EDITION

Designed by SBI Book Arts, LLC

Library of Congress Cataloging-in-Publication Data

Names: Ahmadi Āriyān, Amir, 1979 or 1980- author.
Title: Then the fish swallowed him : a novel / Amir Ahmadi Arian.
Description: First edition. | New York : HarperVia, 2020.
Identifiers: LCCN 2019044942 (print) | LCCN 2019044943 (ebook) |
    ISBN 9780062946294 (hardcover) | ISBN 9780062946317 (ebk)
Subjects: LCSH: Iran—Politics and government—21st century—Fiction.
    Despotism—Iran—Fiction. | GSAFD: Political fiction | Psychological fiction
Classification: LCC PS3601.H5735 T44 2020 (print) | LCC PS3601.H5735 (ebook) |
    DDC 813/.6—dc23 LC record available at https://lccn.loc.gov/2019044942
    LC ebook record available at https://lccn.loc.gov/2019044943

20 21 22 23 24   LSC   10 9 8 7 6 5 4 3 2 1

To my parents,

موسی و زهرا

And indeed, Yunus was among the messengers
When he ran away to the laden ship
And he drew lots and was among the losers.
Then the fish swallowed him, while he was
   blameworthy.
And had he not been among those who exalt Allah,
He would have remained inside its belly until the day
   they are resurrected.

   —QURAN, SURAH AS-SAFFAT 37:139–144

Solitary confinement in prison can alter the ontological
makeup of a stone.

   —JACK HENRY ABBOTT,
      IN THE BELLY OF THE BEAST

CLIMBED THE HILLOCK every day since I took the job at Jannatabad Bus Terminal, but that morning my body begged me to head back home. I paused halfway, lungs on fire and veins throbbing in my head, and looked upward.

A hundred yards away, the rusting, ramshackle terminal gate loomed like the first portal of hell. Under the downcast spring sky of Tehran, I stood with my hands on my hips and arched my back to expand my lungs. I thought of a wisecrack Hamid Fadavi had made in our first meeting: "You'll always know a good bus driver by his flat ass." As soon as this crossed my mind, I was ashamed. Hamid had been languishing in solitary for forty days, refusing food for the last seven of them. With hundreds of bus drivers intending to stage a strike in his support, here I was dragging my feet to the gate and thinking only of his stale joke.

I resumed the climb, but my heart began to race and numbness spread through my legs. It occurred to me that I might be ill. I could simply go home and come back tomorrow with a story about my sickness. I turned to go down.

A group of drivers were marching determinedly up the hill. They had seen me. One of them waved. I waved back and turned around again toward the gate. I pretended to flick some dust off my uniform and started back up.

• • •

The Jannatabad Bus Terminal stretched from Laleh Boulevard all the way up to the south side of Hemmat Expressway. The city had dedicated this massive plot of land to buses at a time when no one could have imagined that Tehran would extend so far west. Even as high-rises grew up around them, hundreds of the identical auburn vehicles fended off incursions into their asphalt territory. Seen from the hilltop's vantage point, the buses formed random geometrical configurations, among which wandered uniformed bus drivers like an army of brown ants. In the mornings, the drivers scattered from their social clusters into the vehicles to start the day shift. But today, I saw them form a conglomeration in front of the management premises, located at the eastern edge of the terminal. As I descended the other side of the hillock toward them, I imagined myself shrinking in the eyes of the men behind me.

The drivers huddled in small circles before the building. Everyone looked better than usual. Their yellowed skins, prematurely wrinkled by the vagaries of Tehran traffic and the effects of chain-smoking cheap cigarettes, had taken on a flush. Their eyes, usually set in dead stares, shone wide and alert. The place was boisterous like a schoolyard. More than half the faces there were new. They had come from other transportation hubs in the city, like the Azadi or Park-e Shahr or Tajrish terminals. But no one was a stranger. Everyone I passed smiled and patted me on the back like we were old friends.

"Yunus!" someone called. I turned and saw Ibrahim waving from inside a small huddle of men. I waved back, and he walked over. In our terminal, his enthusiasm for the strike was unparalleled. He hugged me tightly, like my arrival was the key to his plan's success. His uniform was carefully ironed, his eyes glinted, and his face beamed. He looked as flushed and fresh as a rich man at the beach.

Ibrahim began to bring me up to speed. Hamid was still on a hunger strike in Evin Prison, in critical condition. The news had come out that morning that he had been tortured, and his arm had been broken. Another jailed union member, in Rajaeeshahr Prison, had an infection in his eye, and the guards had denied him medical assistance.

Before Ibrahim could say more, someone called to him. He broke off and rushed away without a goodbye.

A shriek of microphone feedback shocked the crowd into silence. The terminal felt instantly colder, as though the sound had blasted away all the warmth in the air. The noise hurt my ears.

From the sea of drivers, a man emerged and climbed up onto a makeshift platform. In one hand, he clutched a microphone tightly at his chest. Shading his eyes with the other hand, he looked left and right, and his mouth curled up into a triumphant smile. The crowd of brown uniforms stirred and pressed toward him. I was carried like a stray piece of debris on the surface of a river and ended up closer to the platform than I wanted.

"My dear brothers and sisters," he yelled into the microphone. So there were women among us. Or maybe he had said "sisters" out of habit. His thick Bushehri accent amplified the shrillness of his voice. A full beard covered his fat face, and the collar of his wrinkled gray shirt was open down to his chest, divulging a mass of chest hair. Farther down, the shirt stretched tautly over the watermelon-size belly that hung supreme over his belt.

As the crowd quieted down, I could hear female voices whispering behind me. I turned and saw two women. I stared at them in awe and tried to think of a gesture that would express my gratitude for their presence in the strike. A man next to them cleared his throat and frowned at me. I swiveled back.

"We all came here this morning," screamed the man into the mic, "to demand the authorities . . . from the Ahmadinejad administration to the offices of the Supreme Leader . . . to release our . . . jailed brothers." He had stumbled three times in one sentence. The drivers around me shook their heads and grumbled, unhappy with this embarrassing start.

"They are jailed," the speaker continued, "only because they pursued the basic rights every citizen should be entitled to." At this he halted and breathed noisily. The drivers snickered. Some even booed. I felt for him. His wheezing sounded like mine as I struggled to crest the hill. It was time for him to cede the podium. His pained expression indicated that he knew this just as well as the rest of us.

"My dear brothers and sisters," he said, pausing dramatically, "it is my great honor to introduce our speaker for the morning, Davoud Shabestani!"

Admiring moans and an explosion of clapping followed this. I had never heard the name, but I made noises of approval and cheered along with the crowd. A tall, bearded man stepped up onto the platform and stood with composed stillness. The drivers roared even louder. He wore a neat gray suit and an ironed white shirt.

4

"I am sure you all know Davoud," the speaker said. "No one has devoted so much time and work, so much energy, to our union. As you probably know, Davoud spent twelve years in prison before and after the revolution. He understands as well as anyone how our jailed brothers feel."

The speaker handed him the microphone. Clapping erupted again. Davoud held the microphone in a steady grip and impassively regarded the crowd. The man who had introduced him stepped off the stage.

"We have a difficult path ahead," he began, his tone as somber as his face. "We are all on a journey together, one that will never end. For the path toward justice knows no end. The truth is, we all will die before any semblance of what we fight for comes to fruition on Earth. But we shouldn't allow this fact to dishearten us, because the destination is here. The destination is now. As long as you walk this path, you are at your destination. I see before me the hardworking men who risk their lives to serve a sublime cause, and this fills my heart with conviction. I don't need to get anywhere from here. I am where I have always strived to be. Today, standing among you, I feel the mercy of God pulsing through my soul. If you feel it too, then you are where you should be. You are a warrior in our battle against Zolm."

The crowd was silent. I examined myself to see whether something divine pulsed in me, but I didn't sense anything. The coldness that had set in earlier dissipated as Davoud spoke.

"But what is Zolm? The word of God leaves no room for doubt. Zolm is defying the order of the world. It is the imposition of your preferred order on God's design. The Quran is unequivocal on those who commit Zolm: 'The Zalimoun shall never triumph,' promises Allah. 'Woe to the Zalimoun from the torment of a painful day.' My brothers and sisters, we should all look in the mirror every night and ask ourselves, 'Did I commit Zolm today? Did I interfere with the divine design?' You don't need to be well versed in the interpretation of the Quran to know the answer. If you sit in comfort in a ventilated room exploiting a driver who works twelve hours a day in heat and cold, this is Zolm. If your employee demands better health insurance and you call the police, you are a Zalim, a perpetrator of Zolm. If your bank account is swelling and people who work for you go to bed hungry, you are a Zalim."

Someone shouted something. A round of applause broke out. Davoud waited out the clapping with a stonelike face.

"Look at them!" Davoud yelled, pointing at something behind the crowd. Hundreds of heads turned at once.

• • •

In the direction of the gate, where the hillock met the asphalt, groups of uniformed forces had taken up position. It was terrifying how quickly and quietly they had arrayed themselves. The majority of them were police, lurking behind the special guard that formed the front line, huge young men dressed in black, armored from head to toe with only their eyes and mouths visible, like mutated beetles escaped from a lab. The guards held transparent shields and long batons. Plainly clothed militia, Basijis, stood among the police in single-color shirts and cotton pants, brandishing sticks or tapping them on their thighs. They seemed to be the most harmless of the oppressors, yet everyone knew they were the only ones who would be willing to hurt us.

"Look at them!" Davoud spoke forcefully into the mic. "They think I am intimidated. They think their baton-waving thugs and gun-toting cops can scare me off this platform. Listen! I am talking to you back there. You came here to beat up the innocent people who take you to work, who take your children to school every day. You decided to side with the Zalimoun. You are the army of Zolm. I was in the Shah's prison for five years. This regime kept me in jail for seven years. I have met the death angel in flesh and blood. Come here and put a bullet in my head! I want nothing more than to ascend into the embrace of God!"

Davoud stepped down from the platform. The crowd exploded. Cheers and shouts rose from all corners. Men of all ages and stripes yelled and screamed, their faces red, veins bulging on their necks. I jumped up and down, shouting and waving my middle finger in the direction of the guards.

Soon everyone had turned to face the police to yell demands of all kinds at them. Some wanted the resignation of the transportation minister, others the release of political prisoners or accountability from Ahmadinejad. As I repeated the slogans of others, adding my voice to the cacophony, I felt that I was levitating, afloat on the nimbus of rage we were shouting into existence.

The special guards came forward, the sun glinting off the slick surfaces of their armor. They brandished their shields and batons. The Basijis followed them. The police shuffled behind like shy children. They formed a half circle around the crowd and trapped us. Behind the line of forces, the buses sat in silent anguish.

From somewhere behind the guards, a man spoke into a megaphone. "My dear friends, I represent the office of the mayor of

Tehran." Boos and insults met this announcement. I couldn't see who was speaking because the swarm of officers concealed him.

"This morning we had a productive meeting with the members of the city council. We understand you and sympathize with you. We have concluded that your requests should be met, and we are working with the intelligence services to release the jailed drivers."

The crowd jeered and roared like the man was a bad stand-up comedian. He kept talking, but the noise on our side rose so high I could hardly hear him. I first booed along but then decided to listen more. His muffled words did make some sense. They had bothered to meet and discuss and had sent an envoy to negotiate. The strike had already worked. We could give them twenty-four hours and get back to work, and go on strike again if they went back on their promises. But under the influence of the crowd, my rage came welling back and I started to heckle again. "Liar! Scumbag!" I screamed.

The driver next to me tapped on my shoulder and proceeded to recount the story of the mayor's brutal response to the school-teachers' strike. There was no reason to believe they would treat us any better, he said. I nodded as he spoke. Another driver turned to describe the various occasions when the union had trusted the authorities and later regretted it. I nodded at him too. All the while, the envoy kept screaming into the megaphone. As the minutes dragged on, his insistence began to make some impact. I heard new, fearful murmuring in the crowd. "Maybe we should postpone the strike," said one man standing ahead of me to another. "They're all armed. We should negotiate before it gets violent." Others around me started to echo this. I wanted to join in but kept my mouth shut.

A few men pressed back through the crowd to the platform, jostling and elbowing us aside. They drew to a halt around Davoud. Through a crack in the mass of people, I could see part of his face. He was shaking his head at one of the young men speaking to him. Another man started to talk, but Davoud only shook his head harder. Then he responded, keeping his eyes fixed on the ground. He hardly moved his mouth when he spoke. The men seemed to assent to whatever he was saying and dispersed without speaking further.

Shortly after that brief meeting, new chants broke out from small, dispersed pockets in the crowd. "We are here to root out Zolm!" "Political prisoners must be released!" I thought that the men who had spoken to Davoud must have instigated this. They must have been seasoned agitators who knew how to take the pulse of a rally. The chants spread fast. I went along and joined in without thinking about what I was saying. Soon the agitators had drummed up a fresh surge of rage. I recognized this manipulation, but I couldn't keep myself from reveling in it.

The envoy, who had fallen silent, spoke again. His barely concealed frustration made him seem pathetic. "It's a shame you decided to turn down my offer, but I respect your choice. I am not in a position to tell you what you should do. However, I am accountable to the people of Tehran. We can't let you take the buses hostage. Our brothers have volunteered to drive the routes and serve the stranded people in the streets. Please respect them as we respect you."

So that was why they had formed the half circle. They had outsmarted our leaders, who had let us walk into this trap. People yelled angrily at the special guards. The police crept closer, the gaps in their lines rapidly disappearing. I saw a bus coming down the hill from the gate. It parked near our own fleet and disgorged thirty-odd young men, who walked with brisk efficiency toward our buses.

Now the stakes of the conflict shifted. The drivers clashed with the line of guards. Many wanted to squeeze through and attack these strikebreakers. As the drivers yelled and cursed and pushed and punched against the transparent shields, the guards exercised restraint. I spotted my bus and hoped vainly that it wouldn't be taken over like the others.

Engines revved, and the first vehicle rolled slowly out of its parking spot.

Then I saw the woman.

Or rather, I saw a screaming black chador flying through a narrow space between two guards. I didn't know how she broke the line. Now she was past the forces, running on the open asphalt between the guards and the buses, the dark fabric of her dress flapping in the air. From behind, she looked like a mourning angel.

She got in front of the first bus and lay on the ground, faceup.

"Who is she?" I asked the driver next to me.

"Hamid Fadavi's wife," he said.

The bus rolled toward her. The pushing and tugging of the crowd subsided on our side. We watched, frozen in place. The bus slowed jerkily to a stop a dozen feet before the woman.

The driver got out, leaned against the vehicle's door, and stared dumbly at the unexpected roadblock. Emerging from behind the line of guards, five Basijis ran over and surrounded her.

Looming over the prone woman, one of the men yelled something at her. The drivers closest to them at the front of the crowd stirred. The Basiji must have threatened her. Even from a distance, I could see that the man was red in the face. The woman ignored him. He turned to his colleagues and spoke. They seemed hesitant. The man gestured again. As the crowd grew agitated on our side of the human barricade, the Basijis looked at one another. No one wanted to be the first to touch the defenseless woman.

From where I was, the scene looked like it could devolve into gang rape. The hesitation of the men intensified the horror. Now the drivers were cursing and pushing the guards. I managed to move closer and could see the nervous faces of the police. Hamid's wife had thrown them off. They kept one mistrustful eye on us and the other on their colleagues.

Two of the Basijis tentatively took hold of the woman's wrists, and a third one went for her leg. The woman kicked and screamed and writhed around. My face was hot with anger. The crowd was on the verge of explosion. She wriggled her hands out of the uncertain grasp of the men and held them close to her body. They watched her appraisingly and then grabbed her again. We punched and kicked even more wildly than before. The guards dropped their last veneer of composure and pushed back against us with their shields. They also began to use their batons on us.

Behind the guards, one of the Basijis lost his temper. In front of hundreds of witnesses, he lunged forward and kicked the woman in the ribs.

At that, my stomach lurched. Though it was hardly possible through the bedlam, I swore I could hear the sound of her ribs breaking. Pain spiraled around my own rib cage and squeezed a cry out of my body. That was the loudest sound I had ever produced, yet people around me hardly heard it, so thick were the screams of anger and disgust.

The other Basijis released their hold on the woman and stared at the attacker in disbelief. She rolled over, gathered her knees to her chest, and wailed. This deep, atavistic sob rose above the clamor and tore away the last shreds of our restraint. We launched ourselves at the guards with all the force in our bodies. I kicked and threw punches in every direction at anyone whose outfit was not brown. I was ecstatic with anger. The guards also fought with everything they had. They outweighed us in arms. We outweighed them in rage.

I punched a Basiji in the back at the same time a cop in front of me whacked a driver's legs with his baton. I was about to lunge and kick the cop when, out of the corner of my eye, I caught the long, thin shadow of a stick arcing fast across the asphalt to my right. I decided to kick the policeman anyway while he remained a defenseless target. Even when the shadow shortened as the baton reached its zenith before coming down again, I still focused my efforts on the policeman and turned too late to the guard.

When his baton came into contact with my body, I felt no pain. Rather, the blow sent numbness through my limbs. I remained conscious long enough to realize that the stick was electrified.

I looked at the attacker and saw the dark orifice of his mouth rimmed with crooked teeth. I tried to flee but couldn't take a step. My head bobbed disjointedly, and my muscles convulsed. Fire spread beneath my skin, and I collapsed.

From the ground, I watched the darting silhouettes around me. Footwear of all kinds stepped into view in front of my face: sneakers, military boots, worn-out Melli shoes, dirty leather sandals. Some men came very near to me as they stumbled, jumped, and kicked. I sensed that they made contact with me but heard no sound and experienced no pain. My ears shut themselves to the outside world, yet I could hear the squeals of my muscles and bones pleading for help.

The paralysis receded slowly. I couldn't tell how much time had passed, but finally I turned to my side and got up. I staggered, pressing through flailing bodies, across the asphalt to one of the buses, where I sat on the bumper and held my knees. The pandemonium moved over me like a floating pall. I peeked at the fight from behind the bus, knowing that I couldn't be a part of it anymore. The baton had sucked my body empty.

I gathered myself and stepped onto the bumper so I could use the handle of the engine hatch to haul myself up. My other foot found the top of the taillight. From this position, I stretched and grabbed the edge of the roof and with a last burst of strength heaved myself onto the top of the bus.

I lay faceup, dizzy, lungs on fire. The clouds drifted above, softly colliding and merging, sometimes passing briefly over the sun. The sky calmed me. I rolled over to observe the metal roof. I had spent my whole adult life at the wheel, always a couple of feet beneath this surface, and I had never seen the roof up close. My hand trailed across the warm, smooth metal. I put my face on it, closed my eyes, and let its heat soothe me, like a baby laying his head on his mother's bosom.

• • •

The stomp of boots behind the bus jerked me back to reality. A man yelled out an insult. Then something hit his body with a hushed thud. Another blow crushed the words in his throat and distorted them into a wail. More thuds followed, then his groaning stopped. Silence. A pair of feet sprinted away.

I crawled over to the edge of the roof and looked down. The man was twisting back and forth on the ground. A thick layer of blood covered his face. His left arm was bent awkwardly out of shape and his fingers were curled into a misshapen half fist. My stomach turned. Before I could pull back, I threw up. Vomit rained down and splattered over the man's pants. I ducked out of view before he realized what had happened.

I dragged myself to the other side of the roof and watched the fight. The battlefield had spread out, and the violence had intensified. Batons flashed up and down rhythmically, and men fell like chopped trees. The air was shot through with wailing and grunting and thuds and snaps. Blood was everywhere on the asphalt. Some of the wounded men fidgeted spastically.

Half an hour later, things wound down. Most drivers had either fled the scene or hidden behind or between buses. I spotted a few. As far as I could see, I was the only coward who had watched the fight from a roof. Others either had been arrested and were lined up against the bus that had brought the new drivers or were lying injured on the ground.

Ambulances roared into the terminal to carry the wounded away. Those arrested were led into a bus and driven off. I waited until there was nothing before me but empty buses and blood-spattered asphalt. I rolled over again to lie faceup and stared vacantly at the sky.

THE NEXT MORNING I woke up at four out of habit, but I didn't leave the bed. A splitting headache and aching muscles nailed me to the mattress. Pain bored into my head, like someone had hammered nails into my skull in the night. My back and legs had stiffened. With difficulty, I rolled over and cried into the pillow until my mouth went dry.

In the sitting room, I could barely recognize my own possessions. The TV seemed unfamiliar, larger than the day before. So did the couch, the old rug, the yellowing plant, and the table I had found on the street twelve years before. I had never liked it, yet I had kept it all this time. An urge to smash it all up came over me, but my muscles lacked the strength.

In the kitchen, I put on the kettle and stared at the film of dust on the window. It had rained during the night. I thought of Ibrahim. His flushed face and vivid eyes, his childlike excitement when he told me about the prisoners. He was so unlike the deeply depressed man I had known for years. He had faith in what he was doing. He had come alive. Where was he now? Possibly in the corner of a dungeon, writhing in pain.

My thoughts turned to Davoud. I recalled his affected seriousness with loathing. He was nothing more than a political arsonist,

I decided. A monster who knew how to use calculated, cynical stunt politics. His eloquent, firm sentences that stimulated the crowd, quotations from the Quran, all to quench his thirst for blood. "Fuck you, Davoud," I said to the empty room. If we had accepted the deal, none of this would have happened.

I opened the fridge. Its emptiness further enraged me. I kicked the door shut and cursed before shuffling out of the kitchen. I put my forehead against the sitting room window. Blood pulsed painfully through the veins compressed by the glass.

The street was awake. Cars rolled out of garages. People trickled out of buildings. The Afghan man was pulling his grocery stand to his spot on the street and setting things up for the day. Rajab, the blind beggar, had already taken up position on the corner by the curb and laid out his ragged cloth and begging bowl. Everyone was going about his daily routine, as if nothing of any particular import had transpired in the city the day before.

I returned to the kitchen, made tea, and sat at the table. The empty chair on the other side stared at me. I wished someone were sitting there. Not that I wanted to talk. A human voice would have repulsed me. But I longed for the presence of another person, a flesh-and-blood human body sitting there doing and saying nothing, not even moving. I tried to pick up the glass of tea, but it felt immovably heavy.

I went back to the sitting room, overwatered the plant, slumped on the couch, and stared at the black TV screen. Faces and voices emerged, rose up, and died away before my mind's eye. The scream of the woman in the chador reverberated in my rib cage again. I stared again at the snarling mouth of the man who had whipped me into paralysis. Torn clothes. Blood smears. The disfigurement of broken bones.

I had no desire to leave the house that day, but staying in would drive me insane. Last night I had thought I would never drive a bus again, but now sitting in traffic and talking to passengers seemed like the only remedy for my abjectness.

• • •

I knew the terminal would be empty, but its deathly silence startled me. From the hilltop, I saw long lines of buses hunched somberly on the pavement like dogs silently mourning the deaths of their owners. No one was at the gate, but force of habit sent me to the check-in booth. I found the file for my vehicle in a drawer, fixed it onto a wood clipboard, and descended the hill.

They had washed the blood off the ground and reparked the buses. I found mine and began the ritual. I walked around it to see if there were any scratches or smears. The first box ticked. Inside, I surveyed the seats to see if any of them were broken, scratched, or written on. People loved writing lewd shit and insults to politicians. We were supposed to report these every morning, and we couldn't leave the terminal before they were removed. I found "I want to come on your face" and "FUCK AHMADINEJAD." I reported both on the form that no one would see.

I sat down at the wheel and listened. The silence attacked me. I turned on the engine and pressed the gas so the roar would fill the emptiness. I maneuvered the bus stealthily at first, like a criminal sneaking out of a crime scene. At the gate, I got out and put the report in its slot, then got back behind the wheel and began my usual route on the long, straight street that connected Pounak to Azadi Square.

It was west Tehran's third day without buses. Bracing myself for insults and curses, I pulled up to the first stop. The chaos far surpassed what I had anticipated. A throng of people had crammed under the awning to wait for me. Before the door fully opened, they rushed aboard, pushing and jostling. "You assholes finally deigned to work," a middle-aged man yelled. That set things off. Other people lit in with insults about my mother, and the mayor's and the president's. They cursed one another, their families, and whoever runs the world and destined them to be born, of all places, in Iran. I closed my eyes and willed myself to let their words roll off me.

By the third stop, the bus was full. The passengers ignored me, preferring to focus their energy on the fight over space. Now everyone swore and shouted. Several times I opened my mouth to curse back before I stopped myself. I sympathized with them. They had been punished for two days. Most of them did not listen to BBC radio or read blogs. What they knew was that the bus drivers were the face of the citywide ineptitude that poisoned their lives.

At the fourth stop, the bus became a full-blown battlefield. Verbal attacks led to forceful pushing and shoving and elbowing. The youth shamelessly knocked the elderly aside. Men carelessly forced their way past women. The attacks on me increased, and my high-minded tolerance started to run out. By the fifth stop, the passengers on board were squeezed together so that they formed one airtight bulk. The people who couldn't get on shouted in anger, accused the ones aboard of selfishness, and begged them to make room.

When the door finally sighed shut against the compressed mass of human flesh, I cursed Davoud. First in my mind, then under my breath, then out loud. I thought of his immaculate suit and his martyr-like air, his tidy and charismatic self-presentation. Everyone on board was suffering because of his arrogance, and they were the very people Davoud and his ilk claimed they wanted to help. Rich people had cars and had gotten to work already. I hated him and the union and my complicity and cowardice. My hands clutched at the wheel. I imagined grabbing Davoud by the collar in the terminal and dragging him off the platform, kneeing him in the gut, shoving him behind the wheel of a bus, and forcing him to work.

A motorcycle rider nudged his way into a tiny space between me and a Nissan truck on my left and then darted out in front of me. Getting cut off in Tehran traffic was no novelty, but at that moment my body was tense with rage. My shaking right foot slammed on the brakes to avoid an accident. The bus lurched hard, upsetting the precarious balance of its cargo. People knocked each other over like dominoes. Their screaming rose to a feverish pitch before it crested and gave way to quieter swearing. Out of this, one distinct voice rose.

"Stop the bus! You broke my nose!"

The collective attention settled on this new problem.

"Oh, she's bleeding!"

"Give her a napkin! Stop the bus!"

"Her face hit the bar!"

"Stop! You broke her nose!"

I pulled over and opened the front door. In the rearview mirror I saw the mass of passengers cleave itself in two, opening up a path for the injured woman. She huffed her way through and stopped in front of me. Her small, beady eyes glared fixedly above her broken nose, to which she held a blood-smeared tissue.

"What happened?" I asked.

"Are you blind? I guess you are or you wouldn't drive like that."

"I'm sorry."

"You can say sorry to the court."

"It was the biker's fault. He cut me off. I had to slam on the brakes."

"Oh I know that, but I don't care. They should round up all you drivers just for keeping people hanging around like this in the street."

She got off the bus, took a notebook and pen out of her purse, and wrote down the license plate number with a dramatic flourish.

My nerves were totally shot now. Back in the eighties, when problems like this occurred, we didn't have cause to be concerned because we had accident insurance. The transportation administration had a team of full-time lawyers who dealt with people who threatened to sue and a little clinic that fixed up superficial injuries for free. We had this all through the war. Now the lawyers were gone. The clinic was gone. The accident insurance was gone. Five years ago, when a passenger fell and broke his finger, I spent a week in court and paid two months' salary to get out of a lawsuit. Every driver sat behind the wheel in fear of an accident that could ruin him. And we were supposed to just shut up and drive. Of course we went on strike.

I proceeded past the Marzdaran crossroad to the next stop. The fight over space on board had broken out again. Insults and curses from the street reached my ears, as did the complaining of passengers on the bus. I registered it only dimly. I was too far gone down the track of my thoughts. Davoud had a point. We had tried many times to negotiate. They had responded with batons and sticks, their bellies fat off the money we had made them. I watched people in the mirror. We couldn't count on them. They were a selfish mob, politically and spiritually destitute. Obsessed with their narrow interests, their most sublime experiences in life were birth and death. In between, nothing but greed and lies and backstabbing to get ahead in the collective run toward the edge of the cliff. Not a single one of them asked me why the buses were not running. How many of them had ever thought of a bus driver's life? None. Even after being stuck on the streets for two days, they refused to try. It was easier for them to think that we were lazy. Davoud was right. The city needed the shock.

• • •

The bus disgorged more passengers at Aryashahr, the last stop before the Azadi Terminal, but the density of the crowd inside hardly changed. It was like scooping a bowl of water out of a lake. People on the ground outside the door pushed and complained. The ones on board yelled insults back or pretended to ignore them. When they got tired of shouting at one another, they turned to curse me and other drivers. I stared at them, feeling the words out of their mouths hitting me like pebbles. Though my last remnants of empathy had already withered away, I controlled myself. Just a bit more, then I could stop for the day. I would just park the bus at Azadi Terminal and take a taxi home.

Before I closed the door, I turned my head to check the traffic. Then I saw the boy.

He stood by the front bumper, staring at me. He was hardly twenty years old, tall and thin with a well-drawn face. I stared back. He didn't blink.

"What are you looking at, you piece of shit?" I murmured. His expresssion changed slightly, like he had read my lips, and he turned to the people in the line.

"Look at what they have done!" he yelled. His voice was resonant and surprisingly husky.

The passengers turned.

"People are suffering all over the city because bus drivers refuse to do their jobs!"

Like a trained theatre actor, he silenced the bickering with his voice. The jostling and pushing subsided. Now the crowd regarded the boy with interest, perking up at the prospect of drama.

I was ten minutes from the end of the route. I badly wanted to close the door and leave, but people were hanging from the first step, still trying to force their way inside. A thick, human chain formed from the bus to the ground that the door couldn't cut through.

The boy came closer, stuck his head inside, and stared at me like a wild animal.

"You people are a bunch of sleazy assholes," he said matter-of-factly.

At that, people cheered and tittered and made sounds of acknowledgment. Encouraged by the response, he moved away from the door and turned toward the rapt crowd. His hair was trimmed fashionably. His clothes seemed expensive. Not an average bus passenger. It made no sense that he was there. Anyone who could afford a taxi was gone by then. He must be on a mission. Maybe he was a professional agitator, an undercover Ettela'at agent, or a mercenary the government had hired to make a scene.

"Hey!" I found myself yelling. "You watch your mouth down there!"

The boy didn't even deign to turn toward me.

"What the fuck do you know about bus drivers?" I shouted.

"Oh, I know a lot," he said without looking. "The city council agreed to give you everything you asked for. You didn't want it."

"The city council has done nothing but lie to drivers. We trusted them a hundred times before and every single time they failed us. Now, you move along and stop lying to people or you'll regret it."

He turned toward me. "Just be honest," he said. "You guys want to get paid more for less work to free up time for opium and whores!"

I shot to my feet. People rounded on the boy and told him to shut his mouth. The same people who had been egging him on a minute before. Some told me to calm down and to forgive him. The images of yesterday scrolled again before my eyes. Beaten-up bodies, terrified faces, descending batons.

The boy took a step back, hiding his surprise. I pushed my way toward him through the throng of people at the stop. He had retreated behind them to the less busy part of the sidewalk. As I pressed through, people tried to talk me down, but at that point I was a concrete fortress of rage, impenetrable to language. It no longer mattered whether the boy was a sanctimonious brat or a professional mercenary. He had said what he had said. I was consumed by the images of the mangled bodies of my friends and colleagues strewn across asphalt. I could take no more.

I lunged at him. He staggered backward, but my attack was too quick. My fist shot through the air and struck his cheek. The second punch landed harder and caused a fracture. I heard the crack and felt the slight warmth of blood on my knuckles. The boy shrieked like a tormented parrot. His strange cries unleashed a wave of adrenaline within me. I punched him again. The third blow shut him up. His eyes widened in shock. He put up his hands to protect his face. I slipped around him, wrapped my hand around his neck, shoved him down, and squeezed his throat while he writhed and kicked. I secured the headlock, surprising myself at the strength of my grip.

Holding the boy down, I glanced at the bus. Dumbstruck faces pressed against the windows, riveted by the sudden explosion of savagery on the pavement. They were either too stunned or too cowardly to intervene. They moved their mouths and gestured with their hands, but none came forward. I smiled at their pathetic inaction.

I grabbed the boy's hair and jerked back his head to expose his face to the passengers. Then I let go and pushed him away. He stumbled. Blood dripped off his cheek and dotted the sidewalk. His jaw was broken, and his hands groped the air like a blind man without his stick. When he lost his balance and fell, he held still for a second, then rolled to his side and curled into a fetal position. I lunged at his felled body and kicked him in the rib cage. My foot connected with his body where Hamid's wife had been struck. His limbs jerked, and he let out another cry. I walked back to the bus, as elated as a hunter who has just killed a trophy animal.

I smiled calmly at the aghast passengers and sat down at the wheel fresh and rejuvenated. The bus was so quiet I could hear the asthmatic breathing of the fat man the crowd had pressed against the wall behind me. I wondered how long the fight had gone on. Apparently, it was short enough that everyone was still in shock. But someone must have called the police.

I drove in a leisurely manner to the Azadi Terminal and opened the door. I leaned back and listened to the stampede of passengers fleeing and stared at the blue sky.

• • •

The knock on the bus door caught me by surprise. Three police officers were standing watching me through the glass. They were around the same age and had the same haircut, the same white shirts and black jackets and pants, like they were three penguin brothers. I pressed the button and listened to the bus door exhaling open. I closed my eyes and focused on the hiss of the motor swinging the top lever, the rotation of the door to ninety degrees. The background sounds of my life for the last twenty-five years, which I knew I wouldn't hear again for some time.

The one who came up first grabbed my wrist, then pulled

back his hand with a shout. His palm was covered in blood. This reaction startled me off my seat. I moved to help him, thinking that he had somehow cut himself. Then I saw the thick layer of blood congealing on my own hand. Small, reddish smears were all over the dashboard and the wheel, and larger ones covered my uniform like islands in a muddy lake.

The other officers jumped in. One grabbed me by the collar, the other handcuffed me and pushed me off the bus into the back seat of a dark green Peugeot 405. They settled in on either side of me. The first officer sat behind the wheel in front and cleaned the blood off his hand. The car screeched off and joined the traffic of Azadi Square.

"Why did you beat up the boy?" asked the one who had hand-cuffed me. He sounded genuinely curious.

"I don't know," I said.

"You almost killed him."

"I'm sorry." I gazed into his bewildered eyes. He looked away.

• • •

For the first time in the forty-four years of my life, I saw the inside of a police station. It fascinated me. The bland, light green walls and ceilings, the sour smell of sweat and rust. Workers sat at their desks exuding an air of mild depression, sifting through stacks of paper. In corridors, young uniformed men with faces and accents from all over the country led handcuffed goons and drug dealers around.

I was brought to an officer at the end of a corridor. A fat, bearded sergeant glanced without interest in my direction and clicked open a page on the screen in front of him.

"Name?" he asked.

"Yunus Turabi."

"Date of . . ."

He didn't finish the question. From the shift of light reflecting off his glasses I could tell that a page had popped up with information about me. Boredom vanished from his face. He read it carefully. When he looked back again, his eyes glinted with curiosity.

"Take him to that room," he said, pointing to a door across the corridor. "One of you stay with him."

Inside the room, I sat down on a creaky wooden chair across from the officer. When we made eye contact, he would quickly look away. I was not fazed. I felt as though I had quit a job I had hated all along.

Half an hour later, the fat sergeant beckoned us out. We walked back down the hallway to the street. Four men were waiting for me.

THEY BLINDFOLDED ME with a stinking rag and secured my hands with a plastic zip tie that first was comfortable and then grew increasingly tight. A strong hand
grabbed my shoulder and forced me down and into the back seat
of a car. Two bulky men squeezed into the space on either side of
me. The four doors slammed. The same hand grabbed my neck
and shoved my head down between my knees. "Don't fucking
move," the man said. The engine revved and the car veered off
onto Azadi Street.

"Turn on the AC," the man on my right said. He had a thick
accent I couldn't place.

"It's broken," the driver said. "Open the windows."

I'd be in a prison soon. The thought perversely excited me.
After twenty-five years of stillness, day after day charted out by
the same strict routine, my life was now unpredictable. I took a
deep breath. The mustiness of worn floor mats filled my nostrils.
I coughed. The bodies of both guards jerked in alarm. The hand
shifted on my neck and repositioned itself with a tighter grip.

"Do you see the place across the street with the yellow sign?"
said the man on my right.

"Yes," said the one on my left.

"That's the best kebab koobideh in town."

I thought about where we were. We had just left the police station at the corner of Ostad Moein and stopped at two red lights. The kebab place must be the new branch of the chain of restaurants a Tabrizi hotel owner had opened six months before. I hardly ate out but happened to have tried this one. It was terrible.

"No, it's not," said the man on my left. "It's average at best."

"That's the stupidest thing you've said in quite a while."

"Did you ever try the new kebab Bonab restaurant on Jeyhoun Street?"

"No."

"You should. It's a few blocks from us."

"I know where Jeyhoun Street is."

The men had blindfolded and handcuffed me too quickly for me to look at them. The two officers in the front hadn't spoken yet, but the voices in the back were unmistakably young. I imagined them as caricatures of themselves: big young guys with round, full beards and matted hair, narrow eyes, thick thighs, and chubby fingers.

The man on the right fidgeted, and his hand moved on my neck. Its weight bothered me. The places where his skin touched mine began to feel hot. His fingers were sausage-like and settled on my neck awkwardly. His skin was as soft as a featherless bird. Its only roughness was at the tip of his index finger, where his bitten nail jabbed into my neck with every change in the movement of the car.

He shifted his grip again, leaving a sweaty spot where his palm had been. The coldness of air on the damp skin sent shivers of disgust through me. I moved my neck. The man's hard ring pressed into it.

"Can you please take your hand off?" I asked. "I'm not going to move."

His grip became less certain. He must have been silently communicating with others in the car. After a few seconds he released me.

"Okay," he said. "Keep your head where it is."

• • •

The hubbub of Tehran assaulted me through the open windows. The cacophony I had lived in my whole life came to me in strands of sound tangled like yarn: honking of horns, revving of engines, whining tires, pop music pouring out of a car, a barely audible phone conversation. The noises snaked in from all sides, scarring the air, snarling into knots in my head, forming balls of hum and whir. Slowly they merged into an electrifying drone that came from everywhere and nowhere. This left its mark on everything and everyone in the city. It was possible that when Tehranis went to other places they exuded this sound. Maybe that was the reason why people from other parts of the country thought everyone in that city was insane.

A sharp reek filled the car and brought us all to attention. It smelled like a rotten corpse. I gagged. The guards made noises of disgust. I felt them on both sides of my body trying to wave the stink away. I lifted my head up to cough. The hand pushed it down. The car moved a little, but the putrid aroma lingered. I gagged again. Sour bile raced up to my throat.

When I began to breathe normally again, I noticed that my sense of smell had sharpened. The scents now entered my consciousness discretely, the way the sounds did. Smog, smoke, sewage, urine, dust, cheap perfume, cheap cigarettes, rusted metal, overused frying oil, grilled meat.

• • •

The driver slammed on the brakes too late to avoid a collision. The blast of a clash. Its force jolted me forward. My head hit the back of the hand brake. I sat up and reached my handcuffed wrists to my forehead to feel for blood. No one pushed me down. Silent shock gripped the car.

"What the fuck are you doing?" the man in the passenger seat said. "You two stay in," he told my guards. The front doors opened.

I guessed that our car had rear-ended another. Based on feeling alone, it was hard to estimate the damage. We had to stop there and wait for the traffic police. It occurred to me to punch the distracted guards unconscious and escape. But I had no idea how to do that with my hands cuffed. I wasn't even sure if I wanted to get away. The idea of returning to my apartment terrified me.

I heard the voice of an angry woman. The driver was apologizing to her. The other man spoke in a patronizing tone about how the damage to her car was actually minimal, that they were on an important mission, and she could call a number he would give her and they would take care of everything.

"I don't give a shit," the woman said. "I want the police."

"Listen," said the man, "when the police come, I can show them a card and they will go away. You're wasting our time. I told you, just call this number and they will take care of you."

"I don't want that. We're going to wait here."

She wouldn't believe them. Or maybe she did and she was messing with them.

"Look," the driver said, "you are going to get yourself into trouble."

"What did you just say?" said the woman. "You hit my car from behind. Now you're threatening me?"

"Fucking bitch," said the man on my left. He jumped out of the car. The other man pushed my head down, his hand gripping the back of my neck tightly again. He pressed something cold and circular against my temple. "If you move, it ends right here," he said. I froze. My heart was beating savagely.

After some minutes, the men got back in. The engine didn't start immediately, as though the accident had shell-shocked the vehicle itself. An awkward silence enveloped us.

"Mahmoud," said the man in the passenger seat.

"Yes, Hajj Saeed." The man on my left sounded timid.

"How many years have you been doing this?"

"Four years, Hajj Saeed."

"You have been in this job for four years and you still don't know how to use your gun."

"Hajj Saeed, she was—"

"She was complaining because Nasser hit her car from behind. Wasn't that Nasser's fault?"

"Yes, Hajj Saeed."

"When are you allowed to show your gun to unarmed people?"

"But, Hajj Saeed, we were—"

"Did that woman attack you with a weapon?"

35

"No."

The leather of the front seat creaked as Hajj Saeed turned toward us.

"Come to my office tomorrow morning at ten."

"Yes, sir."

· · ·

Before reaching the Yadegar-e Emam highway, the car veered off onto a side street, turned onto another, then turned again. I guessed that we were in the narrow alleys across from Sharif University. The car meandered farther, back down the same streets, then took sharp turns and sped up and slowed down, as if to disorient a pursuer. It must've ended up on Salehi Boulevard before dashing under the Yadegar and turning eventually onto the highway, speeding northward.

They could have gotten onto the highway without making those maneuvers. It took me a minute to understand that I was the one they were trying to disorient. I had heard of this before. Supposedly they were not allowed to take a straight path to prison when they were bringing someone. This amused me. Did they think a bus driver would lose his bearings because of a few extra turns? Even if they had succeeded in confusing me, it would not have made a difference. Everyone in the country knew that the drivers captured during the strike were consigned to Evin Prison.

"You can sit back," the guard said.

I rose, leaned into the seat, and moved my hands. The plastic handcuffs cut into my swelling wrists. My blindfold hitched up a little. I could see the groins of two of my captors. They both wore black cotton pants and buttoned shirts, one pale blue, one dark green.

"Is Wednesday a holiday?" Hajj Saeed asked, trying to shift the mood in the car.

"I'm not sure," the driver said. "Why would it be?"

"It's somebody's birthday on Tuesday, somebody's martyrdom on Thursday. Who goes to work between holidays?"

"I had no idea we were off on Thursday," the driver said.

"Of course we are. You love your job so deeply you lose count of vacation days?"

The man who had pulled his gun on the woman pretended to laugh in the back seat.

We passed the Hemmat Expressway. I knew it from the change in the quality of the air. Away from the clogged downtown, as soon as one entered the northern half of the city, cool, fresh breezes stroked the skin. The car coursed along the roads of the Shahrak-e Gharb neighborhood, and we breathed in some of what the affluent Tehranis got in their lungs every day. Farther up, around Farahzad Valley, the aroma of moist soil wafted in and filled the car. Then traffic again. The car slowed to a stop among other idle, purring vehicles. There was not much other sound. Up here, engines were tuned, windows rolled up, ACs on. The smell wasn't the same either. No trace of the pungency of human life.

Because it was clear that Hajj Saeed was the superior officer in the car, he was the only one of them I was curious about. The others were just there to transfer me. I bent my head farther back to widen the view from under the blindfold. I tried to see more of him, but the space was too narrow. I coughed hard and swallowed the phlegm. The coughing hitched up the blindfold a little higher. I pressed my back into the seat. Now I could see the hand brake stick and the lower half of the dashboard. The car was fairly new. The driver's hairy hand shifted gears. We moved a few yards and stopped. Hajj Saeed's hand settled on his own knee. A tasbih was wrapped tightly around his fingers like a boa strangling its prey. Its beads, shiny green stone pieces strung on a silk thread, slid around his thin fingers. I heard clicks. The tasbih looked expensive, like the heavy, old ones grandmothers used to bring from their Mashhad pilgrimages.

"How's your son, Nasser?" Hajj Saeed asked. I knew that none of the names were real and wondered why they were not more creative with them.

"He is not well, Hajj Saeed," the driver said. "It has metastasized to his lungs." He spoke emotionlessly, the way a doctor would discuss a patient with another doctor. "He needs to go through another round of chemo with a new drug, but that drug is not on the market."

"Why?"

"Because we don't import it anymore."

It was like sitting at the wheel again, listening to desperate passengers talking. During the months leading up to the strike, I heard a dozen complaints every day about how the sanctions wreaked havoc on their lives. During rush hour, when the bus was packed, the passengers were bored, and the roads were impenetrable, someone would bring up how the politicians stole the resources of the country and lined their pockets. That inevitably led to someone else broaching sanctions, which would launch a series of tirades: the price of milk had shot up thirty percent over the week, sangak bread ten percent overnight, the market was full of the garbage Chinese factories didn't want so they traded it for our oil. Someone always went big picture: Bush was mired in Iraq and now took it out on Iran, Putin supported us in public and backstabbed us in his meetings with Europeans. When the facts were laid out, the conversation would eventually lead to a philosophical conclusion: we deserved what we got. We had decided a buffoon like Ahmadinejad was the way out, and he would push us all off a cliff.

The tasbih beads clicked around Hajj Saeed's fingers.

"Didn't you say you have family in Europe?" Hajj Saeed said. "They can get the medication and send it."

"My wife has a cousin in Germany, but the drug is too expensive. He can't afford it."

"Can you afford it?"

"I have scraped up the money. I sold my plot of land in Qazvin and my father sold his car."

"What are you waiting for?"

"Hajj Saeed, you know that banks are under the financial sanctions."

"You know that currency exchange places transfer money?" said the other guard from the back, sucking up to the boss.

"They take a huge commission and don't guarantee anything. If the money gets lost, we have nothing left."

The driver pressed the gas pedal. The car revved loudly in the middle of the traffic.

"I know you are going through a lot, Nasser," Hajj Saeed said. "Everything passes."

"But how?" blurted out the man on my left.

A quiet mutiny was brewing in the car. Hajj Saeed's attempt at softening the atmosphere had backfired. Nasser cleared his throat.

The seat leather squeaked again. Through the gap in the blindfold I saw Hajj Saeed's torso turning to us. The young man's thigh began to shake nervously against my body. Hajj Saeed settled back into his seat. He must have communicated a silent message. The tasbih rolled around his bony fingers, and the beads started clicking.

"Nasser, I understand you," Hajj Saeed said. "It is hard on all of us. But there's no other way. The Europeans lie. The Americans lie. The Russians lie. They all know we have no plans for a bomb. It's all about making a lesson out of us for other countries. They can't tolerate our independence. They know that if we win this fight, a dam will break and other countries will pursue their autonomy. They will torment and starve us to death to make sure no one in this world decides for themselves."

"Hajj Saeed," the driver said, "no one said they like us. It's a matter of who's stronger. When you are attacked by someone five times your size, it's just stupid to fight back. The wise response would be to negotiate, give up something and gain something else."

"Nasser, are you joking? You think we just call the Americans and say, 'Hey, sorry, let's start over,' and they say, 'Okay,' and then we get along? Do you read the news? Did you forget what happened to Saddam? He licked their assholes for decades, fought against us to make them happy, and as soon as he decided to be his own man they fucked him over and killed him. You seem to have forgotten that, as we speak, they have occupied two countries on our east and west and are slobbering over ours. How can you even think of negotiations and concessions to them?"

"But people are suffering. How can you say that they should die because we don't trust Americans?"

I was itching to take off the blindfold and see their faces. Hajj Saeed clashed the beads of the tasbih together.

"We'll be okay," he said. "We are talking to the Russians and the EU. We will find a way. I don't enjoy watching people suffer. But mark my words: if we stop enriching uranium tomorrow and do whatever the hell else they want us to do, they won't lift the pressure. They will find a new excuse: freedom of speech, hijab, human rights, you name it."

"I know that. I am talking about people who—"

"You are not the people's spokesperson. A lot of them are with us. It's true that some here are happy to lay the country at the feet of the Americans. We are surrounded by betrayers and backstabbers, like the gentleman sitting between you in the back."

The sudden address shocked me cold. Hajj Saeed turned toward me. The weight of his stare pressed on my blindfold.

"Everyone knows bus drivers have a hard life," Hajj Saeed said. "I have bus driver friends. I know they don't get what they deserve. They have a right to protest, to voice their concerns. But why now? Why go on strike in the middle of all our problems? The strike has been on BBC and CNN full-time since yesterday.

They talk like a civil war has started. What am I supposed to think? That it's just a coincidence that the union organized this while the government is in the thick of nuclear negotiations? Is it an exaggeration to say there might be the hands of foreign states involved here?"

I sensed a trap. This seemed more like the beginning of an interrogation session than an extension of their argument. I tried to string together answers for questions I thought he would ask me. But I didn't have any. What did I know about the strike anyway? No coincidence is absolutely coincidental. Why did the union pick that day of all days? Why did Davoud insist when the city council offered a way out?

"To your point, Nasser," Hajj Saeed said, "when a bully five times your size comes to beat you up, you have two options: die on your feet or crawl on your knees. We had the revolution twenty-five years ago because as a nation we decided to stand on our feet. Despite our problems, we are stable and independent. Many Arab states decided to crawl on their knees, and they will end up where Saddam ended up. I am proud that we didn't give in. Some people, like the gentleman in the back, want us on our knees. We will defeat them."

• • •

Out of the car, the cool breeze of the Evin hills tickled my face. The highway hummed behind me, which meant that I was now facing the tall, corrugated gate of Evin Prison. The wind rustled through the trees, carrying the voices of people going in and out of the jail.

Like many in Tehran, I had passed by this gate a thousand times. I had an idea of Evin, based on news and rumors, and others had their own conceptions of it. Evin had a way of eluding consensus. Its location intensified the mystery: it was surrounded by highways and streets and tall buildings, yet no one could see it from outside. It sat at the base of multiple steep slopes, smooth stretches of green that plunged from the encircling hills to meet in the bottom of a deep valley. It was the black hole of Tehran.

My heart pounded. In Tehran, few things impressed people more than someone who could say he had been to Evin. Soon, I would have a story of my own. I took a few deep breaths and waited for the gate to open. On TV, I had seen footage of this moment, the gate yawning like the mouth of an ancient beast to swallow a new victim. My turn had arrived. It was disappointing to be blindfolded, but at least I could hear the noise.

One of the guards pushed me. I walked up to the gate. It opened. I heard not the sonorous groan I had anticipated but a pathetic creak. It sounded like the rusted hinges of a toilet door. "Step over the sill," the guard told me. My shoulders bumped into a frame. The gate hadn't opened at all. Instead, I passed through a narrow door built into the larger entrance. I got into Evin the way I would enter a grocery store.

Beyond another outside area, after entering the building, the odor struck first. I recognized wet newspaper, fresh mud, and human shit. Someone put his hand on my shoulder and kept it there while we walked down a hallway. From the echo of the shoes, I knew that only one guard had accompanied me. The alternating pattern of light and dark on my blindfold and the ringing phones and muffled voices hinted at the presence of offices. We paused. The guard opened a door. I stepped over another threshold. Then, the man unlocked the handcuffs and took off the blindfold.

AVAGE FLUORESCENT LIGHT attacked everything in my sight. I blinked and squinted at the whiteness. Another hand landed on my shoulder. "Relax," said the man who had led me there. "You'll be fine." He was not one of the guards from the car. They must have switched at the prison gate. He closed the door. His boots clicked away.

The smell of shit and wet newspaper was less strong in here. After a minute, other colors began to seep back into view, returning shape and texture to the objects in the room: a table, a bed, a file cabinet, a frame on the wall. The mass of unadulterated whiteness in the center of the room eventually resolved itself into a doctor's coat. The light reflected off an immaculately bald head and a pale, shaven face.

"Hello, sir," he said with a beatific smile. "How are you today?"

I said nothing.

"We are going to do a brief examination to see if you need healthcare. It is our responsibility to take care of you while you are here. Do you have any questions?"

I shook my head. He told me to sit down on the edge of the bed. He listened to my lungs and heart and checked my blood pressure.

"Are you on hypertension medication?"

"No."

"Your blood pressure is high. You should see a specialist when you're out of here."

"I don't know when that will be."

He put the blood pressure monitor in a leather bag.

"Why don't you give me the pills now?"

"I can't. Do you have any other issues that you are aware of?"

"No."

"Any form of addiction?"

"No."

I stepped on a scale. He measured my height and weight. I returned to the bed and watched him hunch over his desk to fill out a form. I could read his writing: 5 feet 10 inches, 171 pounds. I had lost some weight in the last few weeks. He checked the boxes for brown hair and brown eyes.

"My eyes are black, aren't they?"

He frowned and moved the paper closer to his body. He was annoyed that I had looked.

"No one has black eyes." His button-like black eyes stared at me from behind his glasses.

Some questions followed. Past surgeries, allergies, regular medication. He dutifully recorded my answers, scribbling meaningless numbers on a page printed with the last drops of an ink cartridge.

"Come here in front of the desk, please." I rose from the bed and stood in the spot where the guard had taken off the blindfold. The doctor pressed a button to call him back.

"Are we all finished here?" asked the officer. The doctor

nodded. The guard put the blindfold back on and led me out of the room.

• • •

We took only a dozen steps down the corridor before we entered another office. The blindfold came off again. This room was half the size of the other one and contained only a desk with two chairs. The furniture was dark gray. So was the man sitting at the desk. His suit and shirt, his hair and beard, all different shades of monochrome as if in coordination with his surroundings. He looked at me like I had suddenly emerged from some dank hole in the ground. Without shifting his gaze, he opened a file, produced a paper, and put it before me. He rested his finger next to each question as he asked it.

"Is this your name and phone number and address?"

"Yes."

"At the bottom of the page, write your email address and password."

"I don't have an email address."

"Within a week you will give it up. You're wasting your time."

"I am not hiding anything. I've never had an email address."

"You have been working with people overseas. We know you have an email address."

"What people?"

He narrowed his eyes and looked directly at me, as if trying to give the impression that he could read inside me.

"Fine. It's up to you. Do you have a post box?"

"Post box?"

"At the post office."

"No."

He put the paper back into the file folder and pulled out a few more stapled pages. He showed me the last one.

"Is that the last message you received on your phone?"

My dear friends, looking forward to seeing you all at the terminal tomorrow morning. If we come together and support each other, Hamid will soon be free.

It was the text Ibrahim had sent to us the night before the strike. For the first time, I was afraid. Up until that moment, things had moved too fast to leave time for reflection. My senses were clouded and numbed. My experiences over the last two days seemed barely real. Seeing those words on the page, straight from my phone, jarred me out of my dream state. Every nerve responsible for detecting danger was singing now.

"Is this the last text you received?" he repeated.

"Yes."

"Did you participate in the strike organized by the bus drivers' union on April 12th, 2005?"

"Yes."

"Are you a member of the bus drivers' union?"

"No."

"You're not?"

"No."

"You know why you are here?"

"Because I was brought here."

He smiled. "Oh, you think this is funny?"

"No."

"Do you know what you are accused of?"

"No."

"'Acting against the national security.'"

That sounded like something that could keep people in jail for years. I wanted to protest but didn't know what to say.

"Do you have anything to add?"

"No."

"Sign here."

I read the form he presented. The answers to his questions were all already there, cleanly typed. They must have had it ready before I arrived. I signed the paper. He snatched it away.

"How long have you been driving buses?"

"Twenty-five years."

"That's a while."

"It is."

"It's a shame you decided to end your career this way."

• • •

The next room was large and brightly lit. Its arrangement closely conformed to every threadbare cliché of bureaucracy. Two desks facing each other across the room, two outdated desktop computers, two worn-out chairs, two men in blue cotton shirts and black corduroy pants, both bearded, potbellied, and young. It was like walking into a satire about bureaucrats. One man was seated before his computer, eyes fixed on the screen, his mouse clicking away. The other one had turned to look at the door. He was watching me with the crude curiosity of an obnoxious teenager.

"Hello, sir," he said when our eyes met. "How are you doing today?"

"I'm fine."

"We're not going to hold you up here. Just a brief examination and basic information. Now, would you take off your clothes for me, please?"

I knew I would have to strip down at some point, but I had never expected it to happen in a room like this. I took off my shirt. The man kept his eyes on me. The other one frantically clicked the mouse and typed rapidly without paying me any attention.

I removed my pants and socks and stood in my underpants. I knew they had to come off too, but I wanted him to have to make an extra request. He made a gesture toward my groin. I pretended not to understand.

"Underwear as well, please."

He opened a drawer in his desk, his eyes fastened on me, and produced a pair of blue surgical gloves. He snapped them onto his hands with a flourish he must have adopted from some movie. He rose ceremoniously as his stare slid down and paused at my crotch, came over to me, took hold of my penis, and moved it left and right and up and down. Fighting back nausea, I looked over at the other man. He continued to steadfastly ignore what was taking place in front of him.

The man's hand slowly slid down the shaft to hold my balls. I inhaled as much air as my lungs could hold. He tightened his grip on my testicles. They shrunk. The skin shriveled in his fingers.

"What are you doing?" The words escaped my mouth. He loosened his fingers slightly.

"You shut the fuck up, okay?" he answered with a shaky voice. Then he cleared his throat, composed himself, and smiled. His fingers squeezed my balls again and let go. Then he stepped back and looked me up and down, like a buyer at a slave auction.

"Turn around and grab your knees," he ordered. I stayed still, more out of shock than disobedience. The man repeated the command. The other man began to type fast again. The fusillade of little clicks increased my heart rate.

I turned around and bent over, taking deep breaths to steel myself against the intrusion of his cold, gloved finger. The man quietly stepped closer.

"Please push out. Like you are farting."

I did.

"Again, please . . . Perfect."

He leaned closer. He was staring into my asshole.

"Thank you," said the man without touching me. "You can stand up."

I rose and turned and came face-to-face with him. He seemed content, innocent even. He opened another drawer in his desk, pulled out a bag, and handed it to me.

"You can put on these clothes."

He sat down at the other computer and began to type. With the short, sharp sounds of both keyboards in the background, I opened up the bag and laid its contents out on top of a small file cabinet. A neatly ironed, light blue prison outfit wrapped in plastic. Meticulously folded blankets. Toothbrush and toothpaste. A white towel.

I put on the uniform. The man who had looked into my asshole stopped typing and regarded me appraisingly.

"Stand against the wall right there."

I flattened my back against the cold concrete. He took a camera out of his desk, got up, and snapped my picture.

"Name." The nasal, high-pitched whine of the other man caught me by surprise.

"Yunus Turabi."

"Date of birth?"

"July 22nd, 1960."

"Birthplace?"

"Tehran."

"Father's name?"

I almost uttered it. My father's name reached the tip of my tongue, halted there, then backtracked down to where it came from. The more I tried, the more impossible it was to say it aloud.

"Name of father?" repeated the voice.

I made another attempt to summon it and failed. The name kept evading me. It retreated far back into the dark corners of my brain and lodged itself amid tissue and blood. I shut my eyes and tried to make out its contours. No sooner had I begun to close in on it than it flitted away into another, deeper groove.

As I struggled to articulate the word, visions came to me of my father at various points in his life. He raged here and smiled there. He frowned here and flinched there. He was a young man in a suit at a wedding, flushed in the face with sweat trickling down his forehead. This must have been what he looked like at the celebration for my cousin. I had been five and remembered him drinking himself unconscious, my uncles dragging him into the car, my mom at the wheel cursing and crying all the way home. Then I saw him in bathing shorts at the edge of a pool, the sky and the water a continuous swath of pristine blue interrupted only by human silhouettes and young sycamores. I saw the water-drops stuck in his chest hair, reflecting the light. I dived into the pool and splashed water all over him.

"Name of father?" the man asked a third time. I was still submerged in the pool. His voice came to me distantly and through burbling distortion. I opened my mouth and emitted a strangled noise. "What?" the other man asked. I didn't reply.

There he was again, in another image, this time in jeans and a T-shirt, at the wheel of our 1978 green Nissan on the way to Ramsar. The car labored up a steep slope into the mountains. From inside, I couldn't see ahead. What if we came to the end of the road and fell off the cliff? My father had a mustache, which suggested that he was in charge and knew how to navigate the twists and turns of a circuitous route.

Another vision of him. Much later, much diminished. He wandered the streets on foot. I followed him from a distance, inhaling the perfume of alcohol he left in his wake. He ranted loudly about the Shah. That was 1974. SAVAK had killed his brother. After that, he barely went out. He stayed home, lighting one cigarette with the butt of the last one, getting fat eating pizza on the couch. He walked around the house, his eyes hard with anger. His intellectualism took off then, and he wanted me to follow in his footsteps. It was the life he thought he should have pursued in the first place. He drank vodka like tap water and, between wet, disgusting burps, praised Sartre, recited Shamlou, and brandished an Ali Shariati book while he yelled incomprehensibly about the destructive consequences of blind Westernization.

Around this time he would sit across the dinner table from me, reading modern poetry out loud, nodding in thoughtful admiration, lifting his head after every stanza to make sure I appreciated the sublimity of it. He had given me an Albert Camus novel about a man who talks to a stranger in a bar about how he fell from grace. He stood over me while I read Ahmad Kasravi's *History of the Iranian Constitutional Revolution*, shaking his head at the narrative of lost causes.

He died not long after, in 1978. This was the year I started and stopped reading. In the last months of his life, he stayed put on a sofa across from the TV, frozen in time and place, absorbing everything the black box oozed out into the room.

The flow was interrupted by an image from the distant past flashing before my eyes. I was three or four. He had picked me up and thrown me up into the air. The sense of weightlessness as I looked down at his young face.

"Are you okay?" asked the man who had squeezed my balls.

"Yes," I said. I was barely in the room.

On the day he died, I woke up to my mother screaming my name. I jumped out of bed and ran to their room. My mother was at the door in her sleeping dress, her chest wet with tears. Behind her, my father was convulsing on the bed, in the throes of a heart attack. His body jerked up and down. He made incomprehensible sounds. Then the rasping failure of his lungs as froth seeped out and accumulated on his lips. The convulsions abated. His body settled into its death, leaving nothing but empty space. Into that empty space, a word, a string of five trembling letters, emerged.

"Abbas!" I screamed.

The man who had checked my asshole startled and bumped the desk. The other one tensed, ready to dive onto the floor should I throw a grenade.

"My father's name was Abbas."

I WAS BLINDFOLDED and led out of the room. On my way to a cell, I examined my new outfit. The light blue shirt was made of good cotton. It had big buttons and a roomy collar, and it hung comfortably over the loose pants cut from the same cloth. It reminded me of my father's favorite pajamas. But I hated the slippers. They were too big for me and made of cheap plastic. The spaces between my toes already felt sore. I stepped heavily so the slippers would clap loudly and annoyingly. The guard didn't care.

The cell door screamed open. From that point on, I would be alone. From the Azadi Street police station to Evin, guards and agents had surrounded me in cars and offices. Across the threshold awaited a coffin made especially for the buried-alive.

The guard pushed me forward. I took two steps and paused. The door slammed shut behind me. Sickly fluorescent light insinuated itself through the blindfold. I listened to the steps of the guard fading down the corridor and adjusted the eye cover to block out the brightness. It was my sole remaining protection against the reality of the cell. I was not ready to take it off.

I reached out to the sides. My right hand touched a wall and my left hand stretched into empty space. The cell width was longer than the span of my extended arms, which was good news.

I shuffled hesitantly toward the wall on the left. I had moved only a few inches before my palm encountered its bumpy and cold surface. I turned and leaned against it and slid down to the floor. A crisp breeze stroked my face. So the cell had a window. Another piece of good news. I wrapped my arms around my knees and rested my chin on my kneecaps.

Except for the guard and one or two interrogators, I was not going to see anyone for a while. The realization triggered a pang of loneliness. Then I thought of the people who had put me here. The man with the gray beard and suit who had accused me of acting against national security. The bald doctor. The officer who had grabbed my hand and found his palm coated with the blood of the beaten boy. The boy himself, whose youthful face I had destroyed. I recalled the worn faces of my colleagues and the countless passengers I had met fleetingly over the years. I had been part of the mosaic of people in the city, participating in the endless small encounters and interactions of daily life. Now I was alone.

Or was I? I had lived by myself for more than half my life. I knew too well what solitude was. This was not solitude. If anything, it was the denial of solitude. Compulsory loneliness was the opposite of the voluntary kind I had cultivated. They had ripped that away from me. If I was to survive this cell, I would need to wrest it back.

• • •

When I did take off the blindfold, I was immediately struck by the cleanliness of the cell. I had anticipated a suffocating shithole blanketed with cockroaches and rat droppings, but it was cleaner than my own apartment. New gray carpet covered the floor. The walls, a shade lighter than the carpet, looked recently painted. That light breeze had come through an opening high up near the ceiling covered by a mesh screen and protected by several oblique plastic blades. A sink was attached to the wall by the door, next to an absurdly small metal toilet bowl, next to a small radiator. The ceiling was as high as two apartment stories combined. A light bulb hung from it, enveloping the objects in the room in a deathly fluorescent halo.

I got up and tried to measure the cell with my steps. About forty square feet, I decided. I opened the plastic bag that had been placed on the floor in the middle of the room and laid out under the window the blankets it contained. I obsessively smoothed their wrinkles. I knew I would not sleep much the first night. The lamp was going to be on the whole time, and even worse, they hadn't given me a pillow. I again examined the walls, the sink, the toilet, and the door, like I was inspecting a property for purchase. Then I lay on the blankets to rest. I looked up and saw the writing.

The letters were too small to read from the floor, but they were undoubtedly words strung together into a sentence right above me on the ceiling. Without a ladder, the writer had to have been tall and exceptionally fit to be able to hoist himself up to the windowsill and must have had an extraordinary ability to maintain balance on his toes on the sill for quite a few seconds.

It dawned on me that more than half the Evin stories I had heard made mention of the graffiti on the cell walls. The light gray paint was recent. It was meant to cover whatever had been there before. Whoever wrote that line had gone out of his way to keep his message out of the reach of the brush. Maybe the man who had painted the walls, the contractor from outside prison, wrote it.

I stood up on my toes and squinted at it. The handwriting was neat, the curves carefully proportioned, the dots in the right spots, the words lined up straight. "You are not alone," I read. "I was here before you. I am thinking about you."

I read those sentences over and over until tears dimmed my view.

• • •

The first sound I heard was that of wheels turning on the floor, accompanied by footsteps. A square hatch opened in the door. The corridor light poured in, and I noticed for the first time the 98, my cell number, written above the doorframe. A head blocked the light for a moment, then the door opened with a loud clang and the cell was illuminated again. A guard entered.

"Hello," he said. He came in and looked around carefully. His straight, black hair was brushed back along the top of his head. His limbs were lightly muscled. A sparse beard covered his angular face. He reminded me of the boy I had beaten that morning, which by now felt like ancient times. In ten years that boy would look like this man, if his face wasn't destroyed beyond repair.

"I am Ehsan," the man said. "I am the guard for the cells in this row."

"I am Yunus."

He nodded. "Would you like some tea?"

"Yes, please."

The cell door opened wide to reveal the corridor. I saw a large cart outside my room carrying only a flask of tea and a dozen disposable cups.

"The row is quite empty these days," Ehsan said, apparently in explanation for why the huge cart carried such a small load. He handed me a cup of tea in an unexpectedly respectful manner, as though he were waiting on me at a fancy restaurant. His kind eyes and gentle demeanor were out of place for Evin.

He nodded and shut the door. I listened to the cart rolling away. The guard didn't pause until the end of the corridor. The cells on my row must have all been unoccupied.

I sat cross-legged on the blankets and stared at the cup of tea. I hadn't drunk any since morning. This was probably the first time in my adult life I had gone so long without tea. The hot bitterness of the first sip dried my mouth. I took another drink and felt the tea assert its dominance over my nerves, forcing them into a calmer state.

I thought of the last cup I had drunk before the strike. The day was started with a Golestan blend. The dark, black hyper-caffeinated liquid would turn my mouth into a desert. That was my way of settling myself before heading out to the terminal. The last five years I had drunk Golestan tea exclusively, big glasses morning and night, in the terminal and at the wheel. But the prison tea was much weaker than that. It was not the tea I'd had with Homa, the first time she came to my apartment. I had bought a pack of expensive Ceylon leaves many years before, only for guests. I opened it for the first time for her. We used to drink it before and after sex while we would talk. She always picked up the glass as soon as I put it on the table. Her lips pressed against the glass rim, returning my gaze as she tipped the vessel upward. She could unflinchingly take large quantities of hot tea.

What Ehsan had brought me in prison was not Ceylon. It was much cheaper, much older, and unmistakably from the north of Iran. The soil by the Caspian Sea makes its mark on tea leaves. It was even worse than what Behrouz had offered me at the first meeting in the basement of the stationery shop, where I was introduced as a new member of a study group formed by bus drivers who wanted to read books and discuss politics. That was the first time I saw an electric kettle and a pot kept warm on a hot metal surface. I immediately hated what I saw. I expected their tea to taste like shit, and I was going to make a comment about it to break the ice and get the other guys to stop staring at me so watchfully. But by the time I took the first sip, I was too nervous to think of a witty remark.

In the eighties, I took a silver thermos to work and refilled it four times a day. I would be at the wheel, wearing frilled trousers and a skimpy green shirt, a head full of curly hair styled in the outlandish fashion of the time, drinking it all day so I could tolerate the sight of the war-stricken city. I would prepare a mix of two packages of Earl Gray and a package of Ahmad. During the years of war, foreign tea was rare. Every other month I would go down to the Grand Bazaar and pester the tea sellers for unexpired bags. Sometimes I even went behind their shops to the storage area and sifted through the packages to find what I wanted. Every morning I put a spoonful of the mix into a thermos, which I refilled over and over with boiling water.

What Ehsan brought to the cell tasted nothing like this. I took another sip and dug further back, swimming into the haze of the past like a foolhardy driver venturing into unknown recesses of the ocean. Then everything came to a pause.

What it did taste like was Shahrazad tea. No doubt about it. The acrid, unmistakable Iranian black tea, which they had decided to mass-produce and dilute down to a pee-like color. I recalled the green paper box adorned with a picture of a black-haired, black-eyed woman peeking over the rim of an ornate cup. This was the tea of my youth, which my mother had brewed at the stove twice a day.

At that point, our kitchen floor was covered with a large woven rug. It was lined with wooden cabinets that held zinc bowls and delicate tea glasses and a thousand different spices. My mom would pour tea from the teapot, then weaken it with the boiled water of the kettle. I used to stand by the kitchen door, lanky and shy. My mom would glance at me expressionlessly in those days, before she walked past me into the sitting room to watch TV.

In the summer of 1979, I turned nineteen. The country was still reeling from the revolution, but we hardly noticed. My father had died in the last days of 1978, relegating the country's exultation to the periphery of our experience. I witnessed the ousting of the Shah and the arrival of Khomeini with a confusing mix of sorrow and joy, acutely aware of my father's absence. It was like watching a film my father would have loved but knowing he never would see it. My mother was in no better shape than I was. We sat passively in front of the TV and observed the country turning inside out. Without him, the import of the news could find no purchase in our home.

During one of the formless days after my father's death, I poured myself tea and took my seat on the sofa in the sitting room. I had angled it so that I could see the TV and my mother simultaneously. She shook out four pills from two different bottles into her palm and swallowed them. By this time, her obsession with cleanliness and her love of cooking had disappeared. She left her keys behind, took the wrong buses, bought the wrong things when she went shopping. After she took her pills, she couldn't walk in a straight line. She moved through the world like an apparition. Nothing stuck to her.

The television screen showed a mullah with a sleep-inducing voice giving a speech about the Ninth Imam. I took my cup of tea to my room and sat by the window. An unexpected spring shower had come and gone, and my favorite moment had arrived: the brief time when the rain has ended but the sun is yet to emerge, when the clouds whiten and sparrows chirp. The sky cracked open and sunbeams stretched toward the earth, but no sound followed and nothing moved. No chatter of birds, no rustle of leaves. Not even a roar from car engines.

Then the door to our house slammed shut right beneath my window. My mom, holding two empty grocery bags, staggered down the sidewalk. She had decided to go shopping. The doctor had emphasized that she should not leave the house right after she took her pills. She remembered this for two weeks, then doubled the dose of the medication without consulting the doctor and forgot about the rule.

Half an hour later, the bell rang, first briefly and hesitantly, then as a continuous, ear-piercing shriek.

Salar, the boy from across the street, lifted his finger off it only when I opened the door.

"What's going on?" I asked.

He opened his mouth but couldn't get any words out. Then, he pointed to the road. I followed the finger and saw a few people gathering around something. Salar turned and ran toward them. I followed him barefooted, the hot asphalt stinging my feet with every step.

The post of a streetlamp had penetrated halfway into the hood of a Chevrolet Nova and was sticking up from its engine like a ship's mast. A man, presumably the driver, was slumped on the curb, crying violently. In the street, five other men had formed a semicircle around a body. Salar joined them and said something. Their heads turned. They were all neighbors.

Lying there, my mom had a relaxed appearance, though a third of her face had gone purple. Her eyes were half open. She stared at the world without seeing it, the way she had followed the revolution on TV. Her left hand was swollen, and her arm met her shoulder at an awkward angle. Her right knee had bent all the way in, her calf pressed hard behind her thigh. I felt an urge to reach down to her and straighten her limbs, but the gaze of those five men paralyzed me. Moreover, she had never liked to be touched. At that moment, I thought of my father's funeral at Behesht-e Zahra cemetery. When they lowered his body down, she had thrown herself on his grave. Clad in black, with sunglasses, she poured dirt on her head, scratched her face, screamed, and punched at the soil.

Why did you do that? I silently asked her mangled corpse in the street. *Why did you get so upset over the death of my father?* It was the question I had wanted to ask and had never dared. That man had turned the last five years of our lives into a living hell. It had been a relief to get rid of him.

One of the men put his hand on my shoulder. The touch rent the thread of my thoughts. I shrugged him off and stepped back. They all turned to me, guilt written on their faces. A bus pulled over at the stop around the corner. People were getting on board, keeping one eye on the accident. I took off running and jumped on before the driver closed the door. People stared at my bare feet. I took a seat by a window.

The revolution had entered my life through TV, and up until that moment I had not seen firsthand how the city had changed. The streets and buildings were familiar, but nothing else was. I didn't know that every kid in our neighborhood was now armed with weapons they had gotten during the fight in the Eshratabad barracks, or that they had taken over the duties of traffic police in the absolute chaos that followed the revolution. I hadn't seen the checkpoints that had popped up on every street to help with the manhunt for the fugitive Shah's people. I didn't know how the number of men with beards and women in chador had skyrocketed overnight.

I got off the bus at the last stop, at a remote corner of Tehran I had never visited. The air was cooler and the empty street was lined with leafy maples that shielded from the strong sun its neat, two-story houses with big front yards. It must have been far north, way above the Vanak line. I crossed the street and sat at the stop on the other side. I got on the next bus that opened its doors without reading its destination sign.

An hour later, another unknown corner of Tehran exposed itself to me. The bus traveled down a highway flanked by vast stretches of sparsely inhabited prairie. My window offered an unimpeded view of the snowcapped mountains to the north.

We followed a westward route through large swaths of empty lands and reached a terminal outside the perimeter of the city. I switched to another bus there and came back into the city, where I caught another bus at Valiasr Square that took me to the Grand Bazaar and Khaniabad.

I got home at three in the morning. I opened the door but had trouble going in. The house smelled of death. I lay down by the shoes in the entryway and fell into a fitful, three-hour sleep. As soon as my eyes opened, I went far enough into the house to grab some money, and then I ran back out to the bus stop.

For the next several days, I spent all my waking hours in buses, traversing the city. I got back to the house after midnight, slept by the shoe rack, and left as soon as my eyes opened. Through the windows of the buses, I witnessed Tehran shedding its old skin. People my age stood at crossroads selling books with red and white covers embossed with the faces of Marx and Mao, recruiting pedestrians into their armed groups. Their yells clashed in the air with socialist Muslims peddling treatises of Mohammad Nakhshab and Ali Shariati. Posters and billboards of the Shah had all been taken down and replaced with images of Khomeini and Yasser Arafat. A citywide effort to defile the deposed Shah was underway. Self-declared street comedians emerged, putting on shows at every corner, mocking the Shah's posh accent, gait, and demeanor for audiences of idle passersby. As a new recreational activity, people around the city set effigies of the Shah and his siblings on fire or propped them up as targets for stone throwers. Among this mad carnival roamed solemn-faced youths, Kalashnikovs hanging off their shoulders.

I couldn't get over how many people there were. It was as if the population of Tehran had doubled overnight. A turbulent ocean of bodies that rose and fell, crashed over curbs, and lapped against walls. Long queues in front of cinemas, vendors squeezed cheek by jowl along all the main streets, packed restaurants and parks. The old was gone and the new was yet to emerge, and people battled for the chance to own the city.

On the fourth morning, on a bus that went from Hasanabad to Baharestan, I sat across from a girl. She was my age, with a round face haloed by a mass of wild, curly hair. She was staring at me with small, black eyes. I returned the gaze, feeling something new for the first time since my mother's death. Her green skirt draped gracefully over her crossed legs, and she wore a long-sleeved shirt.

We both got off in Baharestan Square, in front of the heavily guarded parliament building. She walked up toward the Pol-e Choubi. I had intended to change buses but followed her up the street instead. Three blocks over, she turned around.

"Hi," she said.

"Sorry," I said.

"Why?"

"I don't know. I thought it was inappropriate to follow you."

"Stop following, then. Come walk with me."

I joined her.

"What's your name?"

"Yunus. Yours?"

"Simin."

She walked hesitantly, her head constantly bobbing around, like she was a deer braving a predator-infested terrain.

"This is my last day in Iran," she said.

"Where are you going?"

"America."

"Alone?"

"With my parents and brother."

"I'm jealous."

"I hate to leave."

"Maybe it's good to leave now. It's pretty fucked up here."

"I know. What do you do?"

I gave the question some thought. "Nothing."

"Nothing at all?"

"I just lost my mom."

"I'm so sorry to hear that."

"I lost my dad last year."

She stopped walking. "Who is taking care of you?"

Tears clawed at my throat. I held them down to seem strong. "I can take care of myself," I said.

We walked a block in silence.

"Do you want a drink?" She paused by a kiosk and, without waiting for my response, bought two Coca-Colas.

"So you'll be in America tomorrow. Isn't that crazy?"

"Actually we are going to Israel first."

"Why Israel?"

"I'm Jewish."

"Oh."

She paused, stared at me and took a large sip from her drink without averting her eyes. "Do you have a problem with that?"

"With being Jewish? Not at all."

"You said 'Oh.' "

"I didn't mean anything. Why would I have a problem with that?"

"Jews are not exactly popular these days."

"Really?"

"I don't know. That's what my dad says. I don't know anything about it myself."

We walked another block in silence. On Enqelab Street, the stores were closed and the walls were black with graffiti. A swarm of people got off a bus and enveloped us on all sides before thinning out again. At Ferdowsi Square, she turned into a cul-de-sac and walked to the end of it. I followed her without saying anything. She opened a door and stepped inside. I paused on the threshold, waiting for her to invite me in. She didn't. When the silence lingered long enough to make her intention clear, I stepped back.

"It was nice talking to you," she said. I nodded. She shut the door.

• • •

That night, I opened the door at home and found my aunt Soraya waiting for me. She took me with her. I stayed with her husband and their son for six months. In the meantime, a lawyer sold my parents' house, deposited half the money in a bank account, and bought me an apartment in Aryashahr.

My aunt's plan for her son became her plan for me too. Fancy high school, then an engineering diploma from a Tehran state college. But I had already made up my mind. The buses had saved my life. If that driver hadn't pulled over when he did, I'm not sure

I would've survived the death of my mother. Riding around the city had brought me back to the world.

Behind my aunt's back, I took classes for driving heavy vehicles. The day I got my license, I applied to become a bus driver in Tehran.

THE GRATING OF THE CELL DOOR woke me up. The light from the bulb on the ceiling pained my eyes. For a moment, I thought it was my father. He had the habit of turning on my bedroom light in the morning to wake me up for school. As consciousness returned, I remembered that he was dead, and the brightness surprised me. In my apartment, I never forgot to switch off the light before going to sleep. Only after I became aware of the uniform grayness of my surroundings did I remember where I was.

I looked around the cell. The fluorescent light was on but the sun had managed to force its beams through the slats covering the window, which cast four thin lines of shadow on the wall. The cell was not much brighter than it had been in the night, but there was a feeling of morning. The walls were a little less ashy. Their texture looked coarser in the daylight. I gazed at the writing on the ceiling and read it again to myself.

I exhaled, then became aware that someone was standing in the doorway staring at me. Another few seconds passed before I recognized him. I rolled over slowly like an invalid and propped my body up on my elbows. Drops of sweat slid down my forehead and burned my eyes, blurring Ehsan's form. I blinked the sting away and wiped my forehead with my hand.

"Good morning," he said.

I nodded and lay back down.

"Put on your blindfold, please. Your case officer is going to meet you."

The more this man talked, the more I liked him. My rational mind warned against it. But spending twenty-five years at the wheel, examining hundreds of faces per day, exchanging thousands of little words and brief glances, had exercised my first-impression muscles. Everyone's character is written all over his face and in his tone. My gut told me that those kindly light brown eyes and the honest set of the jaw could not belong to an evil man.

I threw off the blanket and moved to rise, but a sudden coldness around my groin made me freeze. I was shocked to see drying semen gluing the prison pants to my skin and a large wet spot darkening the fabric right around my penis. Moving caused slime to slide down my thigh.

Ehsan noticed and stoically maintained a neutral face. I scrambled to cover myself with the blanket, like a teenager trying to hide a morning erection from his parents. Ehsan averted his eyes and looked down the corridor, giving me time to deal with the fiasco.

"I can't go to the interrogation like this," I said. "I have to clean myself."

Ehsan looked at his watch.

"Get your towel. You have to be quick."

The shower room was far larger than I expected. White ceramic tiles covered the walls of two intimidating rows of stalls. I walked to the end of the row and back. Only one stall was occupied. The sounds of splashing water varied in cadence and intensity as the man went through his washing routine. I went to a stall in the middle that looked cleaner than the others and I turned on the hot water as high as it would go. Ropes of water lashed down on me. The stinging spray simultaneously burned and soothed my skin. I had to take advantage of the few extra minutes Ehsan had given me to get ready to devise an interrogation strategy. I thought back to Habib Samadi.

· · ·

Three days before the bus drivers' strike, we received a message instructing us to leave work early and park our buses in the terminal at 2 p.m. We would then head downtown to the union building. The message emphasized that no more than two people should go together at a time to avoid drawing attention.

The union building had become my favorite place in the city. Decades ago the bakers, who had formed the first labor organization in Iran, saved money one rial at a time to buy a space other unions could share as headquarters. It was a large, two-story building with five rooms downstairs and a sizable conference area on the second floor. An old sycamore, two pines, and a tangle of roses grew outside in the spacious backyard. Miraculously, the building had survived three regime changes and the sharp teeth of construction moguls.

Six months before the strike, I had gone there for the first time. In the conference area, I had sat on a folding chair among fifty other shoemakers, bakers, construction workers, and car mechanics. An old man had handed out copies of the Constitution. Someone else stood up in front of us and introduced himself as a worker's rights lawyer. He went on to explain Articles 26 and

46 and other parts of the Constitution that gave rights to laborers and protesters. From then on, I had attended all the workshops and meetings, gotten friendly with the younger members and union leaders and lawyers, and learned the history of the various unions that met there.

That day, I arrived before the other bus drivers. More than a hundred folding chairs were set up in rows on the second floor. Two large flasks of tea and trays of cookies were laid out on a long, narrow table against the wall.

I went out of the building to watch the evening traffic. Cars on both sides of the road, stretched out as far as the eye could see, coughed out a pall of smoke that spoiled the smooth, spring air. Every day I saw the city from the pedestal of my driver's seat, caring only about what other drivers did insofar as it was relevant to my own maneuvering. From the sidewalk, though, the passengers in the cars were far more interesting. Exhausted taxi drivers pulled hard on their cigarettes and emitted billows of smoke, as if in competition with the tailpipes of their cars. Bored children looked out the back-seat windows at the sea of metal and smog with sleepy eyes. In three days, when the strike would be on and the whole city would turn into a parking lot, these people would be nostalgic for this traffic. A few bus drivers passed by and nodded at me as they entered the building.

Back inside, more drivers had gone up to the second floor. They were sitting around, laughing with each other and sipping tea. A sense of detachment grew in me. I thought about how irresponsible they were, that they had jumped on board without considering the consequences. Finding an easy way to reframe my own fear, I told myself sanctimoniously that joining the strike amounted to tormenting people. After I dithered awhile at the door of the room, I went down the stairs again to go home.

At the entrance to the building, I ran into Ibrahim.

"You just arrived?" he asked.

"Yes," I said like a coward, looking at the crossroad. Had I left a minute earlier, I could have flagged down a taxi and been home before dark.

"The strike is getting bigger by the hour," he said. "I feel like I am living a different life. I never thought I'd be part of something this important."

"I know what you mean," I said.

Ibrahim smoked two cigarettes and talked while I nodded along. Pedestrians passed by and around us like waves sliding past the columns under the piers at the beach.

"How will people react, do you think? Will they support us?" I asked him.

"Of course." Ibrahim looked at me, taken aback. He put out his cigarette, took me by the shoulders and pushed me in. "People will love us. Don't worry about it."

On the second floor, the first row was occupied by people in suits. I had seen some of them in union meetings, but most of them didn't look familiar. A man at the door welcomed Ibrahim and me the way a host welcomes guests at a wedding ceremony and offered us tea and cookies. I picked a chair in the last row with the worst view of the speaker.

More and more bus drivers were arriving. When the room was full, a frail, bearded man stood up in front. He looked at the crowd, taking its measure with satisfaction.

"Dear comrades," he said. The room immediately quieted

down. "Let me start by stating the obvious: it is to the benefit of all that what is said in this room stays in this room. Our committee is sure that we can fully trust every one of you."

He looked around the gathering to gauge our reaction to this. His eyes met mine for a fraction of a second. I responded to his look as coldly as I could.

"Your very presence here indicates that we are on the right track, that we didn't overestimate the sense of solidarity among the members and friends of our union."

People in the first row clapped. The rest of the crowd followed them.

"Now," the man said once the applause faded, "let me be clear. I am not going to minimize the danger we will inevitably face on the day of the strike. It will be hard, and we need to prepare ourselves. So, with other comrades in the central committee, we decided to have this meeting to discuss the potential risks. We also want to talk about what to do if you get arrested. For this, we have invited an old veteran of the union, someone who has devoted his life to our cause: Habib Samadi."

We clapped hard. Among the union people, Habib Samadi was a legend. He was a reclusive hero who had spent much of his life in prison, had fought both regimes, before and after the revolution, and during the hard days of war almost singlehandedly had kept the union alive. We all had heard many rumors about his time in jail. He had gone on hunger strikes and had written long, widely read letters from prison. Some of the more ardent union members knew passages from these by heart. Yet very few people had actually met him. Pictures of him were old and often faded.

Habib rose in the front of the room to a standing ovation. He looked very different from what I had anticipated. He was short and stodgy, with Khomeini-like eyebrows and disheveled, sparse white hair. Decades of suffering had squeezed the life out of his limbs and skin. What vitality remained to him was concentrated in his eyes. He watched the crowd like a sniper and cut to the chase as soon as the clapping stopped.

"First thing you need to keep in mind," he said, "is that you need to be ready for prison every day. As soon as politics touches you, you are contaminated for good. It's a virus that never gets cured. The first and best piece of advice is, if you want to be in politics, zip up three things: your pants, your pockets, and your mouth. Which is to say: Don't fuck around. Don't accept suspicious money. Don't talk to people you don't trust. When the government focuses on an activist, it looks for ways to get leverage. But keeping these things zipped isn't even enough because you had a life before getting into politics. They can always find out about your past and hold it against you. So start with clearing your traces. Think hard about what you have done. If you use email, go through your inbox and shift-delete every message that is remotely provocative or suspicious, including those sent from groups you didn't sign up for. Don't leave comments on blogs and websites. The internet is new, and we still don't fully know how it works or how safe it is. Next step, erase the traces of your activity from your house. They will search every inch of it if they come after you. Never keep letters from political dissidents or lovers. Get rid of drugs and alcohol, porn, and forbidden books."

I went through his checklist in my head. I didn't use email and had never gone online. As for the only lover I ever had, her texts were all deleted and she never sent me letters. No drugs, alcohol, porn, or forbidden books either. I looked at the scared faces of other drivers. Everyone seemed to have something to worry about, to take care of as soon as they left the meeting. No one's life was as barren as mine.

"So let's say you take all those precautions and go to the strike. You go up against the police, you create a crisis in the city. It is going to be dangerous. There is a good chance you will get arrested. Even if you get away on the day of the strike, they might still come after you. The fact that you are sitting here today means they probably have a file on you already."

Habib paused to let these words sink in. My heart banged against my rib cage. I was like a boy playing with a toy dragon that all of a sudden started emitting real fire. Those long hours of union meetings and study group, all the impassioned talk of solidarity and the liberation of the oppressed, none of that had prepared me for this reality check.

Around me, men expressed various degrees of discomfort. The left foot of the person next to me tapped up and down. The man in front of me had wrapped his arms tightly around himself. The guy next to him intertwined his fingers and pressed them together so hard his knuckles were white. Most of these people were like me: well-meaning little guys who enjoyed the union meetings because the bosses pissed them off and they wanted a better life. Like me, they hadn't realized how far in over their heads they were.

"As for the day of the strike," Habib continued, "don't drink much tea. Nothing matters more than focus and control when you are up against the police. A full bladder is distracting."

The people in the first row chuckled. The rest of the crowd remained silent.

"But eat well. You never know. If they catch you, you will have to go without food for at least several hours. Wear comfortable shoes. Do some stretching in the morning. Chances are you'll be forced to run, and your muscles may cramp if you are too stiff. However, it is very possible for you to take all these measures and get caught. If that happens, they will first take you to the police station for paperwork. There you should be respectful and calm. Don't waste your energy on bureaucrats. Then you go to jail. Either right away or they will come and pick you up in a few days. Then you are in Evin."

Habib paused at this. A fearful silence hung over the room.

"Being in Evin is not the big deal that you think it is. There are two reasons for you to be there. First, they want you off the streets. You have identified yourself as a troublemaker, and they want to keep you tucked away until the dust settles. Second, they want to collect information from you about other troublemakers. There are a few more rules about how to survive in prison. I would take note and study them tonight if I were you."

As far as I could see, no one had brought pen and paper. Drivers fidgeted and twiddled their fingers in silence.

"You should never trust anyone in prison. I can't overstate this. Never believe a word of what you hear, especially those uttered by people who seem like the most God-fearing, sincerest, kindest humans on Earth. You should also put together a life story. Take your real one and remove from it anything that would raise suspicion. Write it down and memorize it. Even when they show you concrete evidence that doesn't fit what you said, deny it.

81

Your interrogators are trained to make you contradict yourself, so you have to stick with what you told them. And never lose your temper. They will provoke you. They will humiliate, insult, threaten, beat you. Keep it together. Remind yourself that it's not personal. It's their job. During the interrogations, it always helps to be terse. Never talk or write more than the question requires. Every single extra word can become an arrow in their quiver. Your body language is extremely important. They are trained to notice the slightest movement of your eyes, all your fidgets and twitches. Every time they detect weakness, they will take advantage of it. However, this cuts both ways. Your interrogators are human beings. They have strengths and weaknesses too. Be open to them and see them as humans. This can help you manipulate them."

Across the room a chair scraped. A man stood up and walked around the perimeter of the hall with conspicuous nervousness and poured himself a cup of tea. Another man followed him. Then another one. The crowd had decided that it needed a break.

"The last and most important point," Habib yelled, and the moving drivers froze in place. "Think it through. If you have doubts, and I mean any doubts of any sort, don't do it. If you are not sure, don't go. Don't do something like this just because you don't want to be called a coward."

WHERE ARE YOU, YUNUS?" Ehsan called. "Come out. It's late."

On the way to the interrogation room, I tried to make a mental map of our route. The walk was longer than I had expected. We took two U-turns, and the corridors lightened and darkened. I counted our steps. We took seventy-four before we turned around. Then seventy-four again. Clearly we were walking in a loop. Ehsan was trying to disorient me. I was offended that a prison guard thought he could do that to a bus driver.

Halfway through our third lap around the corridors, Ehsan paused to knock on a door. Its hinges screeched, and the light filtering through the blindfold intensified. From under my eye covering, I could see the shoes of the man who had opened the door. A black leather pair, narrow in the middle and pointed at the tip, disproportionately long, outdated patterning on top.

Ehsan patted me on the back and left. The echo of his footsteps in the corridor soon disappeared.

"I know you can see from under the blindfold," the man said. I immediately recognized the voice of Hajj Saeed.

"Come on in," he said. His pointed shoes retreated from my

view. I stepped into the room, my mind racing over what I remembered about him—his love of holding forth on political matters, his arrogance, his penchant for dominating junior officers.

"Go to the other side and sit down," he said. Then he threw his body onto a chair behind a desk.

The interrogation room was almost twice the size of my cell. As I walked across it, I noted the corner of the withered, wooden desk where he was sitting and the tip of his shoe hanging in the air. I sat down on a folding chair with a tablet arm that faced the wall. The tablet took up the entirety of my constricted field of vision. Words and shapes, layered on top of each other, were carved all over the old, wood surface, engraved over the years by pens and any other blunt objects prisoners could get their hands on. The marks on the wood represented a collaboration by prisoners across generations leaving messages for each other. The tablet was much thinner than it should have been. They must have sanded away layers to remove some of the marks, but it was impossible to obliterate them all. I gazed at the profile of a woman rendered in five broken lines and the muzzle of a dog with its tongue out. Around them letters and half-words and signs hinting at obscure meanings appeared, like ciphers on an ancient palimpsest.

Hajj Saeed put a pile of blank paper and a blue Bic pen in front of me and walked back to his desk.

"You know why you are here?" he asked.

"No."

"You don't."

"Yesterday I was accused of acting against national security."

"Well?"

"I don't know what that means."

He faked a laugh, which tapered into a groan and jumped to his feet. His chair emitted creaks of relief. He marched back and forth in the room, clopping the hard soles of his shoes on the concrete floor as if to help me follow his trajectory. Three steps from my chair to the door. Pause. Three steps across the room. Pause. He retraced the walk and stood over me. From under the blindfold I saw the shadow of his upper body on the paper. His lungs whistled softly as he breathed. He sounded like a lifelong smoker, but he didn't smell like one. He must have quit not long before.

His shadow stayed frozen for a few seconds before it expanded as he bent over me. He came so close I could smell his body. His odor was an aging man's. Hearing him in the car, I had placed him in his mid-fifties. Now he seemed to be at least a decade older than that. As seasoned and battle-hardened as he was, the man was probably incapable of interrogating me for long hours. I should delay and postpone and tire him out.

The shadow kept expanding until it darkened the entire arm of the chair. His warm breath tickled my earlobe. His nostrils droned as he inhaled. He loudly swallowed some saliva.

"What does it say here?" he whispered in my ear, his index finger on the paper. The finger was bony, pale, and smooth. The nail was one week old and clean. My estimation of his age was challenged again. The hand might as well belong to a woman.

"Read it!" he yelled into my ear. My body startled, and I hit the arm of the chair with my knee. The papers slid off and scattered all over the floor.

Hajj Saeed's shadow lifted. Light poured over me again. He

stepped back and hit my shoulder. "Look at what you did. Pick it all up!"

He walked heavily across the room to his seat, which creaked again as he sat down. My body was cramped with anger. I remembered the words of Habib and told myself that I should deny him the pleasure of enraging me. From under the blindfold I tried to see where the papers had fallen, then I pushed the chair away, making as much noise as I could. I got down on my knees and groped around. The man was old, I reminded myself. Be slow and tire him out.

I collected the papers and sat back in the chair. Its joints squeaked. Hajj Saeed walked back over to me and leaned in again, putting his mouth within an inch of my face. He whispered, "What's written here?" and put his finger on the Arabic quote printed at the top of the page.

"*Al-Nejaat fi al-Sidq*," I read with my best pronunciation.

"What does it mean?"

"Be truthful to be saved."

"Salvation lies in honesty!" he yelled, again into my ear. Having anticipated him screaming again, my body absorbed the shock, and my limbs barely flinched. He paused, seemingly disappointed that his trick hadn't yielded the same result this time. He stood up and stepped away. "Salvation lies in honesty!" he repeated. "You know who said that?"

"No."

"Prophet Muhammad himself. But you communists never—"

"I'm not a communist."

The click of his soles stopped. He turned and put his mouth back against my ear.

"What did you say?"

"I just said I am not—"

"Never interrupt me again!" he yelled, so loudly his voice coarsened. My knees jolted up again and hit the armrest. The papers flew everywhere.

"Pick up the papers."

I got down on the ground.

"Yunus," he said.

My hand froze as it reached toward one of the sheets. Hearing my name come from his mouth was nauseating. I wanted to pluck the sound out of the air and shove it back down his gullet.

"Tell me, Yunus," he said, "where are we now?"

"Evin?"

"That's true. What does that word mean to you? When you think of Evin, what comes to your mind?"

"I don't know."

"Yes, you do."

"Well, it's a prison."

"That's exactly the problem. This is not a prison. You are not in a prison. Do you know what this place is?"

I collected the papers slowly, pretending to be thinking.

"A correctional facility. You probably won't believe me, but I am not here to protect the system from you. I know that's what Habib told you in the meeting."

I imagined him in the room where Habib had talked to us. The thought paralyzed me.

"The system is not afraid of you. It wants to help people like you, hardworking folks who have good souls, to get back on track. You need to understand that you are here not because you participated in the strike or beat the shit out of the son of the transportation minister."

Another shock. My grip loosened. Two papers fell to the floor.

"You are here because you have a soul. I know what you have gone through, losing your parents at a sensitive age like you did, working so hard all these years. Do you understand?"

I picked up the papers again and focused on regaining my composure. He walked toward his desk.

"There are a few by the wall to your right," he said. "Do you know Ehsan Tabari?"

"Yes," I said, though I couldn't quite place who he was. Then I regretted the knee-jerk response. I might have stupidly gotten myself into trouble.

"Of course you do. You all talked about him in your study group."

I considered this with a sinking feeling. We did talk about Tabari in the context of someone else's work, so briefly I could hardly remember it. He had something to do with a Marxist who converted to Islam under torture in Evin.

"My old boss interrogated Tabari," Hajj Saeed continued. "I had just started working here and got the chance to follow that case closely. How much do you know about him?"

I tried hard to recall what we had said. Tabari had come up in one of the first meetings I had attended. So they had monitored those from the beginning. I finished collecting the papers and sat back down on the chair.

"We tried a whole new method on Tabari. Before him, we had various ways of drawing information out of the people we hosted here. With Tabari, my mentor decided to get into his brain. We knew that if he came to our side, the Tudeh Party would lose its intellectual powerhouse and probably dissolve. So my mentor read all his books, studied the history of Marxism and imperialism, consulted scholars of Islam, and put together a counterargument for everything Tabari believed in. The interrogation session became a debate between two intellectual peers. I know you people think he was tortured into confession, but he wasn't. My mentor convinced him."

Hajj Saeed's shadow appeared briefly over the pile of papers as he moved to stand right behind me. I struggled to remember more about Tabari. One bit surfaced: Tabari's interrogator was Hossein Shariatmadari. If Hajj Saeed trained with him, I needed to be concerned.

"I witnessed how Tabari changed. I heard him sobbing through the night, when there were no guards around, no pressure on him to act in a way we liked. He repented and prayed and begged God for forgiveness. I know you don't believe that."

"No, I do believe that," I said in an earnest tone, hoping to pacify him.

"That is the method I have followed throughout my career. I want a conversation here. I want to discuss ideas."

"I'd love that."

"Good. But before getting there, I need to know you better and make sure you are honest with me. You have done things that keep me from trusting you right away. The trust needs to be built."

"What have I done?"

He moved away, then returned and walked around me, looking at my profile from both sides, like he had just cut my hair.

"There are a couple of things you need to understand before we start," he said. "Like any other prisoner, you probably think you are being treated unfairly. That's something you should get out of your mind."

He paced around the room in silence. I had learned the pattern: three steps to the end of the room, three steps back, retracing over and over the path to my chair.

"I have been doing this for twenty-five years, as long as you have been a bus driver. You know how many people I interrogated here who were absolutely innocent?"

"No," I said when his long pause indicated that he was actually waiting for an answer.

"What's your guess?"

"I have no idea."

"Zero. Over the last twenty-five years, I haven't met a single person who was brought to this place for no reason at all. Yes, our system is not flawless. Injustice happens, personal mistakes damage the process. But none of the people I encountered in the rooms of this prison were totally innocent. Do you understand me?"

I stared at a shape carved into the tablet arm. I moved the papers over to see its full outline but couldn't tell what it was.

"When Habib told you about in this place, did he mention the writing in the yard in the Shah's time?"

"No."

"Before the revolution, when you stepped into Evin, there was writing on the wall that said, 'There is no God in this place.' Have you ever heard that?"

"No."

"We painted over it after the revolution because, unlike you, we are Muslims and we do believe that God is everywhere. But between you and me, whoever wrote that thing on the wall had a point. I am going to tell you why."

I nodded.

"Now, you are here, for whatever reason. It means that you are standing at a fork. One path goes to hell, the other path to freedom. It is up to you to make your decision. My job is to report your decision to the court. If you are sincere and collaborative, I will ask them to let you go. If you defy me, you are fucked. Do you understand?"

Hajj Saeed moved away from me and paused in the middle of the room.

"I don't have anything personal against you, you know. Actually, I consider myself your protector. If you're honest with me, I will do everything in my power to help you out of here."

He resumed his theatrical pacing and talked as he walked.

"But you can obviously pick the other path. You can try to fool or outwit me, send me on a wild-goose chase. For you, that is the path to hell. So you get to choose. But before you do that, since we are getting along so well, I want to give you a tip: if you decide to fuck with me, I'll destroy you. You will regret what you did for the rest of your life, which will wind up being pretty short. You know why?" He brought his mouth to my ear again. "You know why?" he yelled.

My ears rang, but I didn't flinch. I shook my head, staring at the shadow of his head on the papers.

"Because in this room," he whispered, "I am the god."

The staff in prison loved performance. The man who told me what I was accused of, the other man who checked my asshole, now Hajj Saeed. They all seemed like they were imitating movie characters. Only Ehsan behaved naturally. The half-circle shadow of Hajj Saeed's head grew larger on the papers.

"Did you hear what I said?"

"Yes."

His shoes clicked away. A drawer in his desk groaned open. He returned to me, picked up the stack of papers, and replaced it with a new one. This pile looked the same, and the page on top had the same heading. However, a question was handwritten on the blank paper.

"Answer this. Very simple stuff."

"Okay."

"This is the first step. Keep in mind that you are standing at a fork."

"I have nothing to hide."

"Good." He moved back to his chair.

The question was about family members. Their names and jobs, political affiliations, how they died. My father, Abbas Turabi, was killed by a heart attack in November 1978. My mother, Narges Zafardoust, died in a car accident in April 1979. No, none of them had been affiliated with any political party. No other members of my family ever had been. The next page. Write down what you have been accused of.

"For the accusation question, should I write what I was told yesterday?"

"Remind me what it was."

"Activity against national security."

Hajj Saeed laughed preciously, like he was listening to a child uttering a fancy phrase.

"Write that you are accused of sedition against the Islamic Republic."

I found the pomposity of the new phrasing simultaneously hilarious and frightening. I wrote it down. No, I never had been affiliated with any political party or activist group. I thought of mentioning the union, but the union was not a political party. Don't write more than needed, Habib had advised.

"I'm done," I said.

"Already?"

"Yes."

Hajj Saeed came and picked up the papers. I saw more remnants of words scratched into the arm and another shape I hadn't noticed before. Six jagged lines, four dots, a curve, carved to different depths. It looked like the work of multiple people over the years.

"You disappoint me, Yunus," he said. I wished he would stop saying my name. "After all I said. All I asked was that you not lie to me. I asked you to build trust, so we could develop friendship and I could help you out of here. And you give me this garbage."

"Everything there is true."

"So I must be lying, then."

"No, I didn't—"

"Yunus," he cut me off and started to pace again. "Tell me. Have you ever seen those American movies that are set in a court?"

"I don't think so."

"You probably have. Our TV loves to show them."

"I don't watch much TV."

"I know that. Anyway. You have to take an oath before answering questions."

"Yes."

"You know what it is?"

"No."

"You are required to swear to tell the truth, the whole truth, and nothing but the truth. Why all three? Why is telling the truth not enough?"

"I don't know."

"Because telling a part of the truth means hiding other parts, which amounts to lying."

"I didn't lie."

"You are not listening to me."

"You can go and check everything I wrote."

He bent over me, his breath on the back of my ear. "You know how many people I have interrogated?"

"No."

"Take a guess."

"Seventy-five," I said wildly.

"You are the hundred eighty-fourth," he said, uttering every digit emphatically, giving me time to appreciate the magnitude of his accomplishment. Then he moved back toward his desk.

"I can read every prisoner's character as soon as I see them. Usually even before the meeting, when I go through their file. To tell you the truth, I expected you to be sneaky, suspicious, and untruthful. I wished you had proved me wrong."

"I didn't lie."

Hajj Saeed exhaled noisily, then opened a drawer and rummaged through it.

"You realize that this is the second time you are calling me a liar?"

"I wrote everything I know about my family."

"The third time."

One patch of the tablet arm was curiously black. Idly, I wondered what I would carve there if I had a tool. Hajj Saeed's shadow imposed itself on the spot.

"How about Mustafa and Morteza Golshahi?"

It took me less than a day to learn that Evin was a time warp. It manipulated the order of your memories, messed with your conception of the relation between events. The past could be visible and prominent, the present faded. Memories of my parents came to hunt me down, yet my recollection of my life as a bus driver before the day of the strike had withered away. These names bent time further. Almost thirty years had passed since the last time I had seen my uncles. They had led a widely feared guerrilla group that had fought the Shah. SAVAK had killed them shortly before the revolution, after they had taken over a police station outside Tehran. That was all I knew. I hadn't thought of them once in twenty-five years.

"What about them?" I asked.

"You wrote here none of your relatives engaged in politics."

"They died before the revolution."

"Where in the question does it say anything about whether it's before or after the revolution?"

"They fought the Shah. All the leaders of this country after the revolution fought against the Shah at some point."

"What about the group?"

"What group?"

"The Golshahis'."

"I don't know them."

"They have been in touch with you."

"No. I don't even know who they are."

He smacked me on the back of my head. Something lurched inside my skull. The slap ruined my poise for a second. An urge to rise and strike back seized me. I regained control of myself, my hands clutching white-knuckled at my chair.

"So that you know you can't get away with lying in this room."

Hajj Saeed stalked along his favorite path twice in silence, like a father who regretted beating his son but was not willing to apologize. While he was walking, I thought in silence. Flashes from the news came back to me. The Golshahis had assassinated the Tehran police chief. I remembered the headline. They had killed the former warden of Evin a few years before. Around the same time, they had bombed a market and killed forty people. I had read all those stories in the papers and never made the connection, never thought it might not be a coincidence that they bore my mother's last name.

"I haven't talked to anyone from that group."

"So you know them."

"Now I remember them from the news."

"Have they ever approached you?"

"No. Why would they?"

"You are the only living member of the family."

There are things one knows, yet they never quite register until another person puts them into words. I was my mother's only child. She had three brothers, all killed young. None had children. When I died, a family line would come to an end.

"I have always been just a bus driver. They had no reason to contact me."

"What did you think when you saw them killing innocent people under your mother's family name?"

"I never made the connection."

The shadow receded. Three steps to the other side of the room, three steps across, back to my chair.

"You should know that for even just this familial connection, which you tried to hide, I could keep you here for years. But to show you that I have the best of intentions, I won't hold this against you. Actually, I'm concerned for you. Why did you lie about yourself? You think I don't know you went to the union?"

"The union is not a political organization. We just want our rights. We don't care who is in power."

"Oh, really? You organize a strike and paralyze half the city, and you tell me this was not a political act?"

"We just pursue our rights."

"Now you are insulting my intelligence."

As I opened my mouth to protest, I heard his hand cleave the air a fraction of a second before it reached my head. He hit me in the same place again, with much more force than before. My skull shuddered and my jawbones banged against each other. My eyes rattled in their sockets and black specks swarmed over my field of vision. The blow was like an electric shock. My body shot up from the chair. Acting of their own accord, my hands tore off the blindfold.

A tall, gaunt man with a stubbled face, balding head, and narrow brown eyes gaped at me. I wanted to sit back down, but it was too late. We stared at each other for a while, both transfixed and confused, each of us a deer caught in headlights.

I knew that I had made an irreversible mistake. I had taken the bait the man had thrown me, and spitting it out wouldn't change anything. He had managed to enrage me, to make me violate the most fundamental rule of interrogation. I had laid my eyes on him, on the god of the room. That was sacrilege. Now he could punish me however he wanted.

"You just dug your own grave," Hajj Saeed said softly. He went to the door and signaled to someone in the corridor. I heard another man approach. The two men spoke quietly. Hajj Saeed reentered the room, followed by Ehsan. Both of them stared at me like I was a rare wild animal in a zoo.

"This man doesn't understand his situation," said Hajj Saeed. "We need to make it clear for him."

Ehsan stepped forward. He was and was not the same person. The face that had given me solace now inspired dread. He didn't frown, but he looked different. Maybe it was the cast of his eyes. He wasn't the same person who had let me shower and had patted me on the back before sending me into this room an hour before.

"Squat!" ordered Ehsan.

I kept looking at him, waiting for my only ally in jail to drop guise and save me from Hajj Saeed.

"Squat!" he said again, louder. "Up and down fifty times and keep your hands on the back of your head."

I crouched down.

"Go all the way down. Your ass should touch your soles."

After a dozen repetitions, my thigh muscle cramped. I paused and massaged it. Before I could get down again, Ehsan punched me in the stomach.

The punch brought more shock than pain. I looked at Hajj Saeed, silently demanding him to reprimand Ehsan. Hajj Saeed smiled vaguely.

"Don't rest before I tell you that you can," said Ehsan.

I got myself down again. On my way up, before I had time to straighten my knees, Ehsan kicked at my knee with the tip of his shoe. The blows paralyzed my nerves the way the electric baton had on the day of the strike. I lost my balance and fell. From the floor, Ehsan's shoes filled my dim field of vision. They were identical to Hajj Saeed's.

"Get up!" yelled Ehsan. "Get the fuck up!"

I silently begged him to change back to whoever he had been two hours before.

"Hey, get the fuck up right now!"

Choked up, I crawled to my knees, rose painfully, and stood face-to-face with Ehsan. I filled my eyes with blame and tried to make him feel the weight of my stare.

"Squat!" Ehsan yelled. I squatted down and after two failed attempts got back up. As my legs straightened, he punched me again in the stomach. I doubled over. He kicked me in the same knee and I collapsed fully. He towered over me as I hit the floor. "Get up! Get up!" he screamed. I rolled to raise my body and failed. He dug into my stomach with the tip of his shoe. I tried and failed again and lay supine on the floor like a kneecapped horse.

"That's enough," I heard Hajj Saeed say. His voice was distant and reverberating, as if it came from the bottom of a well. I passed out.

• • •

When I opened my eyes again, an old, bearded man was watching me. I moved and was electrified by a flash of pain. None of my tormentors were in the room.

The new face came closer. I cringed, and the movement hurt even more. The man touched my shoulder. I wanted to slap his hand away but feared a new round of punishment.

"Look what you have done to yourself," he said. He helped me up. Waves of nausea undulated through my body. "Look what you have done to yourself," he repeated. He wrapped my arm around his frail shoulder for support and walked me to my cell.

I SPENT THE NEXT TWO DAYS in a fog. Pain became an electrical fence between the inward-turning realm where I was wandering lost and the outside world. Every time a muscle twitched, a joint hinged, or my lungs tried a deep breath, the sensation crippled my consciousness. It was as though an army of wasps dive-bombed my inner network of nerves and muscle fibers, stinging at will.

Ehsan's barrage of kicks had destroyed my kneecap. When I moved, it slid from side to side and my organs spasmed wildly, causing my heart to contract and expand irregularly and my innards to heave. The pain illuminated the most intricate and minute workings of my body. I marveled at how my muscles had come alive, responding to the slightest of stimuli, how the tendons twanged like overstretched rubber bands, how fast the nerves relayed signals in a desperate attempt to protect the damaged flesh and bone.

For two full days I lay still on the blankets and stared vacantly into the surrounding gray, waiting to heal. I only got up to eat and use the toilet. Akbar, the old man who had helped me to my cell, replaced Ehsan. Every time he put down the food tray and shut the door behind him, I spent a few minutes working up to approaching what he had delivered. First, I would roll my torso over and pause for a few moments there, lying facedown and gathering strength in my upper body so that I could haul myself commando-style across the floor. When I got to the other side of the cell, I would turn and push my body up to lean against the door so I could pick up the food. I would eat as slowly as an ant, aware of the meal's progress down my gullet.

The toilet posed a harder challenge. I maneuvered to it from my blankets and clutched at the rim of the metal bowl. I had to hoist myself up to place my thigh on it and then turn around and settle, my hands pressed against the wall behind me to help with balance. I kept the damaged knee straight, the other bent, with my ass hanging close to the water in the bowl.

The morning of the third day, the pain in my stomach and chest started to let up. The muscles that had absorbed the shock of Ehsan's punches had relaxed, and the act of breathing had stopped hurting. My knee seemed to get worse, though. The kneecap kept sliding side to side, like it was torn free from the rest of the knee. I couldn't straighten my leg at all, as if rigor mortis had set in there and was about to encroach into the rest of my body.

That night I had a dream. I was in a swimming pool with the guard who had checked out my asshole. We were talking in a corner. The man abruptly grabbed my head and pushed me under the water. I flailed and kicked and jerked out of sleep a second before dying. As I thrashed about, I bent my leg at an awkward angle. The pain knocked the wind out of me. A chain of nerves from my chest to my toes burned like a thick streak of gunpowder set ablaze. The bang of my heart against my rib cage grew deafening. The blood in my veins begged for oxygen.

I crawled across the cell and barely made it to the toilet before I threw up. Three gags, and my stomach was empty. Reeking slime spewed out of my nose and mouth. I adjusted my knee on the floor. It hurt, and the pain made me gag again and again.

Finally, I lay faceup, staring at the ceiling. The image of my mother's corpse came to me. Fragmentary dreams of her hands and face and the shape of her distorted fingers had broken into my sleep for years. But at that moment in the cell a new detail from her mangled corpse overwhelmed me. I could not stop thinking about how bloated her right knee had been. I had gotten to the scene only a few minutes after the accident, but it had already swelled to the thickness of her thigh. She probably hit it on the bumper before she flew over the hood. That I could feel a semblance of what she had endured as she lay dying was a great comfort to me.

• • •

On the fourth morning, my eyes opened to four bright lines on the wall. The forceful morning sun had shoved its beams through the window slats, and the cell was brighter than ever. I lay still awhile to absorb the peace in the air. Gazing up at the walls and the ceiling, my eyes settled again on the writing. "You are not alone. I was here before you. I am thinking about you." I whispered it, then read it out loud. I rolled sideways to examine my knee. It didn't hurt as much. I lay back faceup and reread the words on the ceiling over and over. An overwhelming desire to feel the touch of another person racked my body. It was as if I had woken up on the first day of separation from a lover, confronted with her absence after years of sharing a bed. After Homa, I had often felt this way, but I had never experienced such an intense craving.

I turned onto my side again, imagining Homa's naked body lying next to me. It was like I had seen her the day before. I could hear her voice the first time she called to me in the park, the night she talked about her father, the last time she said goodbye. I shut my eyes and imagined how her head and shoulders would rest on a pillow next to me. My hand moved in the air over her invisible outline and paused where the curve of her hip would have been. My penis awoke, which startled me. After she left, I never experienced a hard-on. I had assumed this part of me would be dead forever, but it suddenly had been resurrected. I threw back the blanket and looked down. It kept growing, making a visible bulge in the fabric covering my groin. I watched it reach its full height, standing on my balls like an erect snake. I became embarrassed. I tried to distract myself, looking around for new things on the walls to shift my attention to. But nothing in the cell could compete with the vision of Homa naked. My hand kept gliding in the air over the invisible curves and I remembered her skin, with all its pores and marks, the smoothness of her thighs, those small, colorless hairs on her ass, the calming touch of her low-hanging breasts, and her dry, cracked hands ravaged by the overuse of detergents and the arid weather of Tehran.

• • •

A loud click disrupted my reverie. My first instinct was to scramble for the blanket to cover up the bulge, but it was gone. I had fallen asleep thinking of Homa's hand.

Akbar slid a lunch tray into the room and went to retrieve

my untouched breakfast. He came to the cell three times a day, yet until then, he had remained to me a blurry, one-dimensional presence whose sole function was to bring the food. This morning, as the pain receded and I finally became cognizant of my surroundings, I paid attention to him as he bent into the cell. His thin chest and hunched shoulders barely supported his large, white-haired head. He looked at me. His hand froze in midair.

"You didn't touch your breakfast," he said.

"I just woke up."

"You want lunch?"

I nodded.

"Great." He smiled with what looked like relief. I was confused. As he put down the lunch tray, I remembered the stringent voice of Habib in the union building explaining the significance of untouched meals for prison guards.

"Don't worry," I said. "I'm not on a hunger strike."

Those few days of pain had served as a spiritual detox, a sharpening of my faculty of vision. That morning the cell felt intensely alive. My mind's eye ceased to be obsessively trained on the details of my body. Instead, it turned outward and scanned the cell, surveying the walls inch by inch. Everything around me seemed fresh. Contrasts and contours, bumps and cracks, different shades of gray. The walls offered so much stimulation that I felt I could study them for months. I observed my surroundings in awe and fear, like a child wandering around a forest alone.

I put the lunch tray on my lap. Perfectly round, medium-cooked lentils were disseminated evenly through long, straight grains of rice. The black rounds existed in harmonious complement to the tapered white cylinders. A fine example of geometry in nature.

I put a spoonful into my mouth and chewed carefully. My teeth pulverized the food, making the rice and lentils embrace each other. My saliva bound the mix together into a nutritious mush, as gray as the cell.

Eating made me aware of my body again. I closed my eyes and imagined the downward slide of each mouthful, the slight undulation of the tube that transferred the masticated mass into my stomach, where my body would deploy acid and bacteria to dissolve it. The nutrients would be set apart from waste, and would seep into the millions of passages in the intestine wall, becoming fuel, recharging brain cells, keeping me alive.

I was reinvigorated and emboldened now. The cell no longer meant mere limitation. I could generate my own freedom by recognizing the capaciousness of my surroundings. The toilet didn't have to be just a prison toilet. It could contain all other toilets in the world, be the archetype of a toilet, the abstract, sublime idea of a toilet, of which other toilets were earthly manifestations. As an idea, this small metal toilet bowl perched to the wall of a solitary cell in Evin was capacious enough to include all the ones I had urinated into before, the one in my parents' house surrounded by yellow tiles on the floor that always smelled of detergent and shit, or that disgusting hole in the ground in a shack on the road to Chalus that exuded the foulest reek I had ever encountered, or the toilet in Behrouz's apartment, where I took my first drunk piss ever, or the toilet in the mosque by the terminal, which I had visited at least twice a day for twenty-five years.

I leaned against the door and looked carefully at this archetypal toilet in my cell. I noticed the multiple smears around the metal rim of the bowl. Dry vomit. Saliva filled my mouth. I swallowed it and held my breath and sat up straight to force back a gag. Finding beauty in the beautiful was redundant, I told myself. Finding it in the dull, the abject, was the task ahead.

I crawled on hands and feet toward it. I smelled the dry vomit, rubbed my cheek on it, tasted it with the tip of my tongue. It was sour and bitter. I gagged and my eyes teared up, but I kept at it. It soon ceased to disgust me. It became just another feature of the room. I moved away and examined it from a few different angles.

Then I saw a fly.

The insect, fresh from the free world, was sitting on a slat in front of the open window rubbing its feelers together. It seemed to be deciding whether to come inside or turn around and fly back out. Its body made a dot on the narrow strip of light between the window slats. The position of its black shadow created the illusion that the edges of the slats bent in toward themselves and made the fly look bigger than it really was. It eventually made up its mind and launched itself into the cell. It maneuvered around briefly, took note of the walls and the ceiling, and alighted back on the slat.

"Please! Stay a little longer!"

The words left my mouth before I had even thought of uttering them. The fly stopped rubbing its legs, like it was weighing my offer. Then it tiptoed to the side of the slat and stood in profile to me. I came to my knees and followed its moves closely.

The fly flew into the room again. It floated straight toward me, circled above my head, drifted away, spiraled down, looped back around, and hovered near my face. I closed my eyes and listened with pleasure to its delicate, ear-stroking buzz. Then the fly approached the window but pulled back quickly. It made another turn around the cell and paused over the toilet bowl, carved out short circles in the air, lowered altitude as meticulously as a helicopter carrying wounded soldiers, and landed on the vomit smear. It jabbed its proboscis into the dry vomit and began to feast.

When it had eaten its fill, the fly tore its body off the toilet and took another pass around the cell. It approached the slats three times, pulled away at the last second, and returned to hover over my head. It then sped up and zigzagged, swooped down, and landed on my arm. Goose bumps rose up on my skin under its feet. It tiptoed around, up to my elbow and back to the middle of my arm, and paused there.

I watched it with admiration. It seemed like a perfect machine. Even the coloring was beautiful, with its gradual change from black to gray. Its body was tiny and frail, and about a quarter of it supported the disproportionately large compound eyes that captured the world in a thousand simultaneous, discrete images. Its feelers settled on my skin and rubbed one another at a carefully calculated frequency, gathering data, or perhaps just enjoying the company of the only other living organism in the cell.

"How do you fly?" I asked the insect. "You feed on shit and vomit, but you can go wherever you want. How?"

The legs of the fly stopped moving along my arm. It must have sensed a threat.

"How? How the fuck is that fair?"

The fly took off and flitted around anxiously near the ceiling.

"Look, I'm sorry," I said to the insect. My voice grew shrill. "I didn't mean it. I just want to get out of here." The fly ignored me and continued tracing warped circles in the air. Then it accelerated suddenly, yanked around, and started flying into the walls. It was suddenly desperate to escape but couldn't find the way out. It lurched right before correcting its trajectory toward the mesh of the window screen. In a second, it would find it. I jumped up and moved as fast as I could to block the egress. The fly collided with my chest and dove back into the cell, then flew around hysterically. The sudden jump had hurt my knee. I needed to sit and stretch my legs but couldn't take the risk.

I glared at the fly, offended by its escape attempt. It had fed off my vomit and walked up and down my arm. I could have killed it, and the fly knew it well because it lived in the world of human beings, but I hadn't. It now wanted to go, just because I had asked it a question.

The fly continued on its quest. It checked every inch of the cell for another crack or hole that could offer freedom. The more it tried to escape, the more agitated I got. When the insect had determined there was no other passage to the outside world, it settled on the wall.

"Listen," I said. "I meant no harm. I just want you to stay a little while and keep me company. It's very lonely here."

The fly took off again, spiraling and plunging, making abrupt turns and jags. The pain intensified in my knee. It radiated out from my kneecap, spread and circled around the joint. My body implored me to sit and stretch my legs, but I couldn't give the fly a chance to escape.

It landed back on the wall, its rear to the ceiling, its head at an angle that enabled it to monitor all my moves. I noticed an unsettling tilt to its body, an adjustment that I took to mean it had dedicated the full capacity of its compound eye machinery to discovering a way to break free. I imagined how I looked to the insect, blurred and twisted, refracted into thousands of tiny replicas of myself, all trapped in the cell.

My knee hurt worse. I couldn't stand much longer. Since I had decided not to let the fly go, I had to either kill or catch it. Killing it would have defeated the purpose and catching it would be hard. But I had trapped flies as a child. I would bend my palm into a scoop and hold it parallel to the wall near the body of the insect. The fly would take off when my hand got too close, and then I would pounce on it, keep it in my fist, letting it buzz and struggle to get out. When it stopped, I would put it on the floor. The flies never died, but their wings would usually be damaged beyond repair. The insects would be my pets for about a few hours, before they succombed to their wounds.

I had to take two steps to the wall where the fly was perched. If I took the first one quietly, without scaring it, I would be close enough to attack. I rehearsed the operation in my mind, then slowly set down one foot. The fly rubbed its legs, seemingly unaware of my intentions. Then my other foot sprang forward. My right hand cleaved the air above the insect but didn't reach it. A fraction of a second before I got to it, pain struck. I froze midstep. My leg gave way. My body thudded to the floor.

From there, I watched the fly take off from the wall. It moved erratically through the space over my fallen body. When it had confirmed that I was no longer dangerous, its motion became nonchalant. It floated around, circled the cell, and lingered triumphantly over me. Then it flew through the window slats to its freedom.

I lay there on my back, looking around at the walls, longing in vain for a movement, a sound, anything that would make me feel that I had not been abandoned. From the floor, I cursed and insulted the creature, threatening to kill it the next time it showed up.

Then I lay motionless listening to a silence so thunderous it sounded like a waterfall in my ears, finding the magnitude of my loneliness unbearable. Soon I found myself consumed by a memory, the events of one childhood evening I hadn't thought of in decades.

AS A TEENAGER, I spent many hours sitting by the window in my room on the second floor of my parents' house. In the 1970s, my parents lived two blocks away from Hasanabad Square on a narrow street that was transforming, like the rest of the city, at a manic pace. The surging oil prices had poured money into urban households, and every day I watched out the window how our neighbors, stupefied by this windfall, dedicated themselves to the beautification of the surface of their lives.

Within a few years, massive Cadillacs and Chevrolets with shimmering colors replaced tiny Citroëns and Volkswagens in people's driveways. The demographics of their drivers also changed. Gray-haired fathers helmed old, modest European cars and diligently obeyed the traffic rules. In contrast, brash youth, many of them hardly past the driving age, wheeled around in the showboaty American cars. They parked their giant vehicles wherever they desired and huddled together on the narrow streets of our neighborhood to talk loudly. They sported long hair, wide-leg pants, and tight jackets, even on summer days. On their clean-shaven faces large Ray-Ban sunglasses sat awkwardly. All of them seemed to have come out of the same fashion factory. So did the girls, but as much as I hated the boys' look, I did admire the young women's, with their Googoosh-style pale makeup and shiny red lipstick, Audrey Hepburn haircuts, and short skirts with loose shirts.

The nights on our street were no longer fully dark. We lived not far from Lalehzar, the center of the new Tehran nightlife. A dim aura blanketed the area after dark, a luminous haze created by the thousands of bright lights that turned on at the same time in the evenings to shake the neighborhood out of its diurnal torpor. I was too young to experience the nights of Lalehzar, but in school it was a hot topic. The few kids who had seen it spoke breathlessly of second-floor discos, strobe-lit bodies gyrating to the music American DJs arranged, shaking the ceilings over the burgeoning cabarets. They told of the drunk workers who crammed around small, round tables to ogle scantily clad Israeli belly dancers, next door to coffeehouses where fat men of the Grand Bazaar reclined on wooden beds at the end of the day to eye the cleavage of the big-breasted women serving them hookahs and chai.

During those years, my main source of entertainment came from our neighbors scrambling to catch up with the times. Mr. and Mrs. Fadavi, who had been the very embodiment of piety and modesty in the 1960s, now frequently went out in garish suits and gowns to ballets and concerts. Mr. Sadati, who lived on the other side of us, used to always come home before nine. Yet at that time, I frequently heard his voice around midnight when he would stagger out of his car and drunkenly sing Dariush and Sattar as he struggled to fit the key into his door. Mr. Khiabani, the only man on our street who used to take the bus to work, purchased a spectacular maroon Chevrolet Nova, which he kept cleaner than his own clothes.

Along with this grasping luxury, a new set of faces emerged outside my window. More than a dozen kids had come to our neighborhood to work. Emaciated, sunburned, timid boys carried the shopping bags of the neighbor to our right, cleaned the windows of the one across the street, watered the flowers three doors down. Their bodies were small, their gaits halting, their demeanors shy. They spoke quietly in accents I had never heard before. My father, in one of his dinnertime rants, informed me that they were the children of farmers devastated by the calamity of land reform. Their families had left their villages and ended up in shantytowns that had mushroomed to the south of Tehran, while the city itself was rolling in cash.

In the 1980s, on the rare occasions when I talked to other bus drivers about politics, I told them how I had seen the revolution coming. Looking out the window for long hours at the faces of those kids, simmering with hatred for their rich bosses, I had known something was fundamentally wrong with the country. Underneath the surface of that terrible inequality there were flames, so small that most people never spotted them, but I could see them out my window. Khomeini distinguished himself from other revolutionaries by noticing these flames. He scratched the surface away and blew on them. Then those little flames grew fast, found one another, and became a conflagration.

On that summer morning in 1974, however, the street was unsettlingly empty. No neighbor woman came back from shopping, trailed by a poor, young boy hunched under the weight of heavy bags, no American car roared along the street, no teenagers leaned on a parked car exchanging lewd jokes. There was not even the chatter of birds or the rustle of leaves.

What if the world had already ended?

I had just read a story about a man who survived a nuclear explosion, only because a moment before the bomb had landed he jumped into a sewer to pick up a watch he had dropped, and that sewer happened to be designed in such a way that explosions didn't touch it. He was there when the wave passed and came back up to a world melted into radioactive pulp.

After reading that story, I kept looking from the chair by my window for places to hide from a blast. That day the street was quiet for so long that I wondered whether I had imagined the apocalypse into being. What if the end of the world came and went while I was sitting there looking out the window and everybody died but me? Tehran would turn into the greatest graveyard ever, a vast sprawl of dead zones stretching from the foot of the Alborz Mountains to the edge of the desert, millions of bodies on the streets, millions of corpse-filled apartments and cars. What if I happened to be sitting in the only safe place in the city?

At that moment, my mother turned onto the street, two over-flowing grocery bags weighing her down. Her tidy hair, parted down the middle and brushed over her ears, shimmered under the sun. She wore a white shirt and a brown skirt, both impeccably clean and ironed. This was a few months before my uncle Ahmad, my father's brother, died and my father's mind began to deteriorate.

"Your uncle is coming over for dinner," she announced as she came in. "Go take a shower."

• • •

The doorbell sounded shortly after sunset. My father always finished work at five but never came home before seven. I let him press the bell again and waited long enough for my mother to shout, "Open the door!" Then I shuffled down the stairs and across the sitting room to the entryway.

"Where were you?" my father snapped, an odor of alcohol and cheap cigarettes on his breath. Before I opened my mouth, he brushed past me, dropped his bag, and rushed to the toilet. I heard him unbuckling his pants and unzipping his fly. His pee stream hit the bowl forcefully. He always peed without lifting the toilet seat.

My uncle Ahmad arrived shortly after my father. I never understood how these two men could be brothers. Ahmad was thin and quiet and shy, with sharp cheekbones and a head full of hair. My father was brash and loud like a high school boy. His face was round and his hairline was receding rapidly. Politically, Ahmad supported a unified workers' front that would eventually overthrow the bourgeoisie. At the time, my father was a Mossadeq nationalist, keen on pragmatism and negotiating the hell out of every political problem.

I was the first one at the dinner table. In the sitting room, my dad and uncle were coldly exchanging greetings and banal updates. They could barely disguise their dislike for each other. My mother laid out the plates and the glasses, the salad bowl, the bottle of lemon juice and the pepper shaker, and the pickled cucumbers and mashed eggplant. I was supposed to help, but I didn't, and she didn't insist. When she brought out the basket of bread, the brothers finally deigned to join us. They sat at opposite ends of the table, facing each other like battling kings. At last, my mother emerged from the kitchen with a stuffed chicken on a big tray, a forced smile on her face. She set it down in the place of honor in the middle of the table. The brothers set aside their differences to exclaim appreciatively.

I was the most dedicated consumer of roasted chicken in that household, but that night it seemed more like a carcass than food. The living chicken was staring at me through the meat and bone on the platter, a tall bird with white feathers and beady, attentive eyes that bobbed its head fast, pecked around frantically, and took baths in the dust. Before my eyes my family were acting like Neanderthals, hacking the little bird to pieces and making off with their shares.

The brothers bore down on the flesh. They worked their cutlery into it, pulled the limbs apart, and hoarded organs on their plates.

"Breast or leg?" my mother asked me, dangling a knife over the remains.

"I don't want any right now," I said.

"You haven't touched the food yet."

"I'm going to start with some salad."

I placed slices of tomato and lettuce on my plate and moved them around with my fork in a desultory fashion without eating.

"This is delicious!" my father exclaimed and turned to my

mom. "Where was this chicken hiding, Narges? Do you hoard the good stuff?" He laughed loudly. In those days everyone made jokes about Prime Minister Hoveyda's speech on punishing the hoarders who were taking advantage of inflation and buying goods in large numbers to sell later.

My dad's crack fell flat. I knew what was coming. He often warmed up for his political rants with a bad joke.

"If you ask me," he started, "this is the dumbest administration I've seen in my lifetime. They poured the oil money into the economy and destroyed it. Now that the price of everything has tripled in a year, they're running around, threatening folks who buy stuff in bulk to save money."

I stopped listening for a few moments. On my side of the table, Ahmad was crunching on the gristle and scratching his fork on his plate. I took a few deep breaths to suppress my disgust and turned my attention back to my father.

"Now you see the Shah of the country going around the world saying we are not like those Americans, we are modest, hard-working, we appreciate our share." My father looked around the table for a response. He always inserted these long pauses to make sure we were following him and agreeing with his points. My mom usually interjected a brief remark to refuel him. That night, though, no one responded. My mom was distracted by my refusal to eat. My father groaned and shook his head and returned to his food. I masochistically watched him press his knife into the chicken, cut the flesh away, bring up the clean bone, and gnaw on it like a hungry dog. Then he tore the fat off the top and ground that noisily with his teeth.

I gagged. It didn't make a sound, but it brought tears to my eyes. The brothers were immersed in eating. Only my mother, always alert, had noticed.

My father started up again. "Now the very people who are willing to jail folks over having two sacks of rice instead of one are going to get their hands on an atom bomb. And the Americans are paving the way for them. It's ridiculous."

"I actually think we should have a bomb," Ahmad said dryly, without lifting his head from his plate. He was plucking black veins from the white breast meat with surgical precision. An awkward silence followed.

This was the rule of the game. My father would keep talking until his brother challenged him, then they'd slip happily into a fight. That night, Ahmad's opening move surprised my father and silenced him for a minute. He had never thought his leftist brother would challenge him by defending the Shah.

He finally cleared his throat. "Well. And why is that?"

"Many other countries have the bomb," Ahmad said.

"It doesn't mean it's a good thing to have. And besides, the Shah's understanding of the world affairs is like a teenager's."

"He is not worse than others."

"Since when are you a fan?"

"I hate him more than ever. He is just not worse than other leaders of the world."

"Well, he is. Just think of what he said in Australia the other day, that political prisoners are the same as terrorists. Not very many leaders would say something so outrageous."

"He didn't mean it that way."

"Really? Did you ask him?"

"I didn't have to."

Ahmad didn't lift his head during this back-and-forth. I could detect cynical satisfaction on his face, which puzzled me. He argued habitually with my father whenever they saw each other, but he never said things solely to piss him off.

My father took out his annoyance on the chicken. His knife cut forcefully through the belly, tearing away the skin and meat to reveal the fried vegetables inside.

"The food is great, Narges," said Ahmad. My mom gave him a vague smile. She was focused on me.

"Why don't you eat?" she asked me.

"I'm not hungry."

"Let me cut you a piece."

"I'm fine, Mom."

She bent toward the chicken all the same and selected a piece of white meat from the breast to put on my plate. "It's pure meat," she said. "No veins or fat."

"We are becoming a world power," Ahmad went on. "We can't rely on oil forever. We need new sources of energy."

"The Shah doesn't want a new source of energy. He wants the bomb."

"Really? Did you ask him?" Ahmad said, his face straight.

"Listen," my father said, "we're talking about a fifty-some-year-old baby who thinks lethal weapons are toys and, like other boys, wants all the toys in the world. Why do you think Americans love him so much? He is the definition of a cash cow."

"They don't like him."

The fork and knife were trembling in my father's hands. He had turned red. Drops of sweat beaded on his forehead.

"What they don't like about the Shah," he began, trying hard to hide the shaking of his voice, "is how he wants to revive the glory of the Persian empire, or whatever bullshit he believes in, which might give Iranians the idea that they are actually more than the guards of oil wells for the American companies. Otherwise, he's their best client."

"Either way, we have a right to have a bomb."

"Why don't you eat your dinner?" My father addressed me suddenly.

"I don't want to. It's disgusting that we're eating this." I enunciated the words distinctly, my voice solemn and straight.

"What?" my father said.

"Why?" my mother said.

"Because this was God's creation," I said, maintaining my somber tone.

Ahmad laughed. "That's very nice of you to care about the chicken. I'm happy to burden myself with the sin."

He grabbed the edge of the plate to pull it toward himself. I held on to the opposite side.

"What's wrong with you?" my father said.

"Didn't you just say you were not going to eat this?" Ahmad said.

"Leave him alone. He'll eat it," my mother said.

"Fine." Ahmad let go of the plate.

"I'm not going to eat this," I announced.

"Then give it to your uncle," my father said.

Ahmad's hand reached for the plate again. I didn't resist. I watched him slide it toward himself, a grin stretching across his face. That did it for me. When my uncle had the plate positioned in front of him, I rose and slapped it off the table. The dish hit his chest, and the juices from the chicken breast smeared all over his green shirt. The food landed in his lap, and the plate broke into three pieces on the floor.

My father slammed his hand against the table, got up from his chair, and yelled, "What the fuck are you doing?" He accidentally knocked over a full glass of water, which splashed on the meat. With a smile of satisfaction, I watched the wetness spread across the tablecloth.

Before my lips straightened again, a flash of light shot across my vision. My head jolted back, and the dry sound of the slap echoed in my ears. My father had hit me so hard my mother screamed.

The room went silent. I felt dizzy. My jaw had gone numb, and my skin burned as if it had been exposed to fire. I swallowed my tears, rolled my eyes up slowly, cast my father the most defiant look I could manage, and smiled.

• • •

Lying on my bed in the dark, I listened to the rattle of dishes. They had started cleaning up without speaking to each other. I was torn between guilt and pride. They had just been eating dinner. I had never experienced that feeling of disgust before and couldn't explain where it had come from today. And slapping the dish off the table at a guest. I had no clue why I did it.

My father's mortification made me proud, though. At that age, everything he did was an affront to my dignity, from the long lectures at the dinner table to coming home after sunset to standing up to piss. Defeating him so totally brought me joy. But why had I done this to my mother? Thinking of her, I burned with shame.

The sound of water spattering in the sink rose from downstairs. My mother was washing up. I swallowed down a sob that had been close to breaking free and listened. She turned off the water faucet and walked around in her flip-flops on the kitchen floor. Music from an advertisement on TV obscured whatever else she was doing. Then it was the nine o'clock news. My father and uncle were engaged in their nightly act of masochism. The news anchor said something about the country's achievement in terms of public health. My father cursed.

Two black columns broke up the rectangle of light under my door, and the knob clicked. Brightness flooded the room. My mother's black silhouette, encircled by a fluorescent aura, paused at the threshold. Then she came in and sat on my bed.

"How are you?" she said. There was no anger in her voice. Tears ran down my cheeks. Her hand fumbled on the sheet, found my face, and stroked it. Her fingers paused on the wetness. "You should sleep." She kissed my forehead and left the room.

T**AKE OFF YOUR BLINDFOLD,**" said a man.

My hands moved toward the eye cover but stopped short. It took me a second to identify Hajj Saeed's voice. Over the past four days, which had passed like four months, I had started to forget about him. His voice was warm and reassuring, and it pleased my ears. It was like I was hearing a friend I had deeply missed.

"Take it off. It's fine."

I removed the cloth and blinked a few times to help my eyes adjust. The light bulb in the room seemed to glow more intensely this time. Hajj Saeed was standing near my chair.

"Lift your head," he said. I didn't. "What are you shy about? You've seen me already."

I looked at his pale face. He tilted his balding head, eclipsing the lamp. The flood of light from the ceiling created a yellowish halo around his body.

"How was your week?" he asked.

"Fine."

"I mean in terms of physical health."

"My knee still hurts. It's much better than the first day."

"Ehsan went a little too far. We put him on unpaid leave."

Don't give me that shit, I wanted to say.

"Are you smirking at me?"

I reset my face.

Hajj Saeed paced to the end of the cell and then came back. "You think I'm an idiot, don't you?" he said.

"Not at all."

"You think we're a bunch of paranoid idiots torturing innocent people for fun."

"No."

"Or a bunch of sadists who lock up people and beat them for the hell of it. Well, maybe it's not your fault that you think these things. That is what they tell you."

"Who is this 'they'?"

"Ah, you don't know. I see. Don't worry, we'll get to that." Hajj Saeed moved away and sat down on his chair.

"You don't have satellite TV, so I suppose you didn't see the coverage of your masterpiece. But before you even got home, the strike was all over the Western media. They spent hours talking about it. You think they cover it because they support your cause? Or because they care about the rights of workers?"

"I don't know. I've never watched their shows."

"The Saudis have been suppressing and torturing and killing Shia dissidents for years. The Israelis have killed thousands of Palestinians and demolished countless villages. Do you know how many fucks the Western media gives to those atrocities? Zero. When Saddam was their buddy, they gave him chemical bombs to use on his own people. I can go on and on. In Iran, if in a fight with the police someone gets a nosebleed, their entire media covers it for hours. Do you think it's a coincidence?"

"No."

"They had footage of fights between the police and the drivers. Who gave it to them?"

"How would I know?"

The chair creaked. Hajj Saeed took three long steps, grabbed the back of my head, and banged it against the wall. The blow made only a hushed sound, and my head snapped back. The wall was soft, I realized, covered with layers of soundproofing material.

"Never answer my question with a question again," Hajj Saeed said.

I nodded.

"If you watch these TV channels even for a couple of days you will see the usual gang: Washington-dwelling traitors disguised as human rights activists, sitting in those stupid think tanks, deep in the pockets of the Americans and the UK, lying left and right, holding up every tiny problem as evidence that our government wants to massacre its citizens. Worse than them are the reformists here, that spineless, clueless Khatami and his bunch of castrated sidekicks, shedding crocodile tears for every drop of blood that drips off someone's nose. They don't care if that person was armed and attacked the police. These traitors have muddied the waters so much that now the Israeli leaders have the audacity to make noise about human rights to us. And what do you bus drivers do? You see all this hypocrisy, all these unjust attacks and shameful media coverage, and instead of defending your own country, you pretend to have this noble cause so you can instigate chaos in the city. You provoke the police, and then when they fight back you film them and send it to CNN. Don't you think something is wrong with that?"

"No one I know did that. We just want our rights. Some people might take advantage of our situation, but what does all this have to do with me?"

"Did you just answer my question with another question?"

"Sorry."

"Forget about what Habib Samadi told you. Be honest. Don't talk to me like I'm an idiot."

"I am being honest."

"If you want to know someone, look at the company they keep. Do you agree with that?"

"I guess."

"When I ask you a yes-or-no question I expect a yes-or-no answer."

"Yes, I agree with that."

"I don't know about how your union works, and I don't really care. That's not my job. I am the big-picture guy. I look at the situation from the outside, and I see you and the Western media and the US and Israel on the same side. What am I supposed to think?"

"No matter what you do, there's always someone to take advantage of you."

"I wonder why Israel never tries to take advantage of what I do."

"Because you don't want change. We want to change things. Israel wants change too. We don't want what Israel wants, but whatever we do, they will try to exploit it."

"Who told you I don't want change? Of course I want change. You people think you know so much but you don't know shit about this country. I know a thousand times better than you how many problems we have. But stop deluding yourself. You and the Israelis want the same thing. That is why they support you."

"I don't want to overthrow the system or start a revolution. I want better working conditions for drivers, reform, accountability—"

"Reform!" He jumped in. "Let's talk about reform. What happened to reform in this country?"

"Well—"

"I voted for Khatami."

I turned and looked at him. A smile of triumph emerged on his face.

"That's how much I want reform," he said as he walked back and forth around the room. "Many other guys you see here, guards and officers and paper pushers, voted for him. Now most of us hate him. You like Khatami, don't you?"

"Well . . . I don't know."

"You don't know? What were you doing in the strike, then? You worked so hard with his people to organize it."

"I didn't organize anything."

He sighed dramatically. "You are incorrigible. But fine. Let's leave that for now. As for Khatami, I supported him, then he utterly disappointed me. This whole 'We can't do this or that' and 'We should negotiate with the West' atmosphere the reformists love so much. The way they run around and cry about election fixing. The way they go to such lengths to show the Western companies that we are not savages and if they invest here we'll be their next Dubai. Their wet dreams about how Iran could be indistinguishable from San Francisco. I know for a fact that some of them were in touch with the CIA, asking them to get the US army to come and topple the regime, even after the Iraq war. I hate them because I love this country. They don't. They keep talking about how we should open our fist and shake hands with every bastard who is reaching toward our groin. But they don't want a handshake. They want our open palm so that when we stretch it out before them they can say, 'See? These people are begging for our help.' "

Hajj Saeed came to my chair and rolled up his sleeves. "Look. What do you see here?"

I counted five tiny lumps under the skin on his arm.

"Come on, touch it."

His wrist came within a few inches of my eyes. The protrusions felt hard. Something was embedded deep in the tissue.

"Do you know what that is?"

"No."

"Shrapnel pieces. I picked them up in the war, during the Mersad operation."

I touched the scars again.

"I had a dozen more. The doctors took them out. They couldn't touch these guys because they're too close to a sensitive nerve."

"I'm sorry."

He laughed. "You're sorry!" he said and laughed louder. "He is sorry!" he kept laughing as he rolled down his sleeves.

"That's how much I love this country. Who do you think these reformists are? None of them ever got near the front line for all eight years of the war with Iraq. They just sat on their asses in safe places, took easy oil money and never lifted a finger for anyone else. Your friends—"

"They're not my friends."

"Did you just interrupt me again?"

I said nothing.

"Now, since you're clearly trying to waste my time, I want to show you something that I intended to bring up later."

Hajj Saeed walked to his desk, opened a drawer and reached in. He came back and put a pile of photos in front of me. As I went through them, he watched me closely.

The first one took my breath away. Me and four other drivers, the members of the study group, in a café on Valiasr Street. We were straight out of a meeting. It must have been about six months before I went to jail, a few weeks after I joined the group. I vividly remembered the day all five of us went to that café because we never got together aside from our meetings. It was after a long session on the philosopher Hannah Arendt.

The photo was dim because it was dark inside and the photographer hadn't used a flash. But it was clear enough for me to read the faces. We had been sitting there for three hours, and each of us had ordered several glasses of tea. We had discussed football and childhood memories, ex-girlfriends and how we lost our virginity. We made fun of some of our other coworkers and told obscene jokes.

I brought the photo nearer to my eyes. Hajj Saeed bent forward slightly, paying close attention to my reaction.

Samad's face was the most visible. His mustache, which usually slanted dramatically to both corners of his mouth, in the photo bristled in a thick, straight line that was scaffolded by a wide smile. He had done manual labor since he was ten: as an employee in a cement factory in Zanjan, a supermarket cashier in

Qazvin, and a construction worker in Tehran. He had joined the city transport at twenty-five and spent the next two decades driving buses. He was an unabashed communist, an ardent supporter of Lenin and Mao, and the least diligent driver on the job. His charismatic demeanor and way with words enabled him to project a saintly commitment to the cause. It was easy for him to find colleagues to fill in, even at the last minute, when he skipped out on work for a political action. He was always traveling to remote villages of Baluchistan to distribute food and medicine or holding secret meetings with workers in foundries about the techniques of strikes or attending protests about raising the minimum wage in the state of Ilam.

Behrouz was seated next to him. I swallowed down a growing lump in my throat. The grudge I had held against him since our fight in the street disappeared. All of a sudden I missed him so badly it hurt. He was talking when the photograph had been taken. His hands were frozen in the air. His mouth was so wide open it distorted his other facial features.

I was seated at Behrouz's side, watching him talk. I loved him like a brother. If someone had told me then what was waiting for us down the road, I would have gotten up and walked out of the café and never looked back.

On the other side of the table sat Mehdi, his mouth twisted into a crooked laugh. His right hand dangled in the air like he was about to swat a fly, and his left fingers grabbed the edge of the table. I had always hated him without knowing why. He was a great debater, a Muslim socialist in the vein of Shariati and Al-e Ahmad, a lover of Imam Hussein and other Shia figures who fought the Umayyad and Abbasid caliphates.

Rahman was next to Mehdi. In keeping with his character, he had his back to the camera. I thought of his face, his small, piercing eyes under the shade of his protruding eyebrows, his bony nose, and the thin, pale line of his lips. I had spent long hours with him in the study group, and I never saw him smile or frown. He always put his stool behind the others and watched the bickering from a distance, one thin leg resting on the other, staring owlishly around the room. I never understood his politics, his likes or dislikes, or why he had joined the group in the first place. Yet I had sympathized with him the most. Like me, his longtime solitude had thickened and hardened and turned into a shield.

I slid the first photo to the bottom of the pile and looked at the second one. In it, Samad and I had just stepped out of the stationery store. The group had never left all at once to avoid attracting attention. I always walked with Behrouz and couldn't recall ever leaving with Samad. The street was wet and I was wearing my thickest coat, so it must have been February. Our heads were down and we were not speaking. I flipped to the next photo.

Here Behrouz and I were walking toward the stationery store on a snow-blanketed sidewalk. I was gesticulating and talking in the picture. Behrouz was frowning attentively. I remembered the moment vividly. For the first time I was talking to him about my family. How my father, formerly a banker, became a resentful quasi-intellectual and died miserably. My first encounter with my mother's body after her death. The picture had been taken only a few weeks before he beat me up on the sidewalk. Hajj Saeed prodded me. I moved on to the next photo.

This one was of me with Behrouz and Mehdi, outside the store, conversing with serious faces. It was after the Lenin session, in which a long-simmering battle of egos had come to a head. Mehdi and Samad had screamed at each other from opposite sides of the room, each throwing out wild accusations and insults against the other. In the picture, Behrouz and I were gesturing at Mehdi. We had been trying to calm him down after Samad had called him a snitch. That day the study group had ended.

Something buzzed on the other side of the room. It was the vibration of a cell phone. Hajj Saeed moved to answer it and got halfway to his desk before turning back to snatch the photos out of my hands. He rushed to the desk with them and flipped his phone open.

"Hi, how are you?" he said. "I'm fine. How is Salman's fever? . . . Okay. Okay, great. Pass the phone, please . . . Hi, sweetie . . . I am well. How are you? . . . Daddy is in a meeting, can't talk much. You feel better? . . . I'm so glad to hear that! What did you do today? . . . Nice! But you should get more rest, okay? Thank you. Now, please pass the phone to your mom." The door opened and his voice faded as he moved into the corridor.

I thought about what I had just seen. The photographer, or photographers, had definitely followed us since I had joined the group, and they may have monitored people before that. I was not alone in any of the pictures. Based on what I saw, they had never focused on me. As evidence, the photos were worthless. They captured us walking around and talking. The closest the photographer had gotten was in the café.

Hajj Saeed's voice grew louder again. He was promising to get eggs and milk on his way home. He came back into the room, flipped the phone closed, and shut the door.

"Sorry," he said absentmindedly, like he had forgotten where he was and whom he was talking to. He opened a drawer and rummaged around noisily until he found the papers he wanted. He came to my chair.

The first page was typed up in neat, readable font. It began with Behrouz's name, a colon, and the first words Behrouz had said when he introduced me to the study group. "As I told you last week, Yunus Turabi is joining us today."

I recalled this moment with crystal clarity. Behrouz and I had entered a nondescript, dilapidated stationery store on Ferdows Boulevard. Inside the place was a small counter, a photocopy machine, a meager collection of bestselling novels, writing tools, and postcards. A very old man was sitting by the photocopier. He acknowledged us with a cold nod. Behind the machine, Behrouz opened a hatch in the floor. Surprisingly strong fluorescent light poured out of the hole. We climbed down a narrow, creaky flight of stairs into the cold, musty air of the basement. I glanced at the three people sitting before me on awkwardly small stools. The space was larger than the store above it. Brimming floor-to-ceiling bookshelves covered all three walls and exuded a pungent smell of decaying paper. Mold and cobwebs decorated all four corners of the room.

I knew all the faces and none of the names. They were bus drivers I had walked by a thousand times and exchanged greetings with yet never talked to. I approached and shook their hands.

Behrouz and I settled on two unoccupied stools. With the others, we formed a rough circle.

"As I told you last week," Behrouz had said, "Yunus Turabi is joining us today."

Hajj Saeed had the transcriptions of all our meetings. Every word we had uttered had been recorded. My shaking fingers turned the pages under his gaze. It was like reading a play. All the names were there, followed by colons, followed by unfiltered and spontaneous dialogue, for we had never once considered that someone might be recording us. Some passages were underlined.

It seeemed that one of my esteemed comrades was in fact a snitch.

"Clearly," said Hajj Saeed, "we have a lot to do. But I have to go home and take care of my son. See you soon."

I T BEGAN THE YEAR BEFORE, on September 21st. I knew this because every bus driver in Tehran dreads going to work on this day.

September 21st was when school started. During the summer, buses in Tehran moved around the city with relative ease. Then things changed overnight. Every driver knew what to expect on September 21st, yet it always ended up being worse than anticipated. Exiting the same terminal and hitting the same streets as before, one found the number of cars had doubled. Overnight the city had transformed into an asphyxiating parking lot. The mountainous landscape of the north, which drivers cherished from their high perches through the summer as they traversed the highways, faded as a thickening smog swallowed up the peaks. On board, everyone was agitated because everyone was late. Other drivers blasted their horns and forced their cars through every tiny, open gap. Edgy police officers issued tickets right and left. For a bus driver, working in the city on September 21st amounted to daylong torture.

The September 21st of the year before I had ended up in jail was no exception. As soon as I left the terminal, traffic swallowed the bus like pooling seawater around a foot on the beach. On each pass down the line, the vehicle was full by the fourth stop. It was as though the population of a whole other city had been added to Tehran's own. As the day passed, I let the bus creep along and in the mirror watched the passengers jostle over tiny parcels of space. In the evening, I went home limp and depleted. In the bathroom I inspected my loosening skin, the deep creases in my forehead, and the drooping corners of my eyes. Then I went out for a walk.

My weekly strolls began one evening in 1992, the day I moved into my apartment. After I finished unpacking, I went out to see the neighborhood and walked for an hour. From then on I stuck religiously to the same path every week for the following years.

I never changed the route because I was never bored. Tehran in the nineties kept bloating up like a balloon attached to an air pump that never turned off. The west of the city took the brunt of it. As soon as the regulations were relaxed the real estate developers, having long salivated over the open land, rushed headlong to erect rickety buildings and fill up every square foot of empty space they could lay their hands on. The city, already ugly, became hideous. Tehran deteriorated fast, right before my eyes.

I was the second resident of my half-finished building when I moved in. In 1992, Banafsheh Street was home to four more residential buildings, a dozen large houses with yards and ponds, two gardens of cherry and walnut trees, and a few empty plots of land. Then Karbaschi became the mayor of the city and threw it to the developers, green-lighting their westward rush for real estate gold. In the beginning, my walks took me past scattered houses and aromatic gardens, but before many summers had passed, I found myself wandering through construction pits. My sight was occupied by workers on scaffolds sledgehammering the remains of old homes like an angry rabble destroying the palace of a deposed king. I witnessed the mass-scale chopping down of trees and the mushrooming of dirt holes. Trucks lifted their beds to pour endless streams of concrete, like they were suffering from a fatal diarrhea.

The demographics changed also. The old suburban Tehranis moved out and took with them their arrogance and their dramatic accents. The vacuum they left was filled in waves. First underpaid Azari and Afghan construction workers showed up in droves to take up residence in the ruins, where they erected new buildings as fast as if they were assembling them with Lego bricks. Young hipsters and university students moved in from downtown, and were followed by the lower-middle-class families from other cities.

As I passed along these ever-changing streets on September 21st, 2004, the pollution was suffocating, even there in the outer suburbs, and the traffic hadn't let up. I decided to do something exceptional. Rather than stop by my neighborhood supermarket, I would buy groceries from the place two blocks away.

This supermarket was larger than the one I usually went to. I wandered along the aisles in an aimless fashion. It took me half an hour to fill the trolley. As I approached the cashier, I heard someone calling me.

"Yunus!"

I froze in dread. It was rare to hear my name spoken by anyone who didn't work at the bus terminal. *Don't panic*, I told myself. *It must be a coworker.*

At the sight of Behrouz's pleasant face, I breathed easier.

Behrouz was one of the few people I worked with who I liked. He was pushing a cart overflowing with fruits and vegetables. "Man, what a shitty day," he said.

"I barely survived."

"You live nearby?"

"Banafsheh Street."

"Oh yeah? I had no idea. Are you done here?"

"Yes. I was just leaving."

"Let me pick up eggs and cigarettes. See you at the door."

Outside the shop, he lit a cigarette. I stood with him in silence, leaning against the wall, bags of groceries at our feet. On a different day this would have been the moment for me to make my excuses and go home. But I lingered.

"The fucking school year, man," said Behrouz.

"It's the worst."

"When did you move to the Jannatabad Terminal?"

"Fifteen years ago. You?"

"Five years." He took three hard drags. "I was thinking that I know next to nothing about you."

I took a deep breath. My main rule was to avoid situations in which I would have to talk about myself, but Behrouz's steady manner put me at ease.

"Do you have kids?" Behrouz asked.

"No."

"Are you married?"

"No."

"Divorced?"

"No."

"Do you live alone?"

"Yes."

"Your parents still around?"

"No."

"I'm sorry."

"It's okay. Both died before the revolution."

"Any brothers or sisters?"

"No."

Behrouz lit another cigarette and cleared his throat noisily. "I need to go," he said.

"Okay."

"Let me have your number, Yunus. We should hang out."

Bags swinging in my hands, heart pounding out of my chest, I rushed home like I was fleeing something. Occasional passengers and other guys I worked with had asked similar questions and I had always dodged them or lied. Now, for the first time since my mother had died, I had been truthful about who I was, and my own answers terrified me. My self-image was warped. I always liked to perceive myself as quiet and harmless, steady and trustworthy, a good man who embraced solitude voluntarily, who bothered no one and, in exchange, didn't want to be bothered. That evening, as I had spoken with Behrouz, I realized that I sounded like a sociopath. With no family, no friends, no relatives, I had become an invisible man. I barely existed in this world. For a long time I had been telling myself one story about who I was and had never examined what motivated me to construct it in the first place. Behrouz's innocent queries had shattered that narrative to pieces and forced me to see myself as others saw me.

I couldn't sleep that night. Within two hours I had used the bathroom three times. After decades of avoiding people, maybe it was already too late. Insanity sets in gradually, often unbe-knownst to the insane person, and I had discovered that I might be on the verge of losing my mind. I needed a mirror, the kind that Behrouz had briefly given me, before my tether to reality snapped.

The next morning, as I walked into the terminal and sat down at the wheel, the world felt suffocating. I hated the bus, this metal hulk I had put at the center of my life for so many years because I was too cowardly to face my real self. The bus over the years had become an extension of my body. True, it had afforded me some solace after the death of my mother, but if that constituted a debt, I had paid it off a long time ago. After twenty-five years, I had lost sight of the boundary between it and myself, except that this symbiosis hadn't happened on fair terms. As I had gotten older and more worn out, it had kept getting repaired and refurbished.

I sat with this thought through the day, stop by stop, red light after red light. It was only when Behrouz called in the evening and invited me over for dinner that I felt better.

• • •

He lived in a nondescript building, one of the thousands of four-story condos that had sprung up all over the area over the last few years. Yet for me, having become an alien in the isolation of my apartment, walking up the stairs into someone else's house amounted to visiting another planet.

At the door, Behrouz shook my hand and rushed back to the kitchen to strain the boiling rice. I looked around the apart-ment. An ornate dining table with six wooden chairs at its sides stood on top of one of many Persian rugs that covered the floor. On the wall hung framed Hafiz poetry written out in calligraphy. The open kitchen occupied the middle of the apartment, and at the center of it was Behrouz, dealing with pots on the stove. The door to one of the bedrooms was slightly ajar, and through the gap I saw several potted plants on the windowsill. A woman was watering them.

She bent over slightly, pouring water with clinical precision. She wore a floral skirt and a long-sleeved gray shirt. Her sleek, brassy hair fell all over her shoulders. She didn't seem to have noticed that I had entered her home. I knew Behrouz had a family, but it hadn't occurred to me that I would actually meet them. On top of that, I hadn't seen a woman indoors for years. My communications with them were mostly confined to short exchanges on the bus. For me, eating dinner with a woman was something from a bygone era.

She finished the last pot and turned toward the door of the room. Finally, she noticed me. Surprise flashed across her face, but she composed herself quickly and smiled. She walked out of the bedroom and into the sitting room. As she approached, the lines around her eyes grew increasingly visible. She shook my hand and introduced herself as Homa.

We sat down around the dinner table. Their daughter, Yasmin, emerged from her room. She was a twenty-year-old version of her mother—same eyes, same thick, shiny hair. She went to college in Shiraz and was complaining that the new school year had begun already so she would have to leave Tehran the next day.

The long Lahijani rice, ghormeh sabzi, fresh basil and mint, yogurt and cucumber, and stuffed olives on the table reminded me viscerally of childhood. I ate three times what I would in my own home and spoke more than I had in the last three years. Words poured out, as if a dam in my throat had broken. Behrouz watched with naked surprise as I transformed from a desiccated monk into the life of the party. I hardly recognized myself either. I regaled the group with a wide-ranging series of anecdotes. What random passengers had told me over the years had apparently stayed with me, buried deep, waiting for an opportunity to be recounted. I told them stories I didn't know that I knew. There was once a passenger who, in ten minutes, gave me an extensive account of how he would put Bush and Ahmadinejad in a cage and torture them together. Another man described the odyssey of walking across the mountains into Turkey, applying for refugee status at the UN headquarters there, getting rejected, and walking all the way back into Iran. An old woman broke into tears as soon as she saw me because I reminded her of a son who had been executed after the revolution. I related it all with considerable verve to my attentive audience. Yet a deep sense of sadness lurked in the background of that evening. I could have had the same life as Behrouz, a daughter I watched grow up to be a college student, a wife I cooked with and caressed before going to sleep.

That night, walking down the street back home, I was overwhelmed with love for this family. They had given me the chance to be someone different. And yet, along with gratitude, jealousy began to seep in and tinge the edges of my goodwill. This night, which loomed so large for me, was only one enjoyable evening out of many for them. I wanted all that Behrouz had.

• • •

Behrouz became my first real friend in adult life. We mapped out a new route and decided to walk together two nights a week. Somewhat embarrassed by my performance at his dinner table, I retreated into my accustomed silence. Behrouz took the lead, conversing and steering us past awkward pauses. During our first walks he discussed family, weather, traffic, new highways and streets. Then politics crept in and took up more and more space in the conversation. He painstakingly detailed his disdain for the Ahmadinejad administration and his disappointment in Khatami, his frustration at the unnecessary drama around the nuclear program, Putin's dubious support, and Bush's oedipal obsession with destroying the Middle East in order to finish the work his father had begun. Then one cold, autumn day about a month into our new walking routine, on a dry and polluted evening that made regular breathing a challenge, he brought up the union.

"Are you a member of the bus drivers' union?" he asked.

"No." I hardly knew what it was.

"You should be. What do you know about the union? About what it does, its history, its importance?"

"Very little. Close to nothing, to be honest."

That set him off. For the next two weeks, he talked only about the group.

"The bus drivers' union is one of the oldest and strongest in the country," he said, eyes shining with pride. "After the revolution, they destroyed it, but we fought to revive it, and now it is alive and well, though still far from what it was under the Shah."

One day he brought photos. Faded, yellowing documents from a long time gone. "It's the bus drivers' club," he explained, shuffling through the pictures before I got the chance to see them well. "They had a place of their own, where they gathered with their families, drank, and had fun. The union set it up." One photo showed Googoosh on a stage in a club, singing for a sea of tipsy men. In another, tanned workers thronged around a swimming pool.

"Do you remember the signs on buses before the revolution? 'Capacity: 44, Standing: 10.' It was illegal to board more than ten passengers after the seats were filled." I vaguely recalled this. "That was what the union achieved back then. Also, they got a tax cut for bus drivers because of the working conditions, and extra budget to hire drivers' assistants to collect tickets. They received free milk and cake every day. We had a whole unit just for flat tire operations. No matter what time of day and anywhere in Tehran, if you got a flat tire they would show up within the hour and take care of it. We had house loans, car loans, the best insurance in town, everything. Not that the Shah's people gave up any of it willingly. The union forced them into it. After the revolution, we lost all of the ground we had gained, and then the war happened. But after the war we began to come back."

He shoved the pictures back into his bag and lit a cigarette. He had decided not to smoke while walking, but talking about the union made him forget this.

"Actually," he went on, "the most important work we do, what really makes the biggest difference, is usually what you wouldn't even notice. Do you remember how hard the wheels were ten years ago?"

I did. Turning the steering wheel used to hurt my shoulder. Now that he mentioned it, I realized that at some point my muscles had stopped aching.

"There was a part that makes the wheels hydraulic and we wanted to buy it, but the transportation ministry never gave us the money. Actually, from the revolution to the end of the war they gave us pretty much nothing. The union kept lobbying and negotiating for it. Without that, we would all have had arthritis by now."

After the unofficial lecture, which took up three walks and about six hours, Behrouz brought me texts to read: *Syndicate Rights* by Hussein Semnani, essays and interviews by Yaghoub Mahdavioun, John Steinbeck's *The Grapes of Wrath*, Maxim Gorky's *Mother*. I read everything he assigned, spending long hours poring over every page like I was preparing for an exam. I read at the wheel between trips, in the morning at the breakfast table, and when I finished a book, we discussed it on our walks.

After a few months, he brought up the reading group.

"A few drivers and I have been gathering in a little stationery store in Ferdows Boulevard every other week to talk about books. Every meeting someone assigns a new one. They're all about politics and philosophy and the history of labor organizing around the world."

I said that it sounded great.

"Do you want to join?"

"Of course."

T AKE THE BLINDFOLD OFF," Hajj Saeed said when I entered the interrogation room the next day. I sat down and he put some stapled papers on the tablet. He burped before moving away. His breath smelled like the kebab I'd had for lunch.

"We have so much to do," he said and coughed and cleared his throat, emitting another wave of half-digested meat smell into the room. "Read these pages."

Behrouz's name was on the first page, followed by his introduction of me on my first day at the study group.

" 'Welcome, Yunus,' " I read, hearing my friend's voice in my head. I had felt the weight of his gaze on my skin. Then he had turned toward the others. " 'For today, I assigned two essays by Georges Sorel.' " I had nodded and smiled, trying to signal that I was satisfied and pleased with this choice. I had never heard the name, but it had rolled off Behrouz's tongue so naturally he might as well have said "Khomeini" or "Al Pacino."

I read on, surprised by how many of Behrouz's remarks I remembered verbatim. Elections, he had said, had become nonsensical carnivals set up by governments to distract workers from their real struggle. He had concluded that political organizing would be pointless if its goal was not dismantling the state.

I turned the page. The first passage was highlighted in garish red.

"Read it out loud," ordered Hajj Saeed.

" 'Sorel shows that it is paramount in politics to capture people's imagination, and the best way to do that is to create apocalyptic situations. Just imagine bus drivers stopping work for two days. This city will be dead. People might suffer for a short while, but it's worth it. They'll learn to appreciate our power.' "

"From day one," Hajj Saeed said, "all I asked was that you tell me the truth." Then he made his familiar show of disappointment: the tense pacing, the paternal throat clearing, the sighing and nodding. "This passage alone is enough to accuse all of you of plotting a strike in advance, which amounts to taking action against national security. So stop pretending that you just stumbled into something without understanding the consequences. Turn the page."

Mehdi was talking now. " 'You are prescribing chaos.' " I read his words and remembered his smooth voice, his way of containing his anger, betrayed only by the veins sticking out on his neck. " 'With the general strike, you provoke the security forces and tie the hands of the moderates in the system. We need them as allies.' "

"Go to the next meeting," said Hajj Saeed before I got to the end of Mehdi's comments. I turned three pages and read the first line. We were discussing *The Wretched of the Earth*, which Samad had assigned.

Behrouz had once told me that the best sign that you loved a book is that you could remember when and where you were when you read it. When you thought about certain passages, you might even be able to recall what you wore or the position of your fingers on the cover the first time you read them. I hadn't understood what he meant until I had read that book. Sitting on the creaky chair in the interrogation room, I thought back to how I would pick it up from the bedside table every morning as soon as my eyes opened. I would read it between stints at the bus wheel, in my spare time at the terminal, before going to bed. I devoured it in four days, reread and took notes and thought about it obsessively in the weeks that followed, while passengers filed in and out of the bus. Frantz Fanon showed that the world was as simple as it seemed: the colonized versus the colonizer, one part of the world better off than the rest because they looted and stole. I had gone to our meeting eager to talk about it.

"Read the highlighted passage on this page," Hajj Saeed said.

" 'I wanted us to discuss Fanon,' " I read Samad's words, " 'because it is acutely relevant. We people of Iran, I believe, are colonized by our own state. Everything Fanon discussed here is like our lives. The line between the colonizer and the colonized is as clear here and now as it was in Algeria back in the fifties. The only difference is that here the colonizer and the colonized have the same skin color and speak the same language.' "

"You see what kind of creatures we have to deal with?" said Hajj Saeed. He exhaled through his partly closed lips in an exaggerated manner, practically farting out of his mouth. "The guy is born and raised in a village near Semnan where, like eighty percent of the country, there was no electricity or water before the revolution. After the revolution they got all of that and a school. He got an education there for free and left, worked in a couple of cities before ending up in Tehran. Now he has a good job as a driver—decent pay, insurance, pension. If he were born twenty years earlier he would have died of a heart attack on a farm in his village. And this is what this ungrateful traitor has to say about the system that provided it all for him. What do you think of that? Do you feel colonized?"

"No."

"I thought so. I actually like your response here."

"My response?"

"Turn the page."

My name in bold font, followed by a colon, followed by a long string of words. They were my first remarks in the reading group. Nothing of what I said sounded familiar. I had argued against Samad with an audacity that now shocked me. I said that his analysis was "a gross simplification and misrepresentation of Fanon's argument," because "race and religion disparities are key for him, but those do not apply to our revolution." Also, I pointed out, colonizers invaded Africa, but the Iranian government "emerged from Iranian society." Even the words didn't sound like me. For a second, I thought that for some inscrutable reason they had put those comments there to make me look good.

Hajj Saeed leaned over the chair and flipped through several pages, clearly searching for something. I caught glimpses of words and names on the papers. Over the course of a few months we had read Foucault's *Discipline and Punish*, Al-e Ahmad's *Westoxication*, Marx and Engels's *The Holy Family*, and Bijan Jazani's *Thirty Year History of Iran*. Behrouz's face had been pale and sickly the day he had presented Foucault. Samad's garish pink shirt had been so completely wrinkled in the Marx and Engels meeting that it had made his words seem silly. Mehdi wasn't the best-dressed person either. His ill-advised jeans and disheveled hair usually contrasted with the intensity of his defense of the books he liked.

Hajj Saeed paused at the notes on the Ali Shariati meeting. Mehdi had assigned *Alavid Shiism and Safavid Shiism*, which was my second favorite read after *The Wretched of the Earth*.

During his brief intellectual period prior to his death, my father had managed to scare me away from prerevolutionary Muslim thinkers. But three decades later, Shariati's book had drawn me in from the first page. Shiism was a theory of emancipation, he said. When Islam came to Iran, the underdogs and the oppressed embraced it first, and it was their weapon until the conservative Safavid mullahs corrupted it by colluding with the shahs.

I read Mehdi's comment out loud at Hajj Saeed's order. " 'During the 1979 revolution, Islam was the main victim. The mullahs did nothing but suppress and petrify its emancipatory potential by reducing it to rituals and rules and superstitions. Our job here should be to revitalize the Sarbedaran Shiism against what is now being propagated by the establishment.' "

"You see?" Hajj Saeed said. "You were blatantly conspiring against the system, day in, day out, on all fronts. No other government in the world would tolerate this. You know what would happen if you were a Muslim in America who got together with a bunch of other Muslims to study how to overthrow the government and the FBI found out about it? You would be sent to Guantanamo immediately. You know what Guantanamo is?"

"No."

"Never mind. Turn the page."

The first book I had chosen was Lenin's *The State and Revolution* because it had seemed like a safe bet. I would appear sufficiently revolutionary, and no one would argue about the relevance of the book or the fame of the author. I assigned it and then found a secondhand copy in an Enqelab Street bookstore to study. Over the next two weeks I slogged through the clumsy translation and went to the meeting with a half-full notebook.

Hajj Saeed put his finger next to the end of a highlighted passage of my remarks. " 'Every form of the state is corrupt and should be taken down,' " I read with a thin voice. " 'It follows that every representative of any state who says he or she is in the government to help the poor is a liar and should be dealt with as one.' "

Behrouz had been the first one to comment on this. Then Samad had responded briefly. Then my name again. All my passages in this meeting had been highlighted. My extensive paraphrasing of Lenin, my riffs on the police and jail as two wings that enabled the rich to fly. Every word was damning, yet remembering that day brought me a tinge of pleasure. My small audience had awkwardly squirmed on their stools, astonished at my boldness.

When I had finished speaking, Mehdi attacked. I read his words in silence. "I hate to sound unkind, but I can't say it any other way. You don't know what you're talking about. Your call for an all-out revolution is utterly pathetic and childish. Maybe Lenin didn't know that because when he wrote that book he had never lived through a revolution. We all did and saw firsthand what it delivered." I wondered if he believed in what he said, or if he had just been mounting an attack to put a presumptuous newcomer in his place. "You know what?" he went on. "I think this whole conversation is a huge waste of time. Why do we even care? A Russian man a century ago said a bunch of things about his people in his time. We live in a Muslim country in another century. How am I supposed to get anything important out of this?"

I read Samad's interjection on the page and tried in vain to remember him on that day. "Then why do we read your beloved Mashruteh thinkers?" He was referring to a series of meetings in which Mehdi had made them read up on the constitutional revolution. "Their nineteenth-century Iran was as different from ours as Lenin's world was. And I share nothing in common with Muslims anyway."

Before I could read the rest, Hajj Saeed flipped two pages ahead. From that point on, Behrouz and I hadn't said a word. Mehdi and Samad had soon abandoned Lenin and started their usual fight, which rapidly intensified, until both of them exploded. Samad attacked Islam as the source of all troubles in the country and called Mehdi's reformism "despicably disingenuous." Mehdi accused Samad of wanting to repeat the disaster of the revolution because he got off on smashing and breaking things and couldn't wait for gradual change that would benefit everyone. They had gone on for a good hour, expelling masses of outrage that had long been accumulating. Those passages were highlighted, and Hajj Saeed put his finger on them, but he didn't tell me to read them. He seemed to be rereading them himself.

Hajj Saeed then flipped the page, and for the first time the name "Rahman" appeared. I read his words.

"I think the best way out of this for us is an atom bomb. Imagine it landing right in the middle of Valiasr Square, turning half of this city into ashes. There is too much clutter here, too many humans and things, too much history and misery. We're all messed up beyond redemption. We need a purge. If we go now, future generations might be able to figure things out."

I recalled looking around the basement when Rahman paused, studying the faces of my friends to make sure that what I had heard was not an illusion. Behrouz blinked wildly. Samad's eyes and mouth twitched strangely. Mehdi had frozen in place, hunched and motionless like a poorly carved statue.

"I will volunteer to be the first victim when the bomb drops," Rahman had continued. "Just in case you were going to accuse me of hypocrisy."

The silence that weighed down on us was thick, almost tangible. Rahman looked at us one by one, then he rose from his stool without straightening his back. His hands dangling before his torso, he trudged across the basement, climbed up the stairs, and disappeared without uttering another word. I never saw him again.

"You know," Hajj Saeed said, "I like this guy, his way of keeping quiet all those weeks when everybody else was blabbering, then dropping that bombshell and walking away. I even partly agree with him that we have messed up irredeemably. That's why we need a messiah."

He took three heavy steps toward the door, his pace slower than usual.

"You people think you know us," Hajj Saeed said from across the room. "You think we're just addicted to power. That's your biggest mistake. We are here as safeguards, laying the ground-work for the emergence of the last Imam."

I reread Rahman's words as Hajj Saeed turned around and walked back over to me.

"Now tell me, Yunus. What do you think will happen at the end of the world?"

"I don't know."

"You must have some idea. Have you ever thought about it?"

"No. I am not going to be around to see it."

"You're right about that. Put on your blindfold."

As always, I left the lower edge of the eye cover a little loose to be able to see the corridor that led from the interrogation room to the cell. I pretended to be fully blind and shuffled over to reach Hajj Saeed's desk. Photos were scattered across it. I slowed down and my hands groped. I was buying time so I could take another look at them.

They were the same five photos Hajj Saeed had shown me. Under the direct light from the ceiling, they looked sharper. I glanced at them from under the blindfold and paused on the pic-ture from the café. Now I could see the faces better. Behrouz's expression seemed more enthusiastic to me now. Mine remained stoic. What I had thought was a smile on Samad's face now seemed a gesture of annoyance, more like his usual response to Behrouz. Mehdi was still laughing.

I leaned slightly closer. The door opened. Akbar cleared his throat. I abandoned caution and bent over the desk, blatantly looking at the photo from under the blindfold.

Mehdi's eyes were red dots. He was looking at the camera when the picture was taken.

"What are you doing?" Hajj Saeed said. I ignored him. In the photo, Mehdi, unlike the rest of us, was not looking at Behrouz. He had tilted his head toward the photographer and was looking at the lens, as if to give him a signal.

Akbar grabbed me, tightened the blindfold, and dragged me out of the room.

KEEP THE BLINDFOLD ON," Hajj Saeed said to me the next morning as I was led into the interrogation room. I had already brought my hands to my face to untie the rag. I dropped them back to my sides and shuffled to the chair.

"I was going through the photos again," said Hajj Saeed. "I laid them out on the desk, the ones you saw and others I didn't show you, to study the relationships in the group. Correct me if I'm wrong, but you seem much closer to Behrouz than the other members. Is that true?"

"He introduced me to everyone."

"So you met him first. Is he your close friend?"

"Well, it's complicated."

"What do you mean by that?"

"We met just a couple of months before the study group."

Hajj Saeed's tread beat out a slow rhythm on the floor. I knew what was coming. My mind was in denial, but my body knew it. The shivering set in as soon as he brought up Behrouz, and it grew worse by the second. Soon my legs were twitching uncontrollably.

From the other side of the room, a drawer moaned open. Hajj Saeed was moving at a snail's pace to torment me. He sauntered back and stood in front of me. With the light behind him, his shadow stretched over my chair. He put down another small stack of stapled papers. The text messages I had exchanged with Homa. Every single word, with times and dates, printed in a small, ugly font.

"Read the first line," he said.

"I can't do it."

"Read it out loud."

"I'm sorry, I—"

"Read the texts out loud, word by word. With the times and dates. There aren't that many."

"I can't."

Hajj Saeed sighed. His heels clicked on the floor again as he walked away, but it was not long before he came back.

"What is the point of you resisting? I can just call Ehsan to beat you into reading this."

At that point, I would have welcomed the blows. The sight of the messages had already shot my nerves. My body was heating up from inside, and jags of pain crisscrossed my chest. Physical punishment would at least have been some distraction.

The shadow of Hajj Saeed swung back and forth over the page. He was shifting his weight from one foot to the other.

"Behrouz was released yesterday," he said. The shadow moved away, but the shoes didn't click. "We talked about a lot of things together. He is a brilliant, lovely man. He told me everything about how you hurt him."

Tears welled up. I took deep breaths to hold them back, but they streamed down instead, wetting the blindfold, sliding down my cheeks.

"Take off the blindfold."

I stared at the wall through a blur of tears. Hajj Saeed moved away from me to stand by his desk.

"I told you in our first meeting that I am not here to punish. I want to help. My belief in human potential is unshakable. Everyone is redeemable, even those who commit sins as egregious as yours. This is a fork you are standing at, remember. One way—"

"Okay, I'll read," I interrupted him. His voice grated hard on my ears, tormenting me beyond any physical duress. I would do anything to shut him up. Besides, I felt that I deserved punishment. Reading the catalogue of my sins was something I needed to do for myself.

I read, *It was so—*

"Read the date," Hajj Saeed interrupted.

October 12th, 2004. It was so nice to see you tonight. I imagined her thumbs tapping the words into her phone.

"Where did you meet her?" he asked.

"The first time Behrouz invited me over for dinner."

"I mean when you met her alone."

• • •

After that first dinner, I became a regular weekend guest in Behrouz's house. The couple fed me home-cooked stews, listened carefully to my stories, laughed at my jokes. I was a different person with them. They transformed the rhythm of my life. Now I looked forward to the end of the workweek. Even the long-established route of my nocturnal walks changed. I went out of my way to take the meandering path that ran through their neighborhood park.

One evening I heard my name. When Behrouz had called out

to me in the store, I had been frightened. This time, the voice, feminine and familiar, put me at ease.

"What are you doing here?" Homa said. She was sitting on a bench by the pathway, smiling.

"Oh, I was just walking around. How are you? How are Behrouz and Yasmin?"

"Great," she said. "Father and daughter are hooked on some stupid TV show that I can't stand. I came to hang out here for a little while. Do you watch TV?"

"No, I barely turn it on. Maybe a couple of times a week to watch the news."

"If I lived alone, I would throw it out the window."

With that, we had reached our quota of small talk. Manners dictated that I should wish her and her family a good evening and leave. But I stood there and stared at her face. She stared back. We stayed like this an awkwardly long time. Then she stirred and moved a little to one end of the bench. I crossed the pavement and sat down. My heartbeat rose. I looked ahead at three trees across the pathway, standing tall and erect and identical in diameter.

"It's a nice park," I said.

"Is this your first time here?"

"No, I've walked around here a lot." I didn't say that I had always been with Behrouz when I did this.

From the corner of my eye, I could see her turn her head to look at my profile.

"I come here all the time," she said.

"Alone?"

"Yes," she said. "You live by yourself, right?"

"It's terrible," I said.

"A lot of people live alone," she said.

"Not as alone as I do."

"Well, you can live with other people and be totally lonely. That's even worse."

I inched forward to the edge of the bench. We were getting into uncharted territory.

"I grew up very lonely," I said. "I was an only child and lost both my parents when I was still a teenager."

"Behrouz told me that. That's awful. I'm so sorry."

"I was lonely living with them before they died, then officially lonely after they died." I laughed hollowly.

"My dad worked in Sepah Bank," I continued. "He was a happy, caring man. Then SAVAK killed his brother, who was a Feda-i fighter, under torture. When that happened, he lost his mind, became rude and unbearable at home and messed up at work so much they had to fire him after twenty years. My mom was sweet and put up with him through all of it. He had a heart attack and died when I was eighteen. Then a few months later a car ran down my mom and killed her on the street. Just like that. I got there a minute after she died. Her left hand was black and twisted in a weird way because all her fingers were broken and knocked out of their joints, like this." I twisted my hand behind my back and bent my fingers out of shape to show her. The shock in her eyes jolted me back to reality.

"Sorry," I said. I crossed my legs and laced my fingers on my thigh. My throat felt tight.

"Don't be," she said.

Tears welled up in my eyes. I cleared my throat, cocked my head, and looked away, pretending that something on the other side of the park had drawn my attention to buy time. I couldn't stop crying, though.

I felt the touch of her hand. She tentatively stroked my shoulder, paused a second, and gently pressed with her fingers. I sobbed shamelessly. My whole body shook, and my shoulders convulsed as my last shred of inhibition evaporated. Her hand slid up my neck to my head, and she stroked my hair.

When I could not cry any more, shame returned. I slid myself away to one end of the bench, sniffling and breathing heavily. She moved to the other end, as if to maintain the symmetry of our bodies.

"I have to go," I said.

"Okay," she said. I was vaguely disappointed. I had expected her to ask me to stay. "How do you feel?"

"I feel okay."

"I'm glad to hear that."

"I'm very sorry. I don't know what just happened."

She moved back toward me, reached out, and pressed my shoulder again. Then her hand moved down slowly and grabbed my fingers and squeezed them.

"Don't be silly," she said. "You are a good man."

I nodded and took a few deep breaths.

"Give me your number," she said. "We should keep in touch."

As soon as I got home, the phone buzzed in my pocket.

It was so nice to see you.

"Read on," Hajj Saeed said.

Thanks for bearing with me tonight. I am sorry for being such unpleasant company.

You are a good man, Yunus.

• • •

The next day the traffic on the Pounak-Azadi line was bad, but I barely noticed. I hadn't seen Behrouz in the morning, but I would eventually run into him. Had Homa told him that we had met? They seemed very close, the kind of couple who would talk all the time. Inching along in traffic, I went over the story about last night that I would tell him if he asked.

In the middle of the third trip, the phone buzzed.

I didn't—

"Read the date," Hajj Saeed said.

October 13th, 2004. I didn't tell Behrouz that we met.

OK, don't worry about it.

I don't know why I didn't tell him.

Don't overthink it. It's totally fine.

It feels strange, though. Should I tell him?

I read and reread the message until at some point I realized the cars behind me had begun to honk. The light was green. I had to wait a few minutes until the next stop before writing back. Another text came in the meantime.

Should I tell him? I never hide anything from Behrouz.

Paranoia began to engulf me. What if Homa was trying to cover herself, in case anything went wrong? I realized that I didn't care. My sweaty fingertips smeared the phone screen while I typed.

Don't need to tell him. It's too late. You'll make him suspicious over nothing. Just forget about it.

OK. Have a good day.

Please delete these texts.

I already did.

Hajj Saeed sighed and turned and walked.

"Read on," he said.

October 21st, 2004. Thanks for having us.

• • •

A week later I saw Homa again.

That surprisingly cold autumn afternoon, the study group convened to discuss Ali Shariati's *Alavid Shiism and Safavid Shiism*. The meeting was tense. Afterward, we straggled out of the stationery store like we were returning from an ignominious defeat.

Behrouz stepped in to fix things. "You guys seem pretty thirsty. Let's go to my house and open a bottle of arak," he said before people parted ways. Everyone immediately accepted the invitation.

I entered the house like a thief returning to a crime scene. Behrouz uncorked a bottle. The men gathered around it, and each swallowed down three shots back-to-back to wash away the bad blood. The arak was strong, and our stomachs were empty. Our faces warmed up. The ice broke at once. We began gossiping and joking. We imagined how the fat minister of transportation fucked his wife, made fun of the pants Ibrahim had worn the day before, and told the joke about the mullah masturbating in a forest who saw a bear. I listened half attentively, laughing when the others laughed, my eyes frequently turning toward the door.

An hour later, I stood up, and the furniture whirled before me. I staggered to the toilet. I wanted to vomit, but that would be embarrassingly loud, so I put my head under cold water. I dried off as best I could with a paper towel and returned to the sitting room, water dripping down through the stubble of my beard.

Homa was back.

The light made the scene look surreal. The last sunbeams of the day streamed in through the window, suffusing the sitting room in a hallucinatory orange that only intensified my intoxication. To my left, three drunk men huddled around a table in silence. To my right, Behrouz's narrow back faced me and obscured my view of the narrower torso of his wife. I could see only half of her face behind Behrouz's shoulder. She was staring at me.

We left shortly after Homa arrived. Every time I thought about our affair later, that moment stood out to me. Her gaze over Behrouz's shoulder had thrilled me. The mix of sick sunset light and alcohol had added to its effect. Of course Behrouz had played a significant role. Standing between us, holding Homa tightly in his arms, he had inadvertently started a virility war. I didn't care about his clear affection for his wife. At that moment, he had unknowingly positioned himself as an obstacle between me and what I wanted.

I passed the next day hungover. I daydreamed at the wheel with an erection, imagining myself kissing Homa in a movie theatre, picnicking in Mellat Park, traveling to the shore of the Caspian Sea or going deep into the desert to fuck in the dunes. At noon I wrote her.

October 21st, 2004. Thanks for having us. Everything was amazing.

"Louder," Hajj Saeed said.

It was very nice seeing you.

A long hour passed. Crawling through the traffic, I agonized over what to write back. She made it easy on me.

I have to see a doctor tomorrow evening near your place. If you are home I can bring some food from last night. I cooked a lot for dinner but no one ate lol.

I waited five minutes to write back.

Isn't it too much trouble?

Hajj Saeed laughed.

It's not. The doctor's office—

"Louder!" interrupted Hajj Saeed. "I can hardly hear you."

The doctor's office is near you. I'll swing by around 8. Does that work?

Sure.

See you tomorrow evening. Send me the full address.

Reading the words out loud, I was struck by a realization. She hadn't known where I lived. She knew I was in the neighborhood but could not have known how far from her doctor's office I was. She had probably made up the appointment.

"Read that again," ordered Hajj Saeed.

"Which part?"

"The whole thing. Loud and clear."

I did.

"Do it again."

I did.

"I am going to make sure you will remember that exchange for the rest of your life," he said.

• • •

She slowly took off her coat and sat down on my couch, leaned back and crossed her legs. She wore a white shirt and black jeans. She had makeup on, but her eyes looked tired. I sat next to her and furtively watched her face as she examined the apartment.

168

I didn't know what to do, how to begin. There is a fine line between hastiness and passivity, and only a brief window when you can take action. Before that you come off as horny, after that a chicken. I never had learned how to be smooth. I wasn't even sure if we both wanted the same thing.

"How long have you lived here?" Homa asked.

"Twelve years."

"Your friends must always be asking you to bring their girlfriends over here."

"You're the first woman who has ever entered this house."

She looked at me.

"Behrouz has a girlfriend."

"No, he doesn't." I had spoken the words with total certainty.

"Yes, he does. And you know that."

"No, I don't."

"Of course you do. You are his close friend. You weren't even surprised when I said that. You denied it right off the bat."

"It was out of shock."

"Her name is Golnaz. You know how old she is?"

"How would I know that?"

"She is twenty-three. Twenty-one years younger than he is. Have you seen him with a girl that young?"

"Of course not."

"You don't have to lie to me. I don't care anymore."

"I'm not lying."

She uncrossed her legs and stretched on the sofa.

"How did you find out?" I asked.

"Unlike you," she said, recrossing her legs, "he frequently forgets to delete his texts."

So I was her way of getting even with her cheating husband. I wanted to be offended, but I wasn't. She had given me a chance to make her happy. That was all that mattered. My job was to convince her that the risk she had taken was worth it. That she had come to the right man. I was proud that she had chosen me.

I moved next to her on the couch and put my hand in her hair. I stroked her neck, then leaned in and licked it. Her eyes closed. I grabbed her face, kissed her lips and stuck my tongue in, forcing my way through her teeth to poke into the far corners of her mouth. She tried to back off. I pushed harder. I pulled up her shirt, flipped her breasts out of her bra, and squeezed them. She moaned. I squeezed harder. She moved my hand away. I took off her shirt and unhooked her bra. Her breasts hung down. She covered them and stared at me in confusion. "Slow down a little," she mumbled. I transmuted my embarrassment into anger. Wasn't she cheating on my best friend? She had no right to tell me what to do. I hated her and I hated myself.

I pulled down her jeans and underwear, and she arranged herself on the sofa. I wanted to climb over her and get it done with, but I couldn't. Her nakedness overwhelmed me. I pulled back and looked at her body. It seemed completely alien in that room. I stumbled off the sofa and stood over her, staring at her exposed form. She lay there faceup, perplexed.

HOW DID YOU FUCK HER?" Hajj Saeed asked, the way he would about the weather. "What did you do first? Did you take off her shirt or her pants? How did her lips taste? Come on, just tell me. Don't you regret what you did? Don't you want to be forgiven? That's the way. Confess."

"What do you want to know?"

"How big are her boobs? Did you lick her pussy? Don't worry. It's going to stay in this room. Come on, you remember it all."

I stared helplessly at my hands clutching at the edge of the tablet arm, the knuckles whitening against the wood.

Hajj Saeed grabbed the back of my neck and shook it violently. "Are you fucking deaf? I asked you some questions. What were you thinking when you shoved your dick inside your best friend's wife? Were you proud of yourself?"

He used his grip on my neck to slam my head against the wall. The padded layer did little to soften the blow. My head snapped back and hung down, and my hands let go of the chair. He gripped the back of my head and slammed it against the wall again. "Answer the question. How did you fuck her?"

I felt more relaxed. Every blow released some of the suffocating guilt. I pressed my lips together and hoped for another strike. Hajj Saeed slapped the back of my neck and punched my shoulder.

Then he stopped, perhaps realizing that his strategy had backfired. Finally he moved away from my chair. "Read on," he said.

October 23rd, 2004. Thank you for the food!

You're welcome.

• • •

For the next two months, Homa came over every week on Monday and Wednesday and stayed from 6 to 8 p.m. She told Behrouz that she had signed up for a yoga class.

We quickly fell into a routine. We would go to bed as soon as she arrived and spend half an hour fucking. After, we would lie where we were for an hour and just talk. The time was never enough for us to say everything. We spoke quickly and loudly and interrupted each other. At 7:30 we had to get up to dress. We would have tea and cookies while she got ready to leave. We were like Adam and Eve in there, utterly free and totally isolated from the rest of the world. After her visits I felt lighter. I felt cleaner.

Homa talked a little less then but cried more. She liked to speak about her childhood in Shahroud. Her father was a gardener, her mother a mosque dweller. She had two brothers, one of whom had been killed in the Iraq war and the other a refugee in Sweden. She had escaped her family and come to Tehran to become an actress. Then the revolution happened, and the performers she admired most fled. She abandoned her dream and worked as a bookkeeper for a rug dealer in the Grand Bazaar. She commuted from Pirouzi Street to the bazaar every day, on the bus line where Behrouz used to work. One day, after she passed her ticket to the driver, she opened up her hand to find a note with Behrouz's phone number. She called him two days later and married him after seven months, mostly to silence her parents. "The moment I said yes to that mullah," she told me, "I knew I was making the biggest mistake of my life."

In the second month of our affair, sex started to take a back seat to talking. Homa almost always spoke about her family. For me, the hardest part was listening to her rant about Behrouz. She told me a lot of things that were not my business, but I enjoyed hearing them. I learned that Behrouz was a snorer, that he had symmetrical moles on his hips, that he screamed like a four-year-old when he saw spiders. He and Homa fought over everything, from Behrouz's inability to ever buy the right kind of milk at the grocery store to how to deal with their daughter's boyfriends, of whom there were at least two at a time.

Within a couple of weeks, the awkwardness of talking about Behrouz wore off. I stopped my pretense of shame, and nodded and laughed at anecdotes from their private life. Sometimes I indulged myself and went as far as asking her why, if everything was so miserable, she didn't just divorce him? I told her that she shouldn't tolerate his living like a dirty teenage boy and she shouldn't have to bear the whole responsibility for cleaning the house. Homa occasionally demurred but never rejected what I said outright.

Two months into the affair, for the first time, she missed a Monday.

I can't come today, I read out loud.

It's okay. Did something happen?

I don't know. Behrouz is acting a little weird. I think he's suspicious.

Really?

Yes. Let's see. Maybe I can't come as often anymore.

"You must have shit your pants," Hajj Saeed said.

I hadn't but I nodded.

She didn't show up on Wednesday either. I paid close attention to Behrouz's behavior at work but didn't see any change. Was Homa being entirely honest? I had no way to know, and I was overcome with jealousy. Homa slept next to another man every night. She was raising his child and cooking his food. That was already too much to take. Now it seemed that she had gotten whatever she wanted from me, and she no longer cared about our arrangement.

She didn't come over the next Monday either. On the fourteenth day of her absence, I wrote her.

Are you coming tonight? I read out loud.

No. We have guests. Maybe next Monday?

I remembered every second of the next five minutes. I was in the bus terminal for my lunch break, sitting on a chair in front of the management premises, my eyes glued to the screen. My shaking hand struggled to hold a spoonful of mixed rice steady in front of my mouth. I was working myself up into a rage. She had used me for revenge, I told myself, and now the time had come for her to get rid of me.

I miss you.

Her text came at the worst possible moment. I was burning with anger, and her message only fueled the fire. I wouldn't allow her to sugarcoat her rejection of me with this "miss you" bullshit. I stabbed the spoon into the container of rice and fired off a reply.

Never mind. I have been fucking another woman since last week.

As soon as I sent the text, I wanted to take it back. I reread the words and was mortified. Even if she had used me to get back at her husband, hadn't I used her too?

My last message went unanswered for days. Sometimes I forgot about her for hours, other times I felt superior to her and Behrouz. I had stolen a beautiful woman from her husband, after all. This was an endorsement of my manhood. But those stretches of self-adulation didn't last long. They led to the bouts of longing for the touch of Homa's hand, for the sound of her voice. I stewed in resentment and fixated on the possibility that she had lied to me.

A few weeks after the last message, I was behind the wheel, cresting the Azmayesh Bridge in traffic. At the top of the bridge, a flashback hit me hard.

We were in my bed. I held her from behind as I told her about the moment I had encountered the dead body of my father. When I described the froth on his lips, she pulled herself away and turned around to look at me. She kissed my eyelids and turned back again. "Keep going," she said.

The moment wasn't especially important by itself, but it symbolized all that I had lost. I looked down Sheikh Fazlollah Nouri Highway at the stream of vehicles emitting the pall of smog that engulfed the bridge. I tasted the poisonous exhaust in my mouth. The driver's vestibule became a cage shrinking by the second. I pulled down the window for fresh air, but the pollution flooded in and worsened my sense of suffocation. My ears began to pick up sounds out of the hum with unusual precision. The wet cough of a passenger, the roar of a Toyota engine a few yards ahead of me, a passenger's nail scratching on the window.

At the touch of a hand on my shoulder, I shuddered and jerked around. "Are you all right?" said a middle-aged man. Behind me, people laid on their horns, and in the bus, the passengers had begun to complain loudly. The traffic had moved far ahead. I nodded at the man, drove until I reached the bumper of the car in front of me, and pulled out my phone.

December 27th, 2004. I need to talk to you, I read out loud.

Sure. When?

Come over tonight.

I will see you tonight, but I don't think it's a good idea for me to come over.

Why?

Let's meet in the park. In the same place at 9.

OK.

I sighed and stared at the blank space beneath the last message.

It was a typically irritating, airless Tehran night. Grey haze threw its weight on the city like a fat man slumping on a sofa. Unrelenting traffic encroached into every side street and small square. I arrived early, sat on the bench, and stared around with an empty mind.

She showed up ten minutes late, looking calm and determined. We exchanged cold greetings. She seated herself on the bench. We both stared ahead, like we had the first time we met there.

"We can't go on like this," she said. "I like you a lot, but I have a husband and a child, and I am forty-two. At this age, you just don't abandon things and start from scratch. Do you understand what I mean?"

A very old man walked past us, his cane tapping a careful rhythm on the pavement. He must have been in his eighties. He would be dead soon, I thought. I might have to live this life another forty years before I could join him.

"If it was just me and Behrouz, I would have thought differently about us. But I can't do this to Yasmin. She is at a very sensitive age and is already going through a lot."

The "what about me" card was my only option, but playing it would be pointless. Her mind was made up. Even if I cried or begged, I knew I wouldn't be able to pressure her.

The banality of the breakup bothered me more than the fact of it. I deserved at least a semblance of drama, a few screams and tears. She showed no interest in that. Her lack of passion drained the energy out of me.

The silence stretched as I weighed how to respond. Finally Homa put her hand on my shoulder. "You are a good man, Yunus," she said. She stood up, nodded at me, and left.

• • •

Four nights later, I was walking home from work. The neighborhood was in a bad state. By then, no trace of the semi-idyllic life of my first years there remained. The frenzy of expansion in Tehran had fully altered the character of the remote suburb. The last gardens of walnut and cherry trees were gone, and my route took me past rows of big black garbage bags that stray cats tore into. Instead of the faint whisper of a stream, I heard the occasional squeak of a rat in the gutter and the shriek of hungry crows on tree branches.

Two blocks from my home, a man emerged from the shadows.

I had seen Behrouz the day before and everything had been

normal. Now he looked as though he had just risen from his grave. The whites of his eyes flashed brightly, and his hands seemed to jerk around of their own accord.

He took two long strides toward me and smashed his knee into my diaphragm. The sudden blow knocked the wind out of me. I collapsed. He kicked me in the chest again before I even hit the ground. When I was down, he sat on me, grabbed my neck, and punched me in the face. The first blow knocked my jaw out of place. I didn't feel pain and my mind was clear. He paused, waiting for my response. I didn't move. I had committed a sin and deserved the punishment. I swallowed my saliva and tasted the blood. It tasted good.

Behrouz got off my torso, stood up, and gathered his fists at his chest like a boxer waiting for his dazed opponent to rise. I rolled over, coughed and spat. I clawed at a tree to help me stand and then put up my hands. Behrouz dropped his fists. He looked around and saw a few people watching the fight. "What the fuck are you looking at?" he yelled at them. They didn't move. Behrouz spat on the sidewalk and walked away. I never saw him again.

• • •

Hajj Saeed collected the papers and put them into the drawer. He came back to stand over me, and the shadow of his head moved across half of the tablet arm like a black, setting sun.

"Yunus," he said. The half circle of darkness enlarged slightly and then froze. "Do you know the name for what you did?"

I didn't say anything.

"Adultery," he whispered and resumed his pacing. I thought

his shoes made a slightly different sound on the floor and wondered if he had worn a new pair that day. I tilted my head to try
to see them, but they didn't make their way back into view. "Do
you know what happens to adulterers?"

"I do."

"I'm not sure about that. You have participated in a conspiracy
against the government and beaten the son of a minister within
an inch of his life. That's enough to keep you here a good decade.
But adultery. With a married woman."

His shadow shook its head.

"If you ask me, that's not even the worst part. The law doesn't
distinguish between fucking your friend's wife or a stranger's.
But I do."

He began to walk again.

"I told you that your life is in my hands, and you seem to have
never quite believed that. Now here's the evidence. If I put these
text messages into your file and write a report on how I concluded during interrogation that you committed adultery, you are
fucked. And believe me, I'm angry enough to do that."

He sighed noisily.

"However, I haven't forgotten my first promise. I told you that
I'm here to help people get better. I said that my belief in human
potential is unshakable, no matter how strongly people like you
challenge it. So I repeat the warning I gave you on the first day.
You can decide what you want, Yunus. Either work with me
through this or, well, you know what's coming to you."

"How do I work with you?"

"Tell me the truth."

"But that's what I have been doing."

He paused somewhere in the cell. My lack of emotion in the face of his threats disconcerted me. By forcing me to read those texts, Hajj Saeed had played his last card. He thought the messages would crush me and I would bow to whatever he asked, but the effect they had on me was the opposite. I had a sense of certainty, a feeling of reassurance, that the fall had ended. I had hit at rock bottom, but it was at least a hard surface. I was no longer falling through the air.

"Get up." His voice came from behind his desk. "Come on, get your ass off that chair. Go stand in the corner of the room."

I groped my way to the corner and paused, looking to the wall.

"Turn around."

He slapped me across the face. The second blow landed on my other cheek right after the first one. The third and fourth followed. Then he punched. He pummeled my torso, chest, hands, belly, unleashing his fists indiscriminately and with extraordinary force. I bent and covered my head. The punches stopped, but a familiar pain shot through my leg as his shoe met my kneecap. I lost my balance and collapsed.

HAD A DREAM THAT NIGHT. There were two of me: one standing among a team of surgeons, one on a surgery bed, being dissected. The doctor sawed my head open, pulled out my brain, and rubbed a heated iron on it to smooth out the wrinkles and grooves.

I lurched out of sleep and grabbed my skull. It was unscathed, but my perception of my surroundings had changed. The cell no longer seemed to be one continuous space with walls and a ceiling. It had broken down into meaningless fragments. It made no sense to me that one wall was balanced horizontally atop the four vertical ones. The same went for my body. I tried to put my hands together, but they refused to meet and kept passing above or below each other.

I touched my legs. The right one felt fine, but the left didn't respond. It was numb and dead. I pushed and twisted it to see if it was a real limb. My muscles contracted. The pain made my knee jerk up and hit the middle of my forehead.

I stopped struggling and leaned back against the wall. My body was rebelling against my mind, but my mind would not surrender. It refused to submit to this collapse of what made me who I was.

I forced myself to think of my family. I started with my father.

Abbas. I whispered the name, then yelled it to hear the sound echoing off the walls. What would he think of me in this place? He hadn't raised his voice with me often, so I remembered vividly when he did. Like when he got mad because I told my cousin to go fuck himself. I had never seen him so red in the face. I was ten. My cousin and my uncle were over at our place. The adults were sitting on the couches, talking. My cousin and I played on the floor at their feet. We were squabbling about who should have the toy police car. He snatched it out of my hand, and I told him to go fuck himself, a phrase I had just learned at school. "You shouldn't have said that," I berated myself in the cell. "You should never have said that!" I tried to reimagine the scene, redefine the reality. In the new version, when he grabbed the car from me, I just shook my head to put him to shame. My father didn't get mad, and everything continued on smoothly. His heart rate didn't go up, and this helped postpone his eventual heart attack so he lived a little longer.

Once I started thinking this way, I couldn't stop. That day my father had an accident—crossing the street, a taxi hit him. Both of his hands were in casts for four months. I had never seen him that depressed. That accident must have weakened his heart, and it probably shortened his life. In the new past, I kept him a few minutes longer at home. I asked him, "When did the last dinosaur die?" or "When are we going to watch the Persepolis and Esteghlal Ahvaz match?" By the time he answered my question, the taxi was already gone. No accident, no casts on his hands, no depression. Stronger heart, longer life.

Was the nail in the coffin the day he had a fight at the bank and they kicked him out because he had insulted the Shah? When he received the news that his brother had been executed? He suffered so much in his short life. Maybe even more than I had. He deserved better. He deserved as much peace as anyone else.

Then my thoughts turned to my mother. Her life could have been so different, too. If my father hadn't died like that, she probably would have had no need for the antidepressants that set her off-balance when she walked. What if her teenage son had helped her more, so she didn't always have to go out and do the shopping? She could have stayed in front of the TV that day and survived. The car that hit her would have just come and gone.

I thought of Homa, with her weirdly shaped left toes and the big mole on her back an inch above her ass. Where was she now? She must be with Behrouz, probably happy. Thanks to me, they might have sorted out their problems and were living a better life. Behrouz might have forgiven her and abandoned that young girl-friend. I was sure they would never talk about me. But in solitude, each of them must have had me on their mind a lot. Or maybe Behrouz didn't. He might sometimes remember the night he beat me up and wonder how I felt about that. Not much more, though. But I hoped I gave Homa some sleepless nights.

But maybe there were things I didn't know. She had seemed honest on our last day in the park when she said she would have considered being with me if it weren't for their daughter. She might be regretting her decision now. But who cares. Both of us were going to die soon. In our remaining nights, it didn't matter whether she wrapped her arms around me or Behrouz.

I sat motionless against the wall and spent several hours thinking about the minutiae of my life, combing through memories from before I came to prison. It felt good to retrieve the past. It was like gaining another dimension that gave me the power to keep my thoughts from bubbling out of my mind and floating astray.

I tried to get up for a walk, but the weight of memories in my head kept me nailed to the floor. When I finally did stand, I could barely keep my neck straight. My head kept lolling onto my shoulders. I had to hold it with both hands when I moved. It seemed like its density had doubled and the mass inside couldn't stay balanced. I stumbled around the cell twice, then collapsed back onto my blankets.

The next time I rose, my body felt too light, like gravity now couldn't even act upon it properly. I tried to walk back and forth, but my limbs did not comply. I longed for that strange feeling of heaviness to come back. I wanted to feel material again. I looked around the cell for something to weight me. I picked up my slippers, but they were too thin. I took off my clothes and made a ball out of them and held them in one hand. Then I closed my eyes to focus on the sensation of gripping, to feel the contact of the fabric with the skin of my palm. It was better than nothing but far from enough. The clothes were too insubstantial.

I opened my eyes and examined my naked body. My penis dangled, limp and vulnerable. I hadn't thought about it in days. I spat on my palm, reached down, and started rubbing. I closed my eyes, struggling to picture the bodies of women I knew. The vague images and half-formed silhouettes I tried to summon from the distant corners of my memory did nothing for me. The harder I tried to focus on them, the more ghostlike they became.

I stroked my penis vigorously, but with an empty mind I couldn't make it hard. I kept spitting into my hand and rubbing, making noises that had never before come out of my mouth. The skin on the shaft grew tender and then alarmingly red from the circumcision line upward. The pain in the organ stimulated me. My fingers grew numb. My arm muscles became stiff from the effort. Finally I felt the tickling sensation beneath my balls, the activation of the glands, and the movement of semen. When I came, the white ejaculate spurted out halfway across the cell and splattered on the wall. I collapsed and fell asleep.

• • •

The turn of Akbar's key in the door woke me up. He looked with apparent concern at the untouched breakfast, then with astonishment at me. I waited for him to put down the lunch tray, but he hadn't brought it.

"Why are you naked?" he asked.

Instead of answering, I looked at the drying semen on the wall.

"Put on your clothes. You've got outdoors time," he said.

"What?"

"Twenty minutes in the yard."

I had forgotten about that. Many prison stories I had heard took place in an outside enclosure and involved prisoners looking up at the sky framed by barbed wire and concrete. From what I recalled, prisoners were entitled to open-air time a few days a week.

"Why didn't you take me out before?"

"Your case officer ruled against it."

• • •

I looked up as soon as I stepped outside. The Tehran sky, the blank, blue emptiness, encircled by the barbed wire that decorated the top of the enclosure, was surprisingly untainted by smog or smoke. I searched the sky for something, a cloud or a plane or a bird, any object or living being that would interrupt the monotony. I found nothing. It was like a void, a vacuum that could suck me off the ground and through the bars. I stood up on my toes and opened my arms, feeling the force the blueness exerted on my body, half hoping for levitation.

The four walls that separated these two hundred square feet from the world were tall enough to remind one at every turn that one was still in prison. They were painted a dull white that the passage of time had corrupted into a shade of gray as unexciting as the blue above my head. The ground beneath my feet was clean, save for the inevitable layer of dust.

I looked back up. The sky exercised its pull again, making me feel like a piece of trash about to be sucked up by a vacuum cleaner. My knees buckled, and I grabbed at the wall to avoid falling. I came down on my hands and knees and crawled around like an animal, destabilized by the sensation of gravity flowing in the wrong direction. I crawled across the yard and pulled myself up against the wall on the other side.

There I saw the first signs of human presence. "Eskandar Ahadi, executed on 08-21-1988." The scrawl was barely readable, having been etched into the wall with a blunt tool, probably a pebble. I thought about Eskandar Ahadi. That was the kind of name big men had. If they had killed him in 1988, then he was certainly hanged. Eskandar Ahadi, a tall, proud man with a thick mustache and bright eyes who must have approached the gallows on his own steady feet. That's what the comrades would tell you. They would probably omit the fact that Eskandar Ahadi shit himself when they kicked away the stool, so that he swung in the air like a pendulum with a bulge of excrement in the back of his pants.

The flap of bird wings recalled my attention to the yard. A pigeon was sitting on the barbed wire at the top of the wall. It opened its wings, snapped them back in to its sides, and softly cooed to announce its arrival. It was the kind of city pigeon found all over Tehran, identifiable by its light gray plumpness and speckled neck. Its head was a shade darker than the rest of its body, and its two eyes appeared frozen inside their round sockets next to the tiny red beak.

Something was off about it. It took me a long stare to realize that the bird's head was not bobbing. It sat motionless as if it were embalmed, looking at me sideways. Then it opened its wings again and held them like that, assuming an eagle-like posture. It stood up on its feet, tilted its head slightly upward, and took off. It sharply increased altitude and glided in the air above my head. When it descended, it came down in a spiral and then circled around me some more. The yard walls amplified and echoed the flutter of the wings. On one pass over my head, the pigeon flew so low I felt a breeze on my skin. When it finally ascended again, it passed across the sun, casting a massive shadow at my feet.

The bird landed back on the barbed wire, this time with its

back to me. It cooed, adjusted its position, and cocked its tail. I could see its asshole tighten and then open as wide as a coin. A dropping surprisingly large for a bird of that size slid out and fell in slow motion to the ground. The bird cooed again, opened its wings, and flew away.

I stepped forward and stared at it. It was a tiny thing, but it did disrupt the blue and gray dullness of the surroundings. I squatted over it and examined it carefully. A muddy green cylinder with tapered ends. Thin, yellow streaks ran all over it, and tiny bumps and dents covered its surface. Seeds and bread crumbs and herbs, or whatever the pigeon had eaten, had come together in its stomach and formed this little mass, a token from the world of the free, outside the walls. I felt deeply grateful to the creature for this reminder that life goes on. I brought down my head and sniffed. It smelled like plastic.

• • •

A day later, five chicken cutlets and a dry piece of bread came in on the metal lunch plate. Before that all the meals had been served on disposable plastic dishes. They must have run out of them. I ate the food fast, licked the plate clean, and washed it and dried it with my sleeve so that I could look at my reflection. It was the first time I had seen myself since coming to the prison. There were no reflective surfaces in the cell, and the showers didn't have mirrors, to minimize the risk of suicide.

My beard had grown longer than it had ever been before. This I knew without looking. I had also lost some weight, which I had noticed on my body and expected to see it in my face too. But I didn't recognize my eyes. They returned my look with the baleful stare of a stranger. In the metal mirror, my reflection cursed the day I ran into Behrouz in the supermarket, cursed me for changing my routine, changing the path I had walked for more than a decade. Why did I pause and sit next to Homa in the park? Why did I participate in a strike I had no faith in? Staring belligerently at my reflection, I pitted what I had done against what I should have done, stewing and obsessing until I was overwhelmed. I hurled the plate across the cell.

To calm myself down, I walked. The cell was too small for moving in straight lines, so I went in a circle. Each one took me five steps. I decided to walk five hundred circles. My feet slapped out a steady rhythm on the floor. The cell soon began to revolve around my head. When the first five hundred laps were done, I set out on two hundred more, but I collapsed before finishing this round.

I picked up the metal plate and looked at myself again. My anger had subsided, but now it bothered me that I looked so dirty. Multiple layers of sweat had dried and formed a dark film on my skin. My beard felt greasy. Dirt glued my hair to my scalp and stained the collar of my shirt. My armpits smelled like shit. I scratched the skin of my hand, and black filth collected under my fingernail. They hadn't allowed me to take a shower for more than a week. The cell was disgusting too. Dust had settled on everything. The dried vomit smears still covered the toilet bowl.

I knocked hard on the door. Akbar's plastic slippers smacked the floor as he approached. He opened a small hatch, and a narrow, bright rectangle framed his eyes.

"I need to take a shower," I said.

"The water is cold."

"I don't care."

"It might be very cold. Wait a few hours, it will warm up."

"I have to go now."

The ice water needled my skin. I rubbed the soap bar in my hands and observed the dirty slosh swirling around my feet with revulsion. I rubbed the soap over my body three times, but without a sponge I didn't feel clean enough, so I used my nails to scratch at my skin. More scrapings of filth collected under my nails. I clawed at every inch of skin on my shins and thighs, ass and crotch, torso and back, neck and face. At first I went slowly, then faster and harder. In the third pass over I gouged myself like a distressed animal. The more tender and red and painful my skin became, the harder I pressed. I began to bleed. My nails left long, thin scratches across my chest and thighs. Droplets of blood oozed out and ran like skittering red ants. It burned and hurt. It felt good.

I hid the soap in my towel and went back to the cell. I asked Akbar to bring a piece of rag, which he did with no questions asked. I took off all my clothes and put them in the metal sink and washed them. Then I wrapped the soap in the rag and got down on the floor. I started in one corner and continued to the other side of the room by my blankets, cleaning inch by inch, removing bits of lint and hair, cleansing away all the motes of dust.

• • •

The next morning I woke up missing Hajj Saeed, the way one misses a brother who has emigrated. I needed his company, his voice, the challenge of being in his presence. I thought of our first encounter, his generous offer of a way out in exchange for my truth telling. As a devout Muslim, it must have taken him a considerable amount of restraint to talk to an adulterer, yet he never took his outrage out on me. The more I thought of our conversations, the more his position made sense. Of course the US and Europe were sitting on the sidelines, biding their time for an opportunity to take advantage of everything that went wrong here so they could attack our government, which, after all, was elected relatively democratically. He was right that the strike had given them the chance. The Americans had occupied our neighbor countries and surrounded us with military bases, and we were in the thick of the nuclear negotiations. The bus drivers' union should have been careful about the timing and the form of strike. Or maybe the Americans did have their people in the union. Who was Davoud anyway? I had attended meetings for months and never saw him.

Really, who was I to disagree with anything Hajj Saeed said? He had fought in the trenches against Saddam while I rode around the streets of Tehran in a bus. The sight of his shrapnel-pocked arm should have shut me up. He was a family man, with a wife and son he dearly loved. I should remember to ask about his boy.

• • •

In the afternoon, time stopped. Every day I followed the thin bars of light crawl across the wall. It was the closest thing I had to a clock. That day, the light patches froze in place on the wall. To distract myself, I did the circular walk around the cell. I walked for what I thought was half an hour, but the bars didn't seem to have moved at all.

Akbar's flip-flops tapped out their rhythm on the hallway floor.

"When is my next interrogation?" I asked him as he put the plate of mirza ghassemi on the floor.

"I don't know. You miss it already?"

I didn't reply. He left. I ate as slowly as I could, thinking of ways to keep myself busy and to push Hajj Saeed out of my head. Toward the end of the meal, I had an idea.

The walking in the cell could not satisfy me because it was just motion without destination. I needed to set an endpoint for myself. That would be easy. I had spent my life behind the wheel shuttling back and forth between two points on a line every day. I decided to imagine trips through the city and walk them in the cell.

The first route had to be on Valiasr Street, where the Tajrish–Rah Ahan line runs along the jugular artery of Tehran. This line connecting the north to the south was flanked by wide gutters and gigantic sycamores that softened the summer sun and offered some protection from the snow and rain. It provided a straight channel for life to flow through the city. I had worked on that line for four years and knew it inch by inch. Since I had moved to the Jannatabad Terminal, I hadn't been down there. Here in the cell, I had all the time in the world.

I shut my eyes and imagined a midsummer day at Tajrish Terminal. One of those afternoons when the gates of hell opened out onto Tehran to pour forth a heat that liquefied metal and stone. I thought of the dull symphony of roars from the idling buses, overlaid with the loud voices of drivers who bantered and made jokes, and the occasional revving of engines and screams of weary springs when buses turned. In that terminal one could also hear the rush of the Tajrish River coursing down a steep slope into the echoing tunnel under the terminal bridge.

It was twelve miles from Tajrish to Rah Ahan. I estimated that I could walk six miles a day in the cell, which would come to fourteen thousand steps.

I pictured myself sitting behind the wheel, waiting for the bus to load, taking in the view of the mountains from the terminal. The trail that ran from Darband up to the Tochal summit was lined on both sides with cafés and restaurants and ended at a metal dome that shone blindingly in a valley.

I took my first step in the cell, imagining myself pressing the gas pedal to leave the terminal. I walked the first circles and soon got to the neck of Valiasr Street. Everything seemed expensive: cars, clothes, faces. I soon passed the Parkway overpass and continued down toward the state TV premises. People with a moneyed look appeared less frequently. They were replaced by blue-collar workers with loose button-up shirts and trimmed stubble. Before Mellat Park was where the crazies usually got on board: the drunk-in-the-afternoon older men, the fidgety, sweaty younger guys who never handed over their tickets, the women who always complained that I stopped a dozen feet before or after the sign.

Thousands of circles later, I was past Vanak Square. The heat intensified as I went southward. It shimmered off the asphalt, swallowed walls and trees, bleached the sidewalk. The protective canopy of sycamore branches thinned out, and the cars doubled in number. The memory of that scorching air struck me so hard, I started to sweat in the cell.

Akbar brought food when I got to the Hemmat overpass, but I didn't stop or even look at him. Covered in sweat, I kept counting circles. I remembered an accident I saw there once: a Nissan truck hitting a taxi from behind. Both drivers came out on the melting asphalt to exchange curses and argue over whose fault it was. In traffic, I had opened the window and listened to them. I still remembered their words. Finally, as the murmur of the Valiasr Square fountain reached my ears, I collapsed onto my blankets.

The next day, after breakfast, I took my first steps to start my journey south from Valiasr Square. I felt a slight headache, just as I did every time I drove to downtown. Here the road became confusing. Careless pedestrians walked in front of the bus out of nowhere. Motorcycles howled around in all directions like they were exempt from the law. Horns honked incessantly and set my nerves on edge. When I got there, my listening always sharpened. From downtown southward it was no longer possible to use only your eyes. Drivers had to activate their other senses. Over the years, I had dodged countless accidents by paying attention to the sounds of activities around me. Tracing out my circles, my ears sharpened in the cell too. I heard the caw of a crow from far away, the faint voice of a prisoner singing a gloomy song by Dariush, the loud cry of a man upstairs.

Farther down, Valiasr got narrower and grayer. The buildings became shorter and increasingly dilapidated. The distinct reek of the garbage in the south of Tehran wafted in through the bus windows, mixed with the smell of sizzling hot dogs and donuts frying in stale oil. The odors reached my nostrils in the cell, and I shook my head hard to make them go away.

Thousands of circles farther, I was past the Molavi crossroad.

Here grayness darkened under additional layers of filth. As I approached the Rah Ahan Square, poverty became brazen, out in the open. Unlike in the north, no one in the south tried to hide or beautify it.

The heat affected the body differently in that part of Tehran. Up in Tajrish, it reflected off the sleek surfaces and seemed to dissipate somewhat. Down near Rah Ahan Square, nothing was smooth or shiny. The dark surfaces there absorbed and stored the sun's energy, smothering the area in warmth throughout the day. There, the summer heat got trapped in the body and made you sick. I was nauseated and light-headed as I struggled through the last thousand steps of my journey in the cell, sweating so much the floor beneath my feet was wet.

PAUSE A SECOND AT THE DOOR," Hajj Saeed said. "I have a surprise for you."

I heard the muffled buzz of an electronic device.

"Take off your blindfold."

Across the room, Hajj Saeed was standing by my chair, grinning widely, holding up a camera like he was filming me.

That morning I had come in with high expectations. More than a week had passed since our last meeting. I had obsessed over this man for long hours, putting myself in his shoes, seeing his side of the story, cultivating sympathy for him. When Akbar had called me for the interrogation, I had hoped that Hajj Saeed would be equally excited to see me.

"Why are you still there? Come over here, have a seat! I'm going to show you something. We have so much to do today."

I settled down on my chair.

"How are you holding up? Long time no see."

"I'm okay."

"Glad to hear. Since you spent ten whole days in solitary, we'll take it easy today. We're going to have some fun. When was the last time you went to the movies?"

Without giving me time to respond, he pressed the ON button on the camera.

"Anyway. I like you, and it bothers me to see you suffering in your cell. I also understand that you want to resist, prove a point, help your friends. So I brought something to show you today. It should put an end to all your doubts."

His hand settled on my shoulder.

"Watch this."

A tiny screen opened out of the side of the camera. The man pressed another button and Behrouz's face materialized.

I closed my eyes.

Hajj Saeed squeezed my shoulder. "Keep your eyes open."

Behrouz was staring coldly out at me from the camera. I shut my eyes again.

Hajj Saeed slapped me in the neck. "Keep your eyes open!"

My old friend wore a prison outfit and was sitting against a white wall. He had lost weight. His skin had sunk in and his cheekbones stuck out. Two dark bags hung under his eyes. The change in his face resembled the change I had spotted in my own reflection in the metal plate. His eyes turned away from the camera. He nodded at someone outside of view. Then he spoke.

"Yunus Turabi was my colleague for almost five years, but we didn't talk much." He glanced again at the man and looked back into the camera lens. "The first time we ever exchanged more than a few words was when I ran into him at a supermarket near my house. At the time, I thought it was a coincidence. Now I know that he had planned it in advance." He sighed and shook his head like a bad actor. "I don't know. I don't really know what to believe anymore." He sighed again and looked at the man off camera, probably his interrogator, possibly Hajj Saeed himself.

"I thought a lot about why he, or whoever he worked for,

picked me. Maybe because I am a sensitive, impressionable person. He told me a very sad story about his lonely life, which I totally believed at the time. Now I doubt it was true at all."

Behrouz glanced again at the man off-screen. I wanted to reach in and grab his collar and scream and slap the shit out of him. But how could I blame him? I never had a wife, but if I did and I found myself in his shoes, I might have done worse.

"Yunus talked his way into my life. He came to my house and met my family, broke bread with us. We really liked him." His eyes rolled away from the camera again. "I need a break," he said, his voice shaking. "I can't stand thinking about those days."

The man seemed to be talking to him, though I couldn't hear his voice. They must have removed it from the video.

Behrouz nodded nervously. "Then one day I told him about the study group. It kind of slipped off my tongue. I still didn't know him well, and our study group was very intimate. I shouldn't have trusted him, but I did. When he came in, he began to manipulate our discussions. Up to that point we tended to read philosophy and novels, but he moved the group toward radical politics."

"Why is he saying all this bullshit?" I interrupted. Hajj Saeed paused the video. "Does he know you have transcriptions of all our meetings?"

"Who says we do? I haven't seen them!" He laughed.

"What do you mean?"

"It's up to me to show them to the judge, and you have given me zero incentive to do so. Besides that, even if I did, written documents never trump video confession. In the court this will be the main evidence, not the transcripts."

"But this is a bunch of stupid lies. Other people in the group—"

"Watch to the end." He squeezed my shoulder again.

"He basically used us to connect with the union," Behrouz continued. "He attended all the meetings, quickly got to know all the leaders. Every time he sat down with people, he tried to argue for a general strike, and when he got back to the group, he spent hours talking us into accepting this, to the point that he would talk shit behind your back if you disagreed with him. One day after the meeting we went to a café. He said he had managed to organize about two hundred drivers for a protest and had sorted out the funds for it too. He invited us to a workshop with Habib Samadi."

The timer on the screen showed that Behrouz had been going on for more than five minutes. Halfway through, his initial hesitations and pauses disappeared. He settled into delivering his made-up account, and at times he seemed to enjoy himself. He must have been practicing the false story to render it so brazenly. In the last minute of the video, Behrouz called me a CIA agent who had infiltrated the bus drivers' union and organized the strike. He accused me of receiving large sums of money from foreign agencies to be used for manipulating the drivers. The final thirty seconds I didn't hear what he said. I only stared at his face, desperately searching for some sign of guilt or shame. I found none.

Hajj Saeed pressed a button and the screen slid back into the camera, hiding Behrouz's image among the microchips and circuitry.

"This is all a bunch of lies he said under torture."

Hajj Saeed laughed. "We didn't even arrest him. He wasn't at the terminal on the day of the strike. He came here on his own when he learned that we had you."

This news shocked me even more than the video did, that his hatred for me was so deep he had come here voluntarily just to backstab me. But why did he look like he was in jail? I shouldn't believe Hajj Saeed.

"You know that he has personal reasons for setting me up like that," I said.

"I do indeed."

"And you know that he made up all this shit."

"No, I don't. I wasn't following you guys everywhere."

"You can ask other people in the group. Why don't you take their testimony?"

"Well, that's a good idea."

"Just ask them what they remember. They'll all contradict him."

"Oh, actually"—he pressed the button and the screen opened again—"I forgot to tell you that I did talk to them too."

Mehdi was sitting against the same wall, staring at me through the screen. Going by his brown wrinkled shirt, it seemed that he had not been arrested. He hadn't changed much, except maybe that he was a little fatter in the face. He nodded twice at the man off camera and spoke.

"Mr. Turabi infiltrated our group with a sophisticated agenda." His voice, with irksome pomposity, immediately stoked my hatred for him. He spoke with the same slowness, the same feigned deliberation over every word, the same self-aggrandizement and empty eloquence that he always had. "Mr. Turabi sought access to the highest echelons of union leadership, so he could derail their agenda. I don't know how he pulled it off. He must have made lofty promises. I suspect that he bribed some of them. In any event, he managed to engage the union in subversive activities. He advocated a total shutdown of the transportation system, which would have put Tehran in the headlines all over the world."

Hajj Saeed closed the camera before Mehdi was done.

"Did he also come here to confess and collaborate?" I asked.

"Yes, he did."

"I'm not surprised. He was your guy, after all."

Hajj Saeed took a moment to digest what I had said. Then he laughed. "Is that what you think?"

I didn't say anything. He walked around the room. I looked at the tablet arm and noticed new carvings on the edges. Someone had been interrogated in here while I was stuck in solitary. Maybe Hajj Saeed had questioned him. It could have been Behrouz. They might have detained him while they were working on my case and gotten him to make that video in exchange for leniency with his sentence.

"Yunus," said Hajj Saeed from the other side of the room, "you don't understand this stuff because you have never been married. You would probably have done the same thing if your close friend had had an affair with your other close friend's wife."

"No, I wouldn't."

"You would. You don't know anything. You just don't go out and fuck someone's wife and get away with it. That's not how the world works."

"I don't believe that Behrouz walked in here and said all those things and went home."

"Well, believe whatever you want to believe."

He returned to my chair with some papers.

"Now, today can be the day to finish this thing up. I don't know what's going on in your mind, but as far as I am concerned, this is over for you. You have no chance in court. Now all that remains is your confession, so I can attach it to the file and send it up to the judge."

"I have nothing to add to what I already said."

Hajj Saeed exhaled noisily and cleared his throat. The papers were blank, yellowing, and printed with the "Salvation lies in honesty" salutation at the top.

"Write down everything you know about the strike. Give me a full, detailed account. That's your only way out of here. Give me that and I'll help you get off easy."

"What exactly do you want me to write?"

"Name your contacts, your funders, everyone who communicated with you about this. Explain how you organized the strike, how you transferred the money."

"What money?"

"Who was your contact in the British Embassy? How did you get in touch with the Americans in Istanbul?"

"I've never been to Istanbul in my life. Go check my passport."

"Was there any French or Israeli person at your meetings?"

"I have never been outside this country."

"Put on the blindfold. Move it. Now get up. Get the fuck up and turn around."

I did. He punched me in the stomach. I doubled over. He punched me again. I trapped air in my belly to harden it before his blow connected with my body. Hajj Saeed's clenched fist bounced back. He grunted in surprise and hit again with his other hand.

"How did you get in touch with Americans?"

I laughed. I couldn't hold it. Me contacting American spies in Istanbul sounded like one of the jokes Behrouz would have cracked after a bottle of arak.

"So this is funny to you."

The punches came faster. His fists landed indiscriminately all over my torso. I had made him angry. He kept hitting me, but his lack of focus had diminished the effect. It was almost cartoonish.

Hajj Saeed stopped the beating as abruptly as he had started. "Sit down," he said. "Take off the blindfold."

I did and looked up at him.

"Why do you want me to lie to you?" I said.

He shook his head without moving his stare. "Write the truth here."

"I have nothing to say."

A slap on the back of my neck. "Write the things you have already said."

I picked up the pen.

"How did you get into the study group?"

"Behrouz Sehati introduced me to the group," I wrote. "One day I ran into—"

Hajj Saeed snatched the paper from under my hand, crumpled it, and threw it across the room. "Explain how you got into the study group."

"Behrouz Sehati introduced me to—"

He pulled this page away too. He tore it up and dropped the scraps over my head. "Write the truth."

I wrote the same words on the next page. He punched me between my shoulder blades. He kicked me in the shin.

"Write all of it here right now. How you joined the study group, who introduced you to CIA agents, how much money you got. All of it."

"I can't write about things that never happened."

Another punch in the center of the back. One of his techniques was to hit the exact same spot several times. A slap across the back of my head, which hurt badly. He was hitting with all his force, with bitterness and resentment, which he had not done before. He kicked me again in the shin. I cried loudly to release the pain. He grabbed me by the scruff of my neck and dragged me to the floor. He looked bigger than before. He kicked me in the stomach and thighs until he ran out of breath. I didn't take my eyes off him.

Hajj Saeed called Akbar. The old man paused at the door and looked at me with wide eyes.

"Take this piece of shit out of here," said Hajj Saeed. "I will only see him again when he's willing to come clean."

THAT NIGHT, the prison had a power outage. For the first time since I got there, the ceiling lamp went off and the cell was dark. In the corridors, feet stomped around, doors were flung open and shut. Yells and calls came from a range of distances. Prisoners on other floors banged on their walls and shouted incomprehensible insults. The air was pregnant with crisis, maybe a riot, but I didn't care. The sudden darkness had numbed my senses. I sat cross-legged on my blankets and stared. The blackness that night was absolute and impenetrable, the way one never experienced a night in Tehran.

I held up a hand in front of me but couldn't see it. My body had vanished from my sight, as if the darkness had swallowed it. I touched my arm to make sure it was still there, then extended it again and watched it disappear.

That darkness inside the cell was visible, almost tangible. It seemed to tremble slightly and resist the penetration of my outstretched hand, like I was pushing my fist into black tar. The materiality of the darkness. It was like a protective buffer against the unfolding chaos outside my cell. I lay down, knowing that as long as the electricity was gone no one would bother me, and I fell asleep.

When I woke up again it was still nighttime. The darkness hadn't budged. I could have sworn that a nudge had woken me up, but no one could have entered the cell without making noise. I sat up alarmed and stretched my hand forward. The thick lightlessness closed in around it, pressing against my skin, squeezing the muscle and bone. It became difficult to breathe.

I got up, stretched my limbs, and awkwardly jumped around to break the tension. The darkness slackened its grip and created more space for my body, but as soon as I stopped moving it attacked again, compressing me even more tightly than before. "Help! Help!" I screamed. Then I wondered what I would say to anyone who would come to my aid.

No one came. Drenched in sweat, I kept trying to fight off the blackness, my hands scrambling against nothing, my legs kicking, until I passed out.

• • •

The next time I opened my eyes, the light was back. Thin, bright lines on the opposite wall announced the arrival of a sunny morning. I regarded the patterning with the curiosity of someone seeing an old friend after years of separation, then went around the cell and touched all the surfaces, allowing my fingertips to savor the contact. By now I had catalogued all the major bumps and cracks in the room. When my finger sensed an irregularity, I knew exactly which one it was and could recall its shape and location.

Three feet above my blankets, I felt something I didn't recognize. A tiny, round, black circle, its circumference slightly wider than a nail's head. It hadn't been there the day before. It must have emerged during the blackout.

How? Darkness, thick and strong as it had been, couldn't have penetrated the wall. Several layers of concrete and brick must have shifted of their own accord for my benefit. Why not? The Nile had opened itself up for Moses, and the cave had woven a cobweb across its mouth to protect Muhammad. My predicament was no less unjust.

At lunchtime, as soon as Akbar closed the door, I went at the hole with the bottom of the fork, maniacally hammering at the wall to chip away at it. An hour of work later, the hole looked the same. When Akbar took away the half-eaten dish and the utensil, I peered inside and put my ear on it, trying to catch a sound from within the wall or from farther away. I heard laughter. It was brief and disingenuous, like an audible smirk, the kind of sound Samad would have made when he disagreed with you but didn't respect your opinion enough to argue against it. It went quiet for a minute, but just when I had decided to chalk the whole thing up to my overpressed senses, the hole chortled again.

I punched the wall. "*Khaar-e sag*," I screamed and threw myself onto my blankets. Lying supine, I smelled the dead skin and dried sweat that had seeped into the fabric from my body. What I yelled startled me. I whispered the words again. What was *Khaar-e sag*? Where had the words come from? I must have meant to say two things, "*Khaar-kosdeh*" and "*Pedar-sag*," but anger had made me mash the phrases together. "*Khaar-e sag*." It made no sense and total sense. No Persian speaker in history had ever said that before, but they would all embrace it if I introduced it to them. That could be my contribution to the language, my only achievement that would survive me. The sounds were perfect for an insult: beginning with a heavy, deep *kh*, the utterer should overstress the *s* before coming to an abrupt end at *g*. It could be interpreted in different ways: "sister of a dog" was the literal meaning, but it could also be read as "thorn of a dog," though that would require a pause between the two words, unless one meant to say "a thorn in a dog's side."

I walked around the cell, mumbling the phrase. Every time I uttered it, I moved more energetically until my limbs jerked around in all directions. My head shook wildly, as though it was about to fly off my neck. My body twisted to and fro at a speed my mind could not catch up with, as screams of *"Khaar-e Sag! Khaar-e Sag!"* singed my throat on their way out.

• • •

"Your case officer," said Akbar, picking up the dinner plate, "won't see you again unless you're ready to confess." He paused for my response, which he didn't get. "Are you ready to talk tomorrow?"

I scowled at him in silence.

"What?" he asked.

"Why do you call him a case officer?"

"What am I supposed to call him?"

"Call him what he is. Mr. Interrogator, Mr. Torturer, Hajj Saeed, or just fucking Saeed. What is this 'case officer' bullshit?"

"Let me know when you're ready to come clean," he said and shut the door.

I thought of Hajj Saeed, already regretting the harsh words I had just spoken about him. No matter how hard I tried, I couldn't stay mad at him. He was, after all, what Habib had told us the day before the strike: just an interrogator doing his job. I pictured his gray, thinning hair and long forehead, the hairs in his stubble. There was a black one right at the center of a white patch on his chin. Where the skin curved over his cheekbone, two strands, one white and one black, grew out of the same pore. At that moment, just as the sun had begun to set, he must have been in his house watching TV, his wife sitting next to him on the sofa, their sick child fast asleep. I was sure Hajj Saeed wouldn't watch the Iranian TV channels. They probably had a satellite dish and followed one of those Turkish melodramas my passengers loved to talk about. Their apartment would be old but spacious, in a nondescript neighborhood near downtown, probably Fatemi or Takht-e Tavous. The floor was likely covered with cheap, machine-made Persian rugs. I imagined his wife checking on their son and coming back to Hajj Saeed to tell him that the boy was still sleeping. Hajj Saeed probably waited for her to return, absently flipping through TV channels in search of a better show.

I pictured him watching five minutes of a football game from a league in an Arab country, then switching to another channel without realizing, his senses numbed by the onslaught of trivialities from the screen. This would be the best moment for me to insert myself, to enter his distracted mind and to speak to him. *Hajj Saeed*, I called to him. *Think about Yunus Turabi and his innocence. You know he is innocent. Stop tormenting him. Let him go back to his life.*

Hajj Saeed's hand trembled on his thigh as I addressed him. I tried again, my pleas for freedom hurtling toward him through the air over Tehran. I kept them coming as he turned off the TV, kissed his wife on the forehead, and brushed his teeth. When he went to sleep, I shut my eyes too.

• • •

I woke up the next day wondering if my telepathy had worked and spent most of the morning cross-legged on my blankets, hoping for some change. The prison sounded busy. Doors clicked open in another corridor, others slammed shut upstairs, multiple pairs of flip-flops passed rapidly over a distant floor. Every approach of a sound, human or otherwise, strained my nerves, but nothing happened. Akbar came in twice with the food tray, but he didn't ask if I wanted to confess.

At midnight the rattle of window bars woke me up. First I thought it was a storm, but I didn't hear the howl of wind or rain. It sounded like someone was shaking the window slats hard on the other side. I rose and approached the window, but as soon as I got to it, the rattle stopped. I moved away and it started up again, but it died down as soon as I approached it.

When I went up to the window a third time, the sound changed. Its frequency rose higher until it became a continuous, steady shriek of metal grating on metal. I put my hands over my ears to block it out, but it penetrated my fingers, mauled my eardrums, and jabbed into my brain. I screamed until I had no breath, then I inhaled and howled again with all my power, until my vocal cords were crippled.

When I stopped, I heard another shriek. At first I thought it was the reverberation of my own cry echoing around in my skull. It wasn't. It belonged to someone else. The distinct, raspy keen of an old man was pouring into the cell through the slats. When he

ran out of breath, he started crying in loud, gasping sobs. I stared
at the window, trying, though it was impossible, to see him. He
must be bald and skinny, his back bent, his teeth gone, sitting in
his cell, which was a shithole like mine, weeping away the last
days of his life.

He suddenly stopped. Silence clamped down on the world
around me. Then he yelled, "Help! Help! Help!" Or was it,
"Death! Death! Death!" I jumped up onto my toes and listened.
The word ricocheted off the walls of the cell like a barrage of
bullets. I couldn't tell if he had said "*maaarg*" or "*komaaak*." The
more I listened, the more I kept changing my mind. Finally, he
went quiet.

When the truth hit me, it was worse than the blows I had
suffered during my interrogation. There was no cell behind that
window. No old man could be sitting there yelling. Sometimes
the noise of the highway came through there, or the coo of a
pigeon, or the meow of a cat. The scream of that man was in my
head. It was me, perhaps in five or ten years, alone inside, denied
the means of suicide, sitting and praying that my death would
arrive soon.

• • •

In the morning, time seemed to slow down again. Like a river
exposed to extreme cold, it first became sluggish and thick and
then congealed into a frozen, solid mass. At noon the cell seemed
smaller and darker than ever. The sun was in the sky, but the
four lines of light had disappeared from the wall. I tried to will
time to start flowing again. I walked around the room, tracing
out circular and diagonal patterns. I forced myself to imagine a

trip through the city again, this time from Enqelab to Ferdowsi Square. When I couldn't concentrate on that, I danced and kicked erratically. Nothing worked. Nothing would move the stagnant seconds along. I gave up and lay back on the floor.

From where I was, I spotted a long, loose thread. It floated an inch above the ground, light and confident. I got onto my knees and blew on it. It levitated, danced briefly in the air, and alighted back on the floor a foot away from its initial position. I blew on it again. The thread made gentle, nonchalant movements. Its crooked, frail body settled by my blankets at the very moment Akbar opened the door.

I didn't care to turn around, and remained focused on the delicate fiber. Crouched on my hands and knees, my ass up in the air, I felt the weight of his stare on my back. He picked up the old tray and paused again, waiting to see if I would move or show some semblance of embarrassment.

"Do you want to confess today?"

I puffed some air toward the thread and watched how its flustered takeoff eased into a glide. Akbar slammed the door shut.

• • •

The next day, my eyesight was noticeably worse. The bars on the window were blurry. I couldn't read the writing on the ceiling even when I stood up on my toes. The walls' cracks and bumps and holes had merged into a dull, dotted gray. I spent some time trying to make out subtle suggestions of the shapes of bears and horses and dragons, but it was difficult to see much of anything.

By noon, my listening had also become impaired. The prison had never been fully silent. The doors clanged, and prisoners yelled on other floors. Guards talked to each other, and the wheels of carts rolled up and down the corridors. *Azan* and other religious keening played constantly. In the rare lulls between those sounds, the hum of Tehran crept in, the revving car engines, the vague, constant drone that was a byproduct of millions of people living their lives in close proximity to one another. That day, none of it penetrated the cell. The prison was as silent as a graveyard.

"*Khaar-e Sag! Khaar-e Sag!*" I cried and listened to the echo of my voice in the room. It sounded distant and muffled.

"Do you want to confess tonight?" Akbar's voice jolted me. I hadn't heard the door opening, hadn't seen him putting down the tray. I stared at him in silence. He quickly retreated into the hallway.

• • •

The following morning, after three days of constipation, I sat on the toilet to take a shit.

A baby snake-size turd stuck out its head, spread my asshole wide open, and dropped into the toilet. My body felt lighter instantly. My stomach muscles contracted again, and another large turd came out.

I sniffed the air to detect the stink of my waste, to make sure that at least one sense was working. But nothing hit my nose. Sitting on the toilet seat, I sniffed around like a dog. I picked up the general reek of the prison and the familiar mix of sewage and wet paper, as well as the unexpected, distant aroma of grilled meat. I got off the bowl, my pants down and crumpled around the knees, my ass sore from the pressure of the thick excrement, and looked into the bowl. Two large cylinders were afloat in the water. One smooth and dark brown, the other gnarled and lighter in color. The darker one must have been in the intestine longer.

I put my head into the bowl and sniffed again. I caught nothing, save for the faint stink that was always there. Something must have been wrong with my shit. I cleaned my ass but didn't flush the toilet.

Half an hour later, Akbar showed up. He frowned and looked around the cell, sensing that something was out of place. I watched his nostrils to see if they would flare. He was breathing normally.

"Can you come here, please?" I said.

He put down the tray and took a hesitant step into the cell. He was walking on the tips of his toes like he had stepped into a minefield.

"I don't detect the smell of this," I said, pointing to the toilet. "Do you?"

His head bent forward, only enough to see the floating objects in the toilet bowl. He coughed hard and turned red, then moved quickly toward the door. In his haste, he bumped into the doorframe. "You fucking animal!" he yelled from across the cell.

I attacked him. From the floor, I lunged at him, grabbed his neck, kicked his legs away from under his body, pushed him down, and yelled, "Who is the animal? Answer the fucking question! Who is the animal?" He screamed so loudly he couldn't hear what I was asking. It was surprising to hear so much sound emerge from that fragile body. I kicked him in the chest to shut him up, but he only yelled louder.

Other guards arrived. Two men held me from behind and dragged me back. A third man came around and pummeled me in the face and the stomach. Another person helped Akbar out of the cell.

• • •

They left me alone behind the closed door. For the first two days, they didn't even feed me. The hunger was not the hardest part. I suffered more from the absence of that little routine of seeing a human face three times a day, that small reminder that I was still part of the world of human beings.

On what I estimated to be the fourth day, the door opened and a hand slid in a piece of stale bread and one boiled egg. I devoured the food at once and sat waiting for the next contact with the world outside.

It must have been on the morning of the sixth day when I heard the door to the adjacent cell click open. The guards threw a man in. As soon as they locked the door, he started sobbing. It came so abruptly and loudly that I thought I was imagining things again. But the sound was unmistakably human and was undeniably coming from next door. The man sobbed with his whole body, from the bottom of his soul. The volume of his cries was unnaturally loud, like he was crying into a microphone. He wept for two, three, maybe four hours. They brought food, and he didn't stop. They took the dishes away, and he didn't stop. His incessant crying filled the corridor with so much misery that the guards could no longer take it. In the afternoon, I heard boots approaching along the hall-way and a man violently unlocking the door.

"Why don't you shut the fuck up?" he yelled. "What do you want?" He was not one of the guards I knew.

"I want to see my wife and son," said the prisoner. He had a deep voice and a strong Kurdish accent.

"Oh, really?" said the guard. "The border patrolmen you slaughtered would also love to see their families one more time."

The man began to cry again. The sound of it ran so uninterruptedly that it may well have been from a recorded tape.

"Oh, shut up already. What're you worried about? You're going to fuck a ton of houris soon. Isn't that what you wanted?"

The man was probably an Al-Qaeda fighter. They would never make that quip with a Shia.

"I just want to see my wife again," the man stuttered through a sob.

"Come on," said the guard. "Your wife is some fat aging village woman. You're going up there to your god to fuck houris with big boobs. Isn't that what you were hoping for? They bounce up and down on your dick and cover your face with their tits. Isn't that the whole reason you were fighting, you miserable fuck?"

The guard slammed the door shut and walked away.

The man wailed through the evening and the night. I sat there listening to him all the way through, for almost twenty-four hours, transfixed. Early in the morning, just as the first sunbeams were creeping into the cell, they came and took him away.

I pictured the man as a cliché of an Al-Qaeda fighter: thick beard, piercing black eyes, haggard face. The guards must have taken him to the yard, gotten him up on a stool, and slid the noose down over his head. When they kicked the stool, this man probably shit himself before his soul fully departed his body, like Eskandar Ahadi, whose name was etched on the wall of the outdoors area.

No one would ever know about what happened to him. Whoever knocked the stool from under his feet would get away with it. He would probably do it half a dozen times through the week and lose no sleep over any of it. Hajj Saeed was right. There was no god in Evin. They could take me and kill me at any time if they wanted to, and there would be no retaliation or punishment. The world had already forgotten that I existed. No one would even notice my absence.

• • •

Days later, I woke up and couldn't get to my feet because my clothes weighed me down too much. I took them off and looked at my body with my weak eyes. Large patches of skin had dried out on my thighs and arms. As soon as I noticed them, they began to itch. I scratched them, which only made them itch more. The sensation got worse and spread from my limbs to my back. Like a bear, I rubbed my back against the wall and continued clawing at my limbs. When the feeling became unbearable, I began to howl. Like a wounded animal, I shrieked and punched at the wall and the door and clawed myself until I bled. The sight of blood made me cry louder.

The door clicked open.

A man, only visible in silhouette, entered the room. My eyes were too weak to see who it was.

"Do you want to confess?"

I nodded.

LONG TIME NO SEE," Hajj Saeed said when I entered the room. "Take off the blindfold."

The room felt unreal, like a relic of a life I had forgotten I had lived. I shuffled slowly to the opposite wall, looking all around the room as I attempted to reorient myself. Hajj Saeed observed my slow progress with an air of medical attentiveness.

"You have lost quite a bit of weight."

"I didn't eat much."

"The best thing about being in prison is getting fit. I've never seen anyone leave fat." He laughed.

I settled on the chair and looked down at the tablet arm. Nothing had changed. It occurred to me that I hadn't contributed anything to its graffitied surfaces and thought about what I would write there if I had a pen. Nothing came to mind.

Hajj Saeed came and stood over me. His shadow was reassuring. Everything that harkened back to my life when the world still made sense, before the days of abandonment in solitary, was reassuring.

"I heard that you have decided to talk," he said.

Starved for contact with the world outside my cell, I gobbled up the sight of the cracks in the ceiling and the dust on the floor.

I looked at the moquette layer on the wall that concealed the soundproofing equipment. Fear crept back into me. What if I failed to satisfy the man and he sent me back to my cell? At this point, I preferred a bullet in the head to being left alone again. I thought of ways to commit suicide if Hajj Saeed decided to leave me there. Breaking the lamp and touching naked wires wouldn't work—I knew already that they had reduced the voltage in the jail to a nonfatal level. Maybe I could steal the soap from the shower and eat it? Or bang my head against the wall to shatter my skull?

"Are you listening to me?" Hajj Saeed interrupted my thoughts.

"Yes."

"Well, answer the question, then."

"Can you ask it again?"

"Never mind."

He pressed my shoulder in a friendly way. It made me feel queasy. I wished he had slapped or punched me. Not just because that was what I was accustomed to him doing but because I needed a shock to my system. I needed blows to my organs and limbs to remind them that I was still alive.

Hajj Saeed strode to the other end of the cell. I listened to the rhythm of his soles on the floor. He returned with his papers.

"What do you want me to write?" I asked.

"The truth."

"What exactly?"

"What do you mean?"

"I don't know what the truth is. You just tell me what you need from me."

"Are you ready to confess?"

"I don't know what I am ready to do. I just want to get this over with."

"I'm glad to hear that."

I held the pen in the air over the paper and looked up.

"What are you waiting for?" he asked.

"Where should I begin?"

"Describe how you organized the strike."

"You tell me."

He walked to the end of the cell. His steps were hesitant. He returned to his chair, paused, and cleared his throat. He finally sat down at his desk. I heard a pen scratching out words, then the creak of wood when he rose. He walked over and put the piece of paper on the pile in front of me. This one had a prompt at the top. "Describe the process of organizing the bus drivers' union strike."

Hajj Saeed began to dictate. "Write," he said, his voice growing huskier. His heels clicked out a steady rhythm on the floor. "'There has been a considerable level of discontent among bus drivers in Tehran, especially over the last decade. Given the difficult nature of our job, we were never satisfied with insurance and pension and other benefits, and even though the union pursued those demands, we could never come to a deal with the current administration.'"

I didn't expect him to be taking shots at Ahmadinejad through my indictment. It spoke to an internal tension, a rift between the government and intelligence services. But I couldn't bring myself to get remotely curious about it.

"You wrote it all word by word?"

"Yes."

"Keep going: 'While we were trying to secure our rights, some of us talked to the media and voiced our problems to the public, which received more attention than we anticipated. That must be the reason why the enemies of our country noticed us. I believe foreign intelligence services began to focus on the bus drivers' union in 2003, when the reformist government was still in power. In my view, they had spotted righteous dissatisfaction in a part of the society and began to devise plans to capitalize on this.'"

The drawer in his desk opened. He came over and put an apple in front of me. "Let's take a break," he said and sat on his chair. The apple was immaculately red. The light from the ceiling left a yellow dot on its cheek.

"You can eat that," he said in an instructive tone, like I hadn't seen an apple before. When I was done, he picked it up by the stem and threw it in the trash can under his desk. "Ready?"

"Yes."

"Write: 'Around the time bus drivers got media coverage, we were contacted by top reformists, like President Khatami's brother and the advisor to his Minister of Internal Affairs. Those people set up multiple meetings with the union leaders and encouraged them to go on strike, promising money and logistical support. At the time, I was involved in union activities and attended some of those meetings and occasionally participated in the discussions. This is how I came to the attention of older leaders. Two of them had a meeting with me and asked me to take on more responsibilities. Eventually they put me in charge of organizing the strike in the Jannatabad Terminal.' Did you get it all, word for word?"

"Yes."

Hajj Saeed picked up the paper and read through it. His shadow on the tablet arm nodded in satisfaction. He took the paper away and sat at his desk. I heard his pen scribbling another question on a new page, which he brought over and set in front of me.

"How did the union manage the financial requirements of the strike?" he had written.

"Write," he began. " 'I am not aware of the whole funding process, that part was kept from the organizers. While I was in Evin, through my case officer I learned that some of the money came into the country as cash in suitcases and was distributed among the union leaders. Another allotment came from the George Soros Foundation in the United States.' "

"Georges Sorel, you mean," I interrupted him.

The clicking shoes paused and he came over. "Who is that?"

"The French thinker we studied. I thought you meant him."

He said nothing.

"The person who wrote about general strikes," I added to aid his memory.

"I know who you mean," he said. "That man died a long time ago."

"I know that."

"Then how could he fund a strike now?" he asked. "It doesn't matter. Keep writing."

"Is that true?"

"What?"

"That the union leaders received money in suitcases."

"Do you think I'm lying?"

"No."

"Why do you ask, then?"

"What did they do with the money?"

"They made off with it."

"I don't believe you."

"So you do think I'm a liar."

"I didn't say that."

"If you want to get this thing done, stop interrupting me and finish the writing. There's not that much left."

With the tip of my pen I pressed hard into the wood to protest silently. I wouln't give him a reason to abandon me in solitary again.

"Write: 'Now, having been convinced by the evidence during my stay in Evin, I know that the reformists and their Western masters had launched a project aimed at the forced secularization of Iran.'"

"Slow down, please."

Hajj Saeed repeated the last sentence. When I finished it, he picked up the paper. "Why are you pressing the pen so hard? The paper is full of holes."

"The pen is not good," I lied.

He went to his desk and came back with a new pen, a blue Bic like the one I was using before.

"Try this."

I did. It was exactly the same as the first one. "Yes, I think it's much better," I said.

"Is there anything you want to add? Something I don't know and you want to tell us about?"

"No."

"Okay. Write: 'After initial meetings, I received an email from an unknown address containing a pamphlet on how to organize a strike.'"

"I don't have an email address."

Hajj Saeed sighed, like I had promised him I would set up one but had forgotten to do it.

"It doesn't matter," he said.

"Okay."

"Go on. 'The pamphlet included instructions on how to stage a velvet revolution, as well as a plan for public disobedience and nonviolent action. It suggested ways of convincing people not to do what they are supposed to do, including methods and strategies for organizing strikes. Translating the strategies that brought about velvet revolutions into the Iranian context, the pamphlet encouraged media wars, inflammatory public speeches, sit-ins, silent vigils around the premises of bus terminals, multi-industry strikes, walkouts, martyr making, crowded funerals, and so on. Studying the evidence presented to me in Evin Prison, I realize now that I fell victim to a sophisticated plot orchestrated by intelligence agencies of foreign powers. I regret my involvement in that project. My intention has always been to further the cause of workers' welfare and to contribute to their struggles for their rights. I was not aware of the forces waiting on the sidelines to manipulate our righteous demands and attack not only the legitimacy of our government but our entire way of life.'"

Hajj Saeed cleared his throat and stood motionless over me.

"With those last lines, you won't be in much trouble. You probably noticed that I did my best to help you out. I will also submit
a positive report. Is there anything you want to add or change?"

"No."

"Sign it."

He picked up the confession and looked closely at the signature, then collected the other papers and put them into the
drawer. He paced around some more. His steps were heavier and
his tread was slower than normal.

"You did the right thing, Yunus, believe me. You did what
God Almighty wants you to do."

"I thought you were the god here."

He came over to me, bent forward, and studied my face. "Let
me ask you a question. Do you really think God is on your side?"

"I don't believe in God," I said, unshackled by signing my confession. The man had gotten what he wanted and this was the
small talk before our farewell. I had no reason not to be myself.

"You must believe in something."

"I believe in what I can see."

"You can never be sure about the existence, or lack thereof, of
what you don't see."

"That may well be right. I am just not interested in the question. I don't think much about it."

"Okay, Yunus, I can respect that," he said, like we were colleagues discussing a philosophical problem. "We're almost done
here."

"Okay."

"That's all you have to say?"

"Well. I guess."

"Tell me, Yunus. What do you think of us? What are your thoughts about your time here?"

"I really don't have thoughts at this moment."

"Do you think we were cruel or unfair to you?"

"I was in solitary and got beaten up," I said matter-of-factly.

"The problem with you people is that you just don't know us. You don't even try. We don't enjoy dealing with seventy million unhappy people, most of whom have no idea what's going on. Iranians have changed, Yunus. They have changed so much within my lifetime. They want everything to be just normal without paying any price or working for it, like it's their God-given right. They want the supermarkets to be full of cheap stuff and the absolute freedom to do and consume whatever they want. They have no clue who makes it safe for them to walk around the city with no fear of being blown to shreds by a bomb or shot down by a terrorist. Our people have become shortsighted and ungrateful. They live their lives day to day. But we didn't start off yesterday. There is a history behind us, thousands of years of it. Do you understand?"

"Yes," I said, having no idea where he was going.

"We are at the winter of history, Yunus," he said. "The emergence of the last Imam is near. He will rise with an ax, and his first move will be to chop down the tree of history. It will be painful to watch. The earth will be cleansed of the filthy, the undeserving, and only those faithful to him will survive. Those who join the army of the Messiah will be permitted to survive the chaos and become the society of the future. My job is to save as many people as I can and make them worthy of being soldiers in his army. You have come a long way in signing these confessions,

Yunus. But there is still a lot to do. I am sure if you stay on the right track, which we set you on in here, you will be redeemed at the end of the world. Now you can go."

I pulled down the blindfold before getting up. I didn't want to see his face again.

FOUR DAYS LATER, Akbar opened the door and beckoned me to come out. He acted normally, as if I had never attacked him. We passed the interrogation room and took a long walk down a U-shaped corridor. Human voices came from both sides. Officers and bureaucrats were talking loudly on their phones. Guards laughed and joked as they walked by us. Apart from them, Hajj Saeed and the Al-Qaeda prisoner, these were the first human voices I had heard since I came to prison. The conversation between the torturers and interrogators was music to my ears. One of the men paused and greeted Akbar and asked him about his family. Before the end of his first sentence I recognized his voice. It was the man who had stared into my asshole. I wondered how many other assholes he had checked since I had arrived there.

Akbar took off the blindfold when we left the building. We entered a parking area that stretched from the entrance to the prison gate. I began sweating as soon as I stepped into the yard. It was too hot for a spring morning. It felt like August. I wondered how the cell had remained relatively cool without ventilation.

Several identical black Peugeot 405s were parked haphazardly in the lot. Two men were leaning against one of them. Akbar handed me over to them, patted me on the shoulder, and walked back into the building. The men handcuffed me and put me into the back seat. They climbed in, their large bodies pressing me on both sides. The driver and another man had already settled down in the front. They both rolled down the windows. Like the car that had delivererd me to prison, this one didn't seem to have AC. The men were already sweating. The whole crew looked younger and less professional than the one that had brought me here.

The corrugated metal gate rolled open, and we drove out of the parking lot. They didn't cover my eyes. I saw the cars coursing along the Yadegar highway, the Atisaz residential complex on the other side, trees, asphalt, people. The car rolled slowly through the crowd formed by the family members of prisoners who held up small placards demanding the release of their loved ones. Their faces were flushed with heat, their shirts and scarves wet with sweat. The car went south on the Yadegar-e Emam.

"How are you doing today?" the guard on my right asked. I stared into his face. He looked barely twenty and had a curious, untrained expression. He had used a large quantity of gel to shellac his hair into place.

"I'm very well, thank you."

"What are you accused of?"

"I colluded with the CIA and Mossad to persuade the bus drivers' union to stage a national strike." His eyes widened at every word.

"You are not allowed to talk to the accused," said the man in the passenger seat. He was a few years older than the others and appeared to be their senior officer. He was probably a young Hajj Saeed, apprenticing to become an interrogator in the future.

I looked out the tinted window at the steady movement of vehicles on the endless stretch of pavement in front of us. The idea of moving freely from one point to another made me emotional. It was as if the cars were celebrating my temporary release by escorting me out of the prison into the embrace of the city.

Then we hit traffic. Past the Niayesh Expressway, we paused in the middle of the still river. The heat flooded in. Everything became painfully familiar. The smog weighed down on the metal and glass around us, casting a dark, gray pall over the buildings and cars ahead. I found myself surrounded again by the same miserable faces I had been looking at for the last twenty-five years, these wretches who shuffled between work and home, day after day, in buses and taxis and on sidewalks, exuding a massive cloud of collective depression that pervaded the city.

Pop music floated out of a Toyota Camry into our vehicle. The kids who sold flowers and cleaned windshields for a few coins arrived and encircled the cars around us. After sanctions were imposed, they had expanded their territory from downtown out to the highways north of the city. They somehow knew they shouldn't approach our car.

The man in the passenger seat turned to me. "Show me your papers."

"What papers?" I asked.

"Your defense papers."

"I don't know what those are."

"They say what you're going to tell the court."

"I don't have any."

"You're not going to defend yourself?"

"Probably not."

"Didn't you just say you are accused of collaborating with the CIA?"

"Yes."

He looked at me in silence and turned to face forward when the car moved. His surprise unsettled me, but I talked myself down. Hadn't I confessed to everything Hajj Saeed wanted? How could he not pass on a positive report? Now that I was another victory under his belt, he had no reason to go back on his promise.

The traffic thinned a little, and the car leapt forward. A short stretch of steady movement improved my mood. Tehran was a great city when it gave you the freedom to move through it. I missed looking at the traffic from the bus driver's seat. From up there, when cars were passing smoothly by, driving felt like swimming. On the other hand, when traffic was heavy, it was like being bogged down in thick mud.

The congestion worsened before the Hemmat Expressway interchange. Cars squeezed together tightly, two of them within a few inches of us on either side. In one, a teenager with a shaved head, hardly over the driving age, was tapping a rhythm with his fingers on the wheel. On the other side, a skinny man in a taxi looked ahead with a dead stare as he took long drags on his cigarette. Neither of them so much as glanced in our direction. Everyone knew what a Peugeot 405 with tinted windows on the highway meant.

"Why is it so packed today?" asked the man on my left.

"It's always like this if you come out at this hour," said the driver with a slight undertone of scorn.

The voice of the radio morning show anchor, which I hated

with a passion, came on. For years I had played this every morning in the bus for the passengers to remind them where they were living.

"Good morning, Tehran, and happy Saturday!" said the man. "What a beautiful day. I know it's too hot for spring, but isn't it nice to get a taste of summer early? Think of the fruit we haven't tasted for a year. Yaghouti grapes and cherries! Peaches and mangoes! Delicious!"

The driver turned the volume way down.

So it was the first day of the week. I had apparently decided to confess over the weekend. Hajj Saeed, who never spent his Fridays at work, had come over exclusively for me. I wondered why. Maybe he had more urgent cases to tackle and wanted to get rid of me as soon as possible. Maybe he thought I would change my mind if he left me alone for too long. Maybe he heard that Mehdi and Behrouz were going to take back their statements and wanted to send me to court before they threw a wrench in his plans. I decided that this last theory must be the correct one. The thought made me happier.

As we approached downtown, the traffic slowed again. Cars inched along, jostling their way forward, fighting over every scrap of open space.

"Did you hear from your cousin?" asked the man in the passenger seat.

"Yes," the driver said. "He was moving from Melbourne to Perth. That's why it took him so long."

"To where?"

"It's some other city in Australia."

"What did he say?"

"He said the whole trip costs about ten thousand dollars. We fly over to Indonesia first, then get on boats that take people to Australia. We spend a little while on an island, then get a work permit and visa to enter the country."

"I'm not sure it's as simple as that."

"Thousands of people have done it. When you get there, you're fine."

"You still want to go?"

"I don't know."

"People drown on that journey."

"My uncle's friend died on his way there," said the young man on my right. He gesticulated when he talked. The gel on his hair glittered iridescently. "It's extremely dangerous."

"I know," the driver said. "My cousin says it's worth it. I have family there. If things go wrong, they'll help me out. It's just a matter of getting there."

"You said your cousin works in a restaurant," the man in the front said. "How can he help you out?"

"It's all up in the air anyway," the driver said. "I'm not even sure if I can put together the money."

"But you don't know where you could end up. Your whole family is here."

The driver didn't answer. A drop of sweat slithered down my forehead into my eyes. I blinked it away and looked out the window. The heat had made the world opaque.

"What are you doing?" yelled the senior officer. "You just passed the Hemmat exit!"

"Oh fuck," whispered the man on my right. The one on my left shook his head.

"Sorry. I'll go down and turn around at Hakim," the driver said.

"You don't have to go all the way down and back up again," said the man on my right. "You can take Hakim to the east."

"Hakim doesn't have an exit to Takht-e Tavous Street," the driver said.

"I think it does," the one on my left chimed in.

The driver snapped back at him. "I drive in this city every day and every night. I don't really need your help here."

"Where are we headed?" I asked. The driver looked at me in the rearview mirror. He seemed ready to explode. I cut him off before he opened his mouth. "I was a bus driver for twenty-five years. I probably know."

"Moallem Street," said the man on my right. Sweat was dissolving his hair gel, and his curls now stuck flatly to his head.

"You can take Hakim to the east," I said. "Go all the way to the Sayyad Shirazi Highway. I can show you the way from there."

The car turned onto the Hakim Highway. From there on, all the way to the Shariati Street exit, no one uttered a word. The driver stared ahead in defeat. The others were too hot to open their mouths.

On Shariati Street, a young man selling herbs looked at his watch every other second, silently begging the sun to go down. A couple of women in chador were carrying bags of celery and carrots. A man squatting on a thin curb was smoking. Only the middle part of his soles touched the curb, yet he maintained his balance effortlessly.

Before Takht-e Tavous Street, the accident happened.

I had noticed the Paykan truck before and knew that it would cause trouble. The kid behind the wheel, hardly in his twenties, drove like he was asking for it. In the two minutes I was watching him, he made a few dangerous maneuvers, and when he tried to cut in front of a Kia Pride, he hit a taxi from behind. The clash was not loud, but the way both vehicles jolted suggested damage.

The traffic stopped. All my captors cursed and groaned at the same time. The other motorists laid on their horns, as if creating pandemonium would enable them to blast through the congestion. Both drivers jumped out of their cars and rushed to inspect the damage.

The Toyota on our side broke out of the traffic jam and released a long, deafening honk into the air. The driver insulted the two men before screeching off. Whatever he had said made them snap. Their voices rose, but what they were yelling didn't interest me. Like with other fights I had seen from my bus seat, I followed the body language. I watched the hands flying up and down, the torsos twisting to and fro.

Other people interfered and separated them. We were on our way again. Ten minutes later, the car stopped in front of a massive, ugly building. I could hardly read the sign, damaged by years of exposure to dust and smog: THE COURT OF THE ISLAMIC REVOLUTION.

THE GUARDS, fractious and agitated by the heat, got out of the back seat and led me inside in tense silence.

The building was old, probably early twentieth century, with the highest ceilings I had ever seen in Tehran. It had ornate stucco and well-designed, arched corridors that had been carelessly abandoned to the ravages of pollution and humidity. We walked down a long hallway with benches and office doors on either side of us. Prisoners in various outfits were sitting around, and each of them was accompanied by uniformed guards. All the doors to the rooms were open. Bearded, middle-aged men or women in chador sat inside them at identical desks, with large stacks of files on top. After a while, the guards and bureaucrats and prisoners started to look alike, as if they were part of a never-ending loop of court footage from TV. Occasionally a figure would stand out, usually a middle-aged man in a suit carrying a leather bag, smiling, and talking on the phone. These men would stop here and there to say something to someone in handcuffs, or crack jokes with guards, or stick their heads into offices and chat with people working inside. One of them approached me.

He was a man settling with ease into his mid-forties. His hair was mostly black and still thick, his beard well trimmed. He wore an expensive dark blue suit that didn't hide his protruding belly. He awkwardly shook my handcuffed hand. .

"Good to see you, Mr. Turabi," he said.

"Have I met you before?"

"Unfortunately, no, but I know you quite well. I'm your lawyer. My name is Tamimi."

He shook my hand again and patted me hesitantly on the shoulder.

The man seemed to be the type of lawyer the court hired to keep up the appearance of fairness. He did the job, got paid, and walked away. Yet I felt grateful. Whatever his motivation might be, he had come to defend me against Hajj Saeed. Since the day of the strike, I had not met anyone who would take my side, even if it were just an empty gesture. Or, really, for a long time before that. Maybe since my mother died.

"So I read your case," he said as he unbuckled his briefcase and rummaged around inside it. "It's such an interesting one. I have been looking forward to meeting you. What an extraordinary life you've led."

He looked up at me while his hands continued to rifle through the papers he had brought with him.

"How can you represent someone you've never met?" I asked.

"I've been on your case for a while. You never asked for a meeting."

"No one told me that I should."

"Of course they didn't. They don't want you to meet your lawyer. They hate us. You've got to fight for your rights in prison. Didn't you watch court movies growing up?"

"No."

"Well, every time the cops nab someone, the guy asks for his attorney. You should have done the same." He laughed. "I'm joking. Don't worry. I'm going to take care of you."

Now it seemed absurd, even inexplicable, that it hadn't even occurred to me to ask to speak to someone. But I wasn't used to asking anybody for anything, and I had gotten in over my head so fast. Besides, if this guy cared so much, he could have come to me.

He finally located the file he was searching for and pulled it out. "A lot is going on in your case," he said, glancing through the papers inside. "They used you and made you confess to a bunch of things. Now this puts us in a bit of a tight spot, but you still have a lot going for you. Your biggest advantage is your record. You had no involvement in any political activity before the strike. They tried to dig up dirt on you and found nothing. We should capitalize on that. It makes it hard for the judge to believe all the things you confessed to, because a foreign intelligence agency never works with someone who hasn't been in politics before. But so much is going on here."

He frowned as he read the page. Then he addressed the guards.

"Can I have a private minute with this gentleman?"

Without waiting for their permission, he took my hand and dragged me across the hallway. We sat on a bench.

"Listen to me carefully. We have only half an hour before the trial, and I have to explain a lot to you. Your situation is very complicated. Are you paying attention?"

"Yes."

"This case is cobbled together. It's built on shaky evidence and the confession you made after they left you in solitary and beat you. You were kept in solitary confinement for more than twenty days, which is illegal and amounts to torture. Besides, your interrogator has accused you of espionage, which is a very sophisticated crime, but he has provided virtually no evidence except for your confession and your friends' testimony."

"Why did he do this to me, then? Is it personal?"

"Nothing is personal here. He did it because the government fucked up with the strike and has been scrambling around to explain it away. The aftermath has been huge and extremely damaging. It has caused a legitimacy crisis, so they are trying to spin what happened in a way that's more favorable to them. You showed up at just the right time. They made you the face of the whole thing."

"Why did they choose me?"

"Because you made it convenient for them."

"What do you mean?"

"Why were you arrested in the first place?"

"Because I was at the strike."

"No. You were arrested because you beat the shit out of a minister's son. That's why the police caught you in the first place, right?"

"But my name was in the system."

"You went to all kinds of union meetings and participated in a collective action against the state. Of course your name was in the system. But you were also a blank slate, no connections, no involvement with anything besides work until you started going to that study group, so they could say whatever they wanted about you."

"They knew everything about me already."

"They have access to everyone's phones and emails and shit.

THEN THE FISH SWALLOWED HIM

It takes them two hours to find out whatever they want. And it was even easier in your case since the study group had been under surveillance."

"I still don't understand why they want to make this whole thing about me."

"Look at this through their eyes. You mishandled a strike and beat up working people. The Western media are sitting there like vultures ready to jump on your every single fuckup, and people are glued to their TVs like zombies and believe everything they see. This creates enormous anger. If you're the government, you can't explain it away, but you need to at least have a story to keep your base happy. You understand?"

"Yes."

"Now, listen. The day after the strike, a bus driver who participated in it beats the shit out of an innocent, good-looking young boy who happens to be the son of a minister. Now, that's a great target. If you are so desperate for justification, you take this up and run with it. You say to your folks, 'See? They started the violence. Look what this man did to that poor boy.' If they can make a scenario where you, the villain here, are not just a pawn but the mastermind of the whole thing, then they can say this violent man organized the strike and instigated violence against the police. You follow me?"

I nodded.

"So after the strike they were not looking for you. You got yourself on their radar. I think they came up with the scenario shortly after they caught you. Otherwise, it doesn't make sense that they put one of their best men on your case. Now they are done with you. They have their story. My point is that everyone knows you didn't really do anything. They wanted a face to show to the world and say this is the guy with contacts in the CIA. Last night they did a little news show about you and the strike and showed parts of your friends' confessions on TV."

"What?"

"Of course they did. Why do you think they recorded them?"

"But if they showed it on TV, people will immediately know that this is all bullshit."

"Really? Who do you think you are? People will forget about you in a week. Tomorrow the headlines will be about some financial corruption, the day after they're going to arrest people at some party, the day after that Bush will say some shit about Iran. By the end of the week, no one will remember you."

"If that's the case, why did they bother to do any of this?"

"You're not listening to me," the lawyer said. "This is for their base, not for you and me. As we speak, most of the base is already convinced that the strike was a conspiracy. They don't have to lose any sleep over what happened, and they can just move on."

He waved at a guard who was leading two handcuffed old men past us to the end of the corridor. The guard put on a look-who-I-am-stuck-with face. "I know, I know," the lawyer said and laughed.

"Look. You've served your purpose. What's going to happen is that they will lock you up for a little while and let you go when the strike is totally forgotten. What we can do is reduce that 'little while' by as much as possible. You follow me?"

"I do."

"So"—he looked at his watch—"in ten minutes, you go in there in front of the judge. He knows that you're innocent. He will be lenient if you let him do his job and will probably give you a year. Your good behavior will reduce it to six months, which is shorter than the time you would have served if you were only sentenced for beating the boy. You hang out in there a little while, find friends, have some free food, avoid this cesspool of a city, and then come back to your life. Okay?"

I didn't reply.

"But if you go in there and act all self-righteous and yell, God help you. You understand this?"

I nodded numbly.

"Over the last weekend, I wrote up your defense." He opened the bag and started rummaging around again. "You just need to go in and read this . . . Hang on a second."

His hand paused in the bag and he blushed. He was looking down at the other end of the corridor. I turned around and saw another handcuffed man with two guards coming our way. The lawyer resumed his search for the paper with new urgency.

He pulled it out and handed it to me with a pen. "Read this thing and mark it wherever you think you want to make a change," he said, without moving his eyes away from the other prisoner. "Don't worry about anything. You'll be fine. Just read this paper. I have to talk to another client. I'll be right back." He stood up abruptly and walked quickly toward the man.

I leaned back in the chair and closed my eyes, gathering my strength to look at the document. Being surrounded by so many people, as well as the conversation with the lawyer, had drained me completely. I wanted to lie down and sleep there. At that moment, I would have been happy without a trial. Hardly a day passed since I gave up everything to get out of solitary, but now I longed to get back there. I would not have protested if someone came out of the courtroom and gave me a verdict right then so I could go back to my cell and lie alone on the floor.

A noise made me open my eyes. Guards had come and sat down next to me on both sides. I hadn't heard them. I must have drowsed for a second. At the other end of the hall, the conversation between the lawyer and the handcuffed man was getting loud. The man was emaciated and hunched. From a distance of a dozen yards, I could see the trembling of his hands.

The lawyer raised his voice. He was warning the man of what indifference to his advice might bring about. The prisoner said something I didn't hear, and the lawyer replied with a condescending gesture. The man's bent back straightened. The lawyer's words had shocked him out of his torpor. He produced another paper and read a passage to the man. Then the man snapped.

"Who the fuck do you work for?" yelled the prisoner. His broken voice traveled along the corridor and turned a dozen heads on both sides. The lawyer recoiled, but he quickly composed himself. He patted the man on the shoulder, the way he had patted me when we met. The man slapped his hand away with all the power left in his handcuffed arms. His knees quivered. A noticeable shuddering overtook his fragile body. My legs began to shake too, like we were conjoined.

The lawyer began to talk again. The man interrupted him with a loud "Shut up!" and signaled to the guards to take him away. Before they parted, the lawyer patted him on the shoulder a second time, as if to deliberately get on his nerves. The prisoner let him pat. The lawyer smiled and said something while his hand was on his client's back. When he released his grip, the prisoner's handcuffed wrists flew up, and he grabbed the lawyer by the collar. He kicked the lawyer's shins and forced him down with his shoulder. He moved faster than the guards, forcing the lawyer to stumble back. The lawyer narrowly retrieved his balance, but his bag dropped. Stacks of paper spilled out onto the floor.

The guards dragged the prisoner down to the ground. One threw himself on top of the man. The other one kicked him in the shin, retaliating on behalf of the lawyer, who watched the fight as he picked up his papers. "You ungrateful piece of shit," he yelled before he walked back to me.

"Okay, Mr. Turabi," he addressed me, dusting off his bag. "Did you read the defense?"

I looked at the paper between my index finger and thumb and read the first line. "In the name of God, the Compassionate, the Merciful. Certain incidents took place on April 12th, 2005, in Jannatabad Bus Terminal in Tehran, which pained the heart and soul of the great people of Iran."

"We only have five minutes," he interrupted. "Did you read the text?"

"Yes," I lied.

"The whole thing?"

"This is only two pages."

"What do you think?"

"I think it's okay."

"You have nothing to add or remove?"

"No."

"Excellent. Good luck with the trial, then. I have to go. I'll check in with you later."

"Wait, you're not coming in with me?"

"No."

"Aren't you my lawyer? Who is supposed to defend me in there?"

"That's why you have that piece of paper, my friend. This judge hates lawyers. I can come in with you and talk. Frankly, it would have been easier for me to do that, but I spent time and energy writing this thing because I don't want to fuck up your trial, and I want you to get a lenient sentence. I don't expect a pat on the back. I just did my job. But don't disrespect me with this tone, like me not coming with you in there is because I don't care."

He waved at the guards. One of them came and took hold of my arm and began to march me toward the courtroom. "Good luck," the lawyer repeated.

THE ROOM SMELLED LIKE DEPRESSION. It was spacious and empty with a dozen rows of old, wooden benches and a podium at the far end. Scratches and bumps and traces of moth teeth marred the elaborate woodwork on the furniture. Between the benches and the podium, two flimsy, thin-legged tables were set up to separate the accused from both the spectators and the judge. In the jury area, the most abandoned part of the room, thick dust and cobwebs covered the seats.

Walking through the space between the rows to the end of the room felt like moving through a movie scene empty of its actors and extras. The guards led me to one of the tables. I sat on an ugly plastic chair that looked jarringly out of place next to the rest of the magisterial furniture. The officers sat in two seats in the row behind me. None of the doors opened, and the other men were so quiet I turned around once to make sure they were awake. We waited there for half an hour, but despite the silence, I wasn't bored for a second. Coming from the gray of the solitary cell, the courtroom was extremely stimulating and colorful. Twin portraits of Khomeini and Khamenei hung right above the podium. Both looked down with frowning faces, like wrathful gods supervising the judge. A wrinkled Iranian flag drooped in its mount on the wall. Large chunks of plaster had fallen from the ceiling.

When the door finally cracked open, the man who entered defied all my expectations. He was skinny and stooped. A worn suit two sizes too large for him hung off his shriveled frame. With one hand he adjusted his glasses and scratched his sparse beard, and with the other he carried yet another file full of papers jutting out unevenly. He shuffled across the room without looking at us, sat down at the small table by the podium, produced a fountain pen from his pocket, and slowly examined it. Then he opened the file and leafed through its contents in total silence, still without even bothering to glance in our direction. He must have been the secretary.

Before he got to the end of the file, the door opened again, and a stodgy mullah came in.

"Get up," whispered the guard behind me. The mullah, indifferent to our gesture of respect, proceeded to the podium. His robe was too large for him too, and it dragged on the floor behind him like the train of a bride's dress. His black turban, a size larger than usual, looked like a car tire pressing down on his head. It caused his forehead to crease up. He sat up at the podium and stared at me with eyes as piercing as Khomeini's. He took several breaths, wearily heaving his chest up and down. He was tired in a way I fully understood. The afternoon exhaustion of all nine-to-five workers, probably the only thing he shared with the bus driver sitting across from him.

"Is this a party?" he addressed me.

"Excuse me?"

"You are leaning on that chair like we have thrown a party for you."

I scrambled to fix my posture. The secretary got up and handed the file to the judge, who read the first few pages with care. His interest seemed to wane after that. He skimmed the document until he got to the second half of the file. A glint of interest returned to his eyes, and he paused over one page. I watched him reread it and then pull it out of the folder to look it over again. From the outline of the black letters on the back of the paper, I thought it must be a letter. It had the indentations of official correspondence and a large stamp at the bottom. It could be Hajj Saeed's final assessment of my case.

He finally put the letter back with the other documents and took out a few stapled papers and began to read. Right away I recognized the statements I had written. When he was done with those, he reclined in his chair and looked at me.

"Come here," he said. His eyes didn't follow mine as I rose. They remained fixed on my crotch as I approached the podium. The judge turned around the confession papers and slid them toward me.

"Did you write this?"

My handwriting surprised me. I had put down my final confession, dictated by Hajj Saeed, so neatly like I had copied down my favorite poem for class.

"Yes," I said.

"Is this your signature?"

"Yes."

"Go back to your chair."

Neither of the guards took any interest in these proceedings. One smothered a yawn, and the other stared fixedly at the floor.

"Get up!" the judge yelled as soon as I had sat down. "Read the indictment," he said to the secretary. The man rose. His height changed so little he might as well have kept seated.

The indictment began with a long survey of what the Islamic Republic had achieved over the last few years. It emphasized its unquestionable legitimacy manifested in the impressive turnout for every election, the steady rise in the quality of life for the working people, and how the country was at the cutting edge of medical and nuclear science. Then it described the success of the nation on the global stage and its astute foreign diplomacy, which had forced the Saudis and Israelis to scramble for new alliances. As a result, the indictment contended, the enemies had launched a new campaign to damage the government by recruiting people from inside the country, especially from the more vulnerable sections of society.

Only the last paragraph was about me. Paraphrasing my own confessions, the prosecutor had depicted me as a naive man manipulated by nefarious foreign agencies into organizing the notorious strike.

"I'm going to read the accusations the indictment raises against you. Say yes or no to my questions."

"Okay."

"Is your name Yunus Turabi?"

"Yes."

"You are accused of collusion with the enemies of the Islamic Republic. Do you accept the charge?"

I went cold. I had heard various versions of the accusation before but never uttered by someone with such total authority. I had let circumstances pull me in this or that direction, without really putting up a fight. This was my last chance to assert my will, to act with integrity by refusing to go along with them. The lawyer had advised me to admit my guilt. He had reassured me that everything was taken care of and warned me against gainsaying or provoking the judge. But my instinct ran counter to this. A voice from inside warned me against confessing to a crime I had never committed.

The judge repeated the question, impatience creeping into his voice. Then again, what was the point of taking a stand here, I wondered. I had written and signed the confession. The lawyer had made it clear that this was just a charade, and they would let me go soon. If I resisted, they might send me back to solitary. I was certain, however much I might long for it now, that I would not survive another round in there.

"Yes," I said quickly, before I could waver again.

"You are accused of conspiring against the national security of the Islamic Republic of Iran. Do you accept the charge?"

"Yes."

"Do you have a last word for the court?"

"I do," I said. I unfolded the pages the lawyer had given me.

In the name of God, the Compassionate, the Merciful.
Certain incidents took place on April 12th, 2005, in
Jannatabad Bus Terminal in Tehran, which pained the
heart and soul of the great people of Iran. Unfortunately, the

strike, which was meant to strengthen the rights of working bus drivers, thanks to provocations by certain figures who infiltrated the event, took on an iconoclastic tone and insulted everything this country and its people deem sacred, which was not the intention of the organizers.

As a proud citizen of this country, I am aware that safety is a rare privilege we enjoy in a tumultuous, dangerous region, and for that we all need to be grateful to our government. I am also aware that the hostile Western countries have yet to digest the fact that Iran is no longer their puppet. As a result, they are constantly planning to undermine our independence and inject negative energy into our society. They provoked Saddam Hussein into an eight-year war with us, imposed the harshest regime of economic sanctions in recent history, and when it turned out that the great people of Iran would not buckle under those pressures, they started to infiltrate our social movements and manipulate our civic activities. It is incumbent upon us, as citizens who benefit from the protection of the Iranian state, to neutralize these schemes and expose the perpetrators.

Prior to visiting this court I spent some time in solitude, which allowed me to reflect deeply on what I did. Also, I discussed the events leading up to the strike and on the day of the strike with my case officer. Through these discussions I developed a new insight into what happened. As I stand here before this court today, I know that my actions, while taken with the best of intentions, were harmful to myself and my people, and didn't help the causes I had claimed to support. Here before this court I announce that I regret my activities, *and ask forgiveness from the great people of Iran and our Supreme Leader.*

Finally, a few words about the bus drivers' union. I was a member of the union for six months, but it took me numerous sittings with my case officer to completely understand its dynamics. I believe that the union, although established with good intentions to pursue the righteous demands of bus drivers, has been infiltrated by elements who do not have the love of Iran and its people in their heart. They have succeeded in driving this organization off the right path. Therefore, I hereby announce my resignation from it.

I am grateful to Your Honor and the court for providing me with this opportunity.

I folded the paper. The secretary was already working on another file. The judge had produced a tasbih while I was reading and kept fiddling with it for a while after I finished. When he finally lifted his head, his face expressed nothing but midday tiredness.

"You can leave," he said. He picked up the file, descended from the podium, and marched out of the room. The secretary remained seated, occupied with the papers in front of him. The guards kept their distance from me as we walked to the door. They didn't say a word all the way back to Evin.

Outside, the sun continued to grill Tehran. The world was bleached. The asphalt sparkled with heat and seemed to be approaching a melting point. People dragged their feet around, looking at each other with dead eyes.

• • •

The next few days I mostly slept. The trip to the court had drained all my energy. I woke up every day dizzy and wandered around the cell, tired as though I had stayed up all night. Then I would fall asleep again until noon, only to be jolted awake by the meal the new guard would bring me. I ate without tasting the food and usually slept a few hours again until dinner. This new guard, a prematurely bald man who looked forty but must have been in his late twenties, didn't exchange a word with me. I thought of asking him to tell Hajj Saeed that I wanted to see him, but I knew it wouldn't happen.

About a week after the trial, he took me out of the cell. We walked past the interrogation room toward the front yard. Halfway down the hall, he opened a door and signaled for me to go in. I stepped into a small room with a desk and two chairs. A man with gray hair and a gray beard looked up at me when I entered. He seemed like someone I knew from a previous lifetime. It took me a while to remember him. This was the same man who had told me what I was accused of on my first day in the prison.

He pointed to a chair and watched me sit.

"I've got the news," he said as soon as I was in the chair.

I looked at him blankly, not quite realizing what he was talking about.

"Are you nervous?" he said.

Then I understood. I had thought the verdict would be announced in the court, that I would take another trip through the city to hear it. My heart began to pound, but I kept my face straight, determined to deny him the pleasure of messing with me.

"How are you holding up?" he said.

"Very well." I feigned a smile. "I've been sleeping a lot over the last week."

"Glad to hear that." He cleared his throat and opened the folder in front of him. "You're a lucky man. For what you have done, people usually get a life sentence. Did you know that?"

"I didn't do anything."

He exhaled dramatically. "Mr. Yunus Turabi, you are sentenced to four years in Rajaeeshahr Prison."

"Four years? Four years?"

"You were lucky to have a kind judge."

FOUR YEARS IN PRISON had ruined my sense of direction. I used to work out where I was just by looking at the mountains. With just a glance I could estimate my distance from Tehran's main squares. The day I was released, I had no notion of how the world was laid out now. As I stepped out of the Rajaeeshahr Prison gate on the hills of the city of Karaj almost thirty miles west of Tehran, I was nothing but the past. The rasp of the metal door closing behind me sounded exactly the same as when I had heard it entering the prison.

The day I got out, the chaotic sprawl of the city down the hill made no sense to me. The place I used to know had metastasized and grown into a shapeless monstrosity. The Tehran-Karaj Highway lay down there and the trains ran parallel to it, keeping pace with the cars on the road. Far to the east, the smog hovered stubbornly over Tehran. I set down my bag, put my hands on my hips, and bent my back to give my lungs room to expand, before descending the hill.

I had to ask five people for directions to the Gohardasht Bridge. There I found a parked shared taxi waiting for passengers to ferry to Tehran. I slid into the car. My bus driver's uniform, two thousand tomans, and the keys to my apartment were my only worldly possessions. I had carried them into Evin with me, and from there to Rajaeeshahr. When I had entered the second prison, the guards had confiscated my belongings. They had taken me to a cell with two bunk beds and two cellmates. There a ravenous god bit off a four-year chunk of my life and left me with an aged body, high blood pressure, failing kidneys, periodic migraines, and bad breath.

I wondered what had happened to my apartment. Water and electricity must have been cut off years ago. By then rats and cockroaches had probably overrun the place. I pictured a gnawed-on sack of rice and a blanket of dust on the furniture, then realized it would likely be much worse than what I was imagining. Four years is an eternity in Tehran. I would hardly recognize my neighborhood. They might even have already torn down the building. The developers had probably searched for me so they could buy the apartment, and when they found out that I was in prison, had gone ahead and destroyed it. Even if the place was there and I could make it livable again, what was I supposed to do with my life? The city transportation department wouldn't hire me. I was permanently disqualified from government jobs. Maybe I could drive a truck. Private companies were usually desperate for workers. I could spend the rest of my life on the road.

A young man got into the taxi. The first human being sitting near me in public after all this time. He had no idea how special his life was. Prison had changed me. I no longer despised people like I did when I was a bus driver. Without the company of others I would not have gotten through those four years. Especially my first cellmates, Meysam and Sadjad. Meysam was in jail for proselytizing Bahaism. Sadjad was a nuclear physicist accused of leaking sensitive data to Mossad. They told me their life stories over our first dinner and laughed at me for panicking about my sentence. Meysam was in there for fifteen years and Sadjad for twenty. Meysam took me to the public area inside the prison called the Hosseinieh and introduced me to the others. A man who had strangled his wife and son. A leader of a dervish sect. The former CEO of Mellat Bank, accused of embezzling billions of tomans. People of all stripes, some innocuous, some insane.

The boy next to me in the taxi pulled out one of those new phones that were all screen and no keypad. I knew them from TV but had never seen one up close. Little, brightly colored squares were laid out in a neat grid, and when he touched one, a new window would open. He pulled up page after page and scrolled up and down. A virtual keyboard popped up. The man typed something on the tiny field with magical dexterity, shaking his head and murmuring. He suddenly turned to me.

"Were you in Tehran today?" he said.

Having not been addressed by a free person for four years, I became tongue-tied and dumbly shook my head. He looked back at the device. I missed the ease of communication that my prison friends and I had shared. I could talk to people like Hajj Abdollah, the portly former MP who watched TV day and night and had mastered the art of reading between the news lines. Or the elderly member of the Feda-i guerilla group with a seemingly endless store of implausible accounts of his armed struggles against the Shah. I even missed Mash Gholam, an eighty-five-year-old man from Rasht, thrown into jail because he couldn't afford the alimony for his forty-two-year-old ex-wife. He would sing loudly and stop only when he peed himself. One day he died of a heart attack right before my eyes. Talking to men with death

sentences—the two Kurdish Al-Qaeda affiliates, those Khuz-
estani separatists bragging about their connection to a Saudi
prince, even the mujahid fighter who had infiltrated the national
TV station and stolen its archive—seemed easier than speaking
to this boy. He could never know me the way they did.

A woman got into the front seat of the taxi. As soon as she sat,
she pulled out her own phone, which was similar to the young
man's, and shook her head as she scrolled up and down.

"On Facebook," the man said, to no one in particular, "it says
more than a million people showed up."

"On what?" I asked.

"Facebook." The man repeated the same word so naturally
that further inquiry would have made me look like an idiot.

"One of my friends," said the woman from the front seat,
"writes that her cousin, who is a cop, saw the crowd from a police
helicopter and estimates that it's over two million."

"It's amazing," the man said.

The driver got in and turned on the engine. "I'm not going all
the way to Azadi Square. The crowd has come onto the highway.
I'll drop you guys off at the Ekbatan exit."

"Wonderful!" said the woman. None of my passengers had
ever seemed so excited about not getting to their destination.

After some silence, the young man looked at me and spoke.
"You're a bus driver, right?"

"I am."

"What have you seen over the last couple of days?"

"I've been away traveling. I didn't follow the news."

The man's eyes slid down and stayed on my uniform.

"I am going straight to work now," I clarified.

"You mean," said the woman, "you don't even know what happened after the election?" She turned back and stared at me. The driver was also looking at me in the rearview mirror. It felt like being back in the interrogation room, under pressure to divulge another piece of information I didn't actually possess.

While I was in prison, for the first time in my life I had experienced what it meant to be the center of attention in a large group of people. A few months after my arrival, the TV there had shown a documentary about the union strike, featuring me and Davoud Shabestani. It made all the familiar claims: the CIA had orchestrated the strike and co-opted the bus drivers, the Soros Foundation had funded it, and I was their link to the union.

The Rajaeeshahr prisoners had watched in silence. Even after the end of the documentary, no one dared to look at me for a while. Then Hajj Faraj, a veteran reformist, asked me for details. I told them the truth, but no one believed me. From that day on, if I was in a group and politics came up, they turned to me for an opinion. They asked me about behind-the-scenes deals, the latest CIA plans for Iran, or the results of upcoming presidential or parliamentary elections. I first shied away, then told them as much as I knew, which was almost nothing. But my platitudes were received with keen attention. When I confessed my ignorance, they interpreted it as me being tight-lipped and professional. So eventually I had embraced their interest and confidently held forth on every subject.

But out here, in the world of the free, the discussions moved past me. The day before my release, I had heard that the election was a mess, but I had no idea what had happened in its aftermath.

"No," I said as nonchalantly as I could while frantically trying to recall snippets of conversations I had heard in the Hosseinieh over the last few weeks.

"They stole the election from Mousavi and handed it to Ahmadinejad," the woman informed me eagerly. I nodded.

The driver let out a dramatic sigh. "Who cares? They're all cut from the same cloth."

"Oh, don't start that, please," the woman said.

"Why not? I tell you why. Because you know it's true, but you don't want to face it. You can go through this charade because you don't have to work twelve hours a day to feed your kids."

"You're struggling," the young man said from the back seat, "because Ahmadinejad destroyed our economy. We can't afford four more years of that."

"You guys are just young. I've lived this shit my whole adult life, all thirty years of it, and I'm telling you that this system is sick down to its roots. This after-election thing is just another show by the Americans to keep the mullahs in their place."

"It says here two people have been killed so far," said the young man. They had decided to ignore the driver and had returned to their devices. The news generated no response in the car.

What do you know about death? I wanted to scream. They had never stepped into a prison. In there, I had been surrounded by it. The mujahid member, who ran laps around the yard every day during outdoors time, was hanged two weeks after my arrival. A month later a young man, walking in front of me in the yard and laughing at something, paused and pressed his palm to his heart. His laughter turned to gasps for breath before he collapsed, his dark red face distorted into a monstrous grimace. Shortly after that, a middle-aged man somehow managed to climb to the top of an electricity post in protest of having his weekly visit with his wife suspended. He threatened to kill himself while the guards begged him to climb down. The prisoners laughed and dared him to jump. Then he did. I watched him fall like a sack of rice, but I turned my head away before he hit the ground. I forgot to cover my ears, though. The sound of his bones exploding on the concrete made me vomit on the grass.

I looked out the taxi window to the mountains in the north and the smoggy outline of Tehran, which was sluggishly expanding on the horizon. Half of me looked forward to being back after all this time. The other half longed to return to the safety of my cell and my friends.

· · ·

The taxi parked at the Ekbatan exit, even though the traffic ahead of us didn't seem that bad. While I was looking at the mountains through the window, the young man had wrapped a green strip of fabric around his wrist and the woman had exchanged her black shawl for a green one. There was a tiny park by the highway. A scattering of grassy patches, young sycamores with sooty leaves, uncomfortable metal benches. An unmistakable vestige of Karbaschi's time as mayor. I hadn't missed it at all.

I took a walk around the park and sat on a bench, looking at the skyline of the Ekbatan towers through the tree branches. Two pigeons fluttered down from above and landed right by my foot. They paraded around my shoes fearlessly, seeming to wait for something I was supposed to deliver.

One day during my final spring in prison, I took the last bit of my breakfast with me to the yard and threw it to a fat, waddling bird that looked much like the ones before me now. From the surrounding trees and bushes, others had appeared, platoon-like, arriving to ambush me. They bore down on the food and battled over every crumb. I went back in and brought more bread. They gobbled it all up in a flash.

From that day on, I went around the section before outdoors time to ask for the remains of people's breakfasts. The birds quickly learned to gather around the bench as soon as I sat down. After a while, I knew each of them, not so much by appearance as by attitude. I could tell the timid apart from the aggressive, the greedy from the modest, and I threw the bread pieces down in a way that would deliver justice. Eventually they dropped their guards completely and would come close to sit on my lap and shoulders. They first perched gingerly and politely, then naturally, as if I were a tree. Becoming a birdman added to my prison celebrity. Every day a crowd of onlookers gathered to watch me and my avian friends. Some of them got into pigeon feeding too.

Now, in this park, the birds behaved as though they had heard the news about me from their Rajaeeshahr kin. I didn't have food, so I left to avoid their demanding stares.

I walked down on the sleeper lines of the Karaj Highway. A few other people accompanied me in the direction of Tehran. A larger crowd moved along the other side of the road, coming back from the city. It was not that unusual to see groups here. The Azadi Stadium was a mile away, and after Esteghlal-Persepolis matches one frequently encountered throngs of young men on foot, brandishing their red or blue flags and chanting. The crowd that day was made up of the kind of people you never see in prisons, another species altogether. They were very young and held flags, all green, along with their shirts and wristbands and shawls. More than half of them were women.

This foreshadowing of the dramatic scene in Azadi Square was not sufficient preparation for what I was walking into. From the narrow sidewalk on the Jenah overpass, I looked down upon the largest gathering I had ever seen in my life. Thousands upon thousands of people had occupied the square, stretching from under the white bulk of the monument, which stood over them like a protective mother, to the perimeter of the space, and from there into all the streets that led to it. From the overpass, the quiet crowd formed a body that, unbeknownst to its individual components, fidgeted and undulated, as if coordinated by an invisible conductor.

I descended the walkway from the overpass into the square. Hardly an inch of unclaimed space was left. People had occupied benches and stone walls, grass and concrete, sidewalks and pathways. Cars had to carefully nose their way through masses of human bodies to get anywhere on the streets surrounding the square.

I walked around, growing increasingly astonished. Middle-aged women in chador were sitting next to barely veiled girls with heavy makeup, all holding pictures of Mir Hossein Mousavi. A blind man in a wheelchair wearing a cap decorated with a picture of Khatami and Mousavi smiling together was flanked by three young men in identical green T-shirts and gelled hair. The square was mostly quiet, but here and there chants would erupt briefly. "You liar, where is your sixty-three percent?" "Where is my vote?" and, less frequently, "Down with the dictator." Everybody had the phones I had seen in the taxi, and many of them were holding them up. Soon I realized that the phones had cameras in them, and people were filming and taking pictures of the rally.

At the Azadi Street entrance, I ran into an excited group of young people who had just arrived. They were jumping up and down and shouting to attract attention.

"We saw Mousavi! We saw Mousavi!" they yelled. People ran over to them and huddled around. They talked over each other in half sentences, their voices shaking with exhilaration. They had seen him at the Jeyhoun crossroad. He had shown up out of nowhere, gotten on a makeshift platform, and addressed the protesters with a portable microphone. The newcomers hadn't heard his speech well, but the gist of it was that he had promised to stand with the people until the authorities gave them a satisfactory answer. Those who had surrounded the excited newcomers dispersed, running around to spread the news. It quickly reverberated through the masses and voices grew louder with excitement. I was still trying to make sense of the situation when someone tapped me on the shoulder.

"You're a bus driver, right?"

"Yes."

The man hugged me tightly. I recoiled but let him finish the embrace.

"Nothing warms my heart more than seeing working people among us."

"Of course," I murmured. He was in his early twenties, possibly a college student. The air he put on with his posh accent made him sound like a character from a TV comedy sketch.

"You know," he said, "they've already started to write on their websites that this movement won't go anywhere because working people don't take part in it. If we show them folks like you are here in the square, it'll shut them up. Please bring more of your friends next time. It's going to be a long fight, you know."

"Sure." I nodded and smiled. Then I froze in place. Was he an infiltrator who knew my past? Why was he talking to me when there were millions of other people there?

"Can I take a selfie with you?"

"A what?"

"A selfie for our website. I will send you a link."

"I don't know . . ."

He ignored me, slid over to my side, and pulled out his phone. I only understood what he wanted when he said, "Smile, please."

"No!" I yelled.

A dozen heads turned toward us. The young man jumped aside and held up his hands to indicate that he would back off. I fled, elbowing people away and stepping haphazardly over the ones sitting in the grass. I left the square and didn't stop moving until I got to an uncrowded side street.

• • •

Around the corner, a large group had gathered along the street that intersected the one I was walking on. The cameras were out, recording the incident unfolding in the middle of the block. The crowd was too thick to get through. People nearby were screaming and cursing.

Two men in front of me started talking.

"Did he really shoot him?"

"No, it was tear gas."

A third man jumped into their conversation. "What do you mean, tear gas? The guy was holding a real Kalashnikov."

"No, he wouldn't dare. That was tear gas someone else threw into the crowd. Even if he used his gun, it'd be loaded with plastic bullets."

"He's right," said a fourth man. "We shouldn't panic. They're trying to scare us away."

"He moved back from the edge of the roof!" a voice yelled from the front. "Move ahead! We shouldn't let him get away!"

"What's happening?" I asked a woman who was listening to the conversation like I was.

"There is a Basij base on this street," she said. "They are armed and on the roof. One of the Basijis just shot at the crowd."

"With real bullets?"

Before she could answer, the crowd pushed us forward. I turned the corner onto the other street. Now I could see the base. It was a nondescript, two-story building, a remnant of the second Pahlavi era that had miraculously survived intact. A small sign on the door marked it as militia-owned. There was one man on the roof. He wore a strange helmet with flaps that hung over his ears, a blue shirt, and military pants. He held a Kalashnikov in his hands. He waved threateningly and shouted at the people who were kicking at the door. They ignored him. He held up the gun, targeted something across the street, and fired.

The crowd dispersed in a flash. People ran in all directions, yelling and screaming. I stood where I was, transfixed by the sight of a gunman shooting at people in broad daylight. The packed street quickly became half empty. Smoke enveloped everything. I could see fire leaping out of the yard behind the building, depositing soot on its white facade.

A young man with frightened eyes was running in my direction. A few steps in front of me, he put up his hands. Both his palms were covered in blood. He continued by without saying a word. Then I saw a body by the wall. A bald man lay on the ground, his limbs splayed out at awkward angles. A few men appeared from different corners of the street, each taking hold of the unconscious person to help lift him. Now I could see a large blood smear on the side of his shirt. "Allah Akbar!" the carriers of the body began to shout. "They killed him! They killed him!"

The gunman had disappeared. I smelled tear gas, and my eyes began to burn. I turned around and ran, bypassing the crowd at the square, until I got to Azadi Street.

• • •

I walked down the middle of the road, against the massive tide of silent demonstrators. The street was covered with pictures of Mousavi and Zahra Rahnavard in all sizes and postures, "Where Is My Vote?" flyers, newspapers, and pamphlets. Countless green rags and flags flapped around. The protesters, mostly young, made Vs with their fingers in the air.

Near the Azerbaijan crossroad I came upon a park, and I went in to rest. It seemed there were no cars on the streets until Enqelab Square, and I would have to walk the remaining few miles. I needed to save energy. The park was strangely quiet, though only a hundred feet away people were flooding past. I walked around, trying to understand why this place seemed so untouched by the events of the day.

Behind a thick cedar I ran into two men. The homeless of Tehran. Now I was practically one of them. Both squatted on the grass, their sneakers torn, their ragged clothes covered with stains, and their haggard faces blackened with dirt and soot. One of them was holding a piece of aluminum foil over the flame of a lighter while the other one inhaled the smoke with a straw. They both looked up at me with empty eyes, too battered by life to care what I thought.

As a bus driver, I had seen this a thousand times in Tehran and had always looked away, shaking my head. Before being in jail, I had had no clue what they were feeling and why they were using heroin. Now I could relate.

In my third year in Rajaeeshahr, they had decided to renovate our section and scattered us across the prison. I parted ways with Meysam and Sadjad and entered a new cell. There I shared the space with Soroush, a counterfeiter, and Fazel, a drug dealer. We were in the dirtiest room I had ever seen. Smears of feces covered the four corners of the ceiling, and cockroaches ran wild over everything.

Soroush had studied Persian literature and ended up in jail because he had forged traveler's checks. He was too depressed to talk to us. Except for when he ate, he stayed in his bed, muttering about his wasted youth or doodling disfigured portraits in a notebook. Fazel was one of those people who grow up and die in prison. He got caught selling drugs at the age of sixteen and served two years, went out and got caught again in three months. After he served five more years, he left but was back ten months later. I met him on the eve of his thirty-fifth birthday. By then prison was his only home. There he felt comfortable and had everything he needed, including heroin. I would sit and watch him lining up the gray powder on a scrap of aluminum foil and moving the mild flame of a lighter underneath it so he could take in the smoke with a paper pipe. When he asked if I'd like to try it, I said yes.

Thus a new ritual came into my life. I would have a few puffs first thing every morning, which softened my jaw muscles and made me talk. I'd joke and laugh and tell stories from the time I drove buses around Tehran. Fazel would laugh and nod and smoke and talk about his own adventures. He had dealt with Afghan traffickers at the border in Baluchistan and escaped a border patrol car in his Toyota truck across a desert.

As soon as I started using heroin, I stopped going to the yard. I grew fond of the new cell. The feces and the cockroaches ceased to bother me. Sometimes I went three full days without leaving. Fazel never asked for money or any help with smuggling the drug into the prison. He seemed happy to have someone trustworthy around him when he was high.

One of the rare days when I went into the yard to get fresh air, I ran into Meysam. He pulled me aside. "Yunus, why don't you come out anymore? Why have you lost so much weight?" I shrugged off the questions and tried to walk away, but he followed me and kept asking. I finally told him that we were using heroin, which I enjoyed greatly and in fact preferred to wandering around the yard, and that it was nobody's business.

The next morning, the guards raided our cell. Four men in black uniforms kicked the door open. They strip-searched all three of us and inspected our books, checked all the dishes and cutlery, all our clothes, and finally found Fazel's stash in his mattress. They took him away. I never saw him again.

The withdrawal symptoms kicked in immediately. Within a few hours, my nose began to run and my eyes teared up uncontrollably. I coughed and shivered like I had a severe flu. Then the diarrhea began. Pain spread fast through my whole body. My muscles got tight. Even the slightest movement was an ordeal. The sensations receded in a week, but I never became the person I had been before doing drugs. I felt old and stiff, sedentary and isolated.

· · ·

I pulled a one-thousand-toman bill out of my pocket and dangled it in front of their faces. One of them nodded. "Five puffs," the other one said. I squatted next to them, took my turn, and left. It all happened in less than three minutes.

Enjoying the serenity the opioid unleashed in my body, I walked back out of the park. The crowd was still flowing along Azadi Street, silent and determined, fingers making an ocean of Vs in the air. I walked lightly on the sidewalk, my muscles soft, my legs more agile than before. I came upon a falafel place that I had been to in my previous life. The sight of the shop got me hungry. I hadn't eaten anything since the breakfast in prison. I walked in.

"It's insane out there!" the man behind the counter said as soon as he saw me, as if I were an old friend.

"It is. I had no idea what was going on, then I got caught up in it. Can I have a falafel sandwich?"

"You got it. Which line do you work?" he said as he dropped the balls into the hot oil.

"Azadi-Pounak." The line I used to drive, as if the last few years had been a brief daydream behind the wheel.

"What's going on up in Pounak and Aryashahr?" he asked.

"I didn't work today."

"To be honest, I'm enjoying this, even though it screws up business. You know how many people came through this door today? Four. You're the fifth one."

I shook my head in sympathy. He scooped the falafel out of the oil and shoved it in sandwich bread. "But what's a few days of bad business if these kids are getting rid of mullahs?" He laughed heartily.

"I don't know," I said, taking the sandwich from his hand. "I'm just exhausted."

Outside, I bit ravenously into the food and stood watching the never-ending stream of protesters passing by. I turned my back to the avenue and walked down a side street, then another narrower one, until I ended up in a different small park. I sat on a bench, eating and listening to the silence.

A pigeon fluttered its wings, took off from the tree behind me, and landed by my foot. I tore off pieces of the sandwich and threw them at the bird. Before the fat creature could get to them, other pigeons and sparrows showed up and wolfed down the crumbs. I went to the grocery store across from the park to get more bread.

ACKNOWLEDGMENTS

Joyce Carol Oates has been an incredible mentor since my first day at NYU. My wife, Katie, has been my biggest supporter since the day we met. She spent many hours reading and editing and giving me feedback on the manuscript despite her demanding job. Salar Abdoh has been my older brother in New York, on both personal and professional fronts. My agent, Jessica Craig, was heartwarmingly present and supportive at all stages.

I am grateful to the Axinn family, whose support made it possible for me to start a career in the US, and to everyone at NYU, especially Deborah Landau and John Freeman.

Researching this book, I talked to about a dozen Iranians who spent time in solitary confinement. Many of them are still in Iran or travel there. I can't name them. Of those I can, Mohammad Tootkaboni, Roozbeh Mirebrahimi, Rahman Boozari, and Alborz Zahedi were indispensable.

I am indebted to numerous bus drivers who generously chatted with me on the streets of Tehran despite their grinding job, and to Mohsen Osanlou for talking to me about the history of the bus drivers' union.

Over the past decade I lived a hectic life that spanned three countries on three different continents before settling in the US. My parents took the brunt of this uncertainty. Dedicating this book to them is the least I can do.